THE
GIRL IN
THE
MIRROR

ROSE CARLYLE is a lawyer and keen adventurer. She has crewed on scientific yachting expeditions to subantarctic islands and lived aboard her own yacht in the Indian Ocean for a year, sailing it from Thailand to South Africa via the Seychelles. Rose was awarded first class honours in her creative writing Masters at the University of Auckland and was a Michael King Writer in Residence in 2020. She lives in Auckland with her three children. *The Girl in the Mirror* is her first novel.

ROSE CARLYLE

THE GIRL IN THE MIRROR

CORVUS

First published in Australia in 2020 by
Allen & Unwin, Sydney, Australia.

First published in Great Britain in 2021 by
Corvus, an imprint of Atlantic Books Ltd.

2 4 6 8 10 9 7 5 3 1

A CIP catalogue record for this book is
available from the British Library.

Paperback ISBN: 978 1 83895 195 5
E-book ISBN: 978 1 83895 196 2

Printed and bound by CPI Group (UK) Ltd, Croydon, CR0 4YY

Corvus
An imprint of Atlantic Books Ltd
Ormond House
26–27 Boswell Street
London
WC1N 3JZ

www.corvus-books.co.uk

In memory of my brother,
David Carlyle

PROLOGUE

For the first twelve days of our life, we were one person. Our father's brains and our mother's beauty swirled into one blessed embryo, the sole heir to the Carmichael fortune.

On the thirteenth day, we split. It was almost too late. One more day and the split would have been incomplete. Summer and I would have been conjoined twins, perhaps sharing major organs, facing a choice between a lifetime shackled together and a surgical separation that might have left us maimed.

As it was, our rupture was imperfect. We might look identical, more than most twins, but we're mirror twins, mirror images of each other. The minute asymmetries in my sister's face—her fuller right cheek, her higher right cheekbone—are reproduced in my face on the left side. Other people can't see the difference, but when I look in the mirror, I don't see myself. I see Summer.

When we were six years old, Dad took a sabbatical from Carmichael Brothers, and our family sailed up the east coast of Australia and into Southeast Asia. Our home town, Wakefield, is the last safe place to swim before you enter croc territory, so Summer and I and our younger brother, Ben, spent a lot of time on that cruise playing inside our yacht.

I loved everything about *Bathsheba*. She was a custom-built sloop, her sleek aluminium hull fitted out with the best timbers—teak decks, oak cabinetry—but what I loved most of all was the ingenious double mirror in the bathroom. The builder had set two mirrors into a corner at right angles, with such care that I could scarcely discern the line of intersection. When I looked squarely at either one of these mirrors, I saw Summer, as usual. But when I stared between them, past that line, into the corner, I saw a non-reversed image. I saw my true self.

'When I grow up, I'm going to have one of these mirrors in my house,' I told Summer, watching the solemn blonde girl in the mirror mouth the words in time with my voice.

Summer put her little hand on my chest. 'But, Iris, I thought you liked pretending to be the right—the other—way round,' she said.

'Mirrors don't change what's on the inside.' I pushed her hand away. 'Besides, my heart *is* on the right side.'

We were the most extreme case of mirroring the doctors had ever seen. It wasn't the facial differences, barely detectable without calipers. They had scanned my abdomen when

I was a baby, and my liver, pancreas, spleen, all my organs, were on the wrong side of my body. This was how the doctors knew that we had split so late. When I lay still and watched my bare chest, it was the right-hand side that rose and fell in a rhythmic flutter, proof that my heart was misplaced.

Inside Summer, though, everything was as it should be. Summer was perfect.

PART I
IRIS

CHAPTER 1

THE MIRROR

I wake in my twin sister's bed. My face is squashed between plump pillows covered in white cotton. It makes me feel like a kid again, swapping places with Summer, and yet everything has changed. We're adults now, and this is Adam's bed too.

I roll over and survey the marital bedroom. Everything is oversize and lush; the colours are creamy and airy, but the carpet is the colour of a ripe peach. There's something illicit about lying here, even though Summer and Adam are thousands of miles away, not even in Australia anymore. Someone must have changed the sheets since they left, but I can smell Summer. She smells of innocent things: suntan lotion, apples, the beach.

This room breathes Summer, so it's jarring to remember that she didn't choose these furnishings. Adam owned this house when Summer married him, not long after his first wife, Helen, died. The room looks much the same as it did on Summer's wedding day last year. It's just like my sister to mould herself into the life that another woman left behind. She's easy-going to a fault.

The super-king bed is nestled into a bay window with decadent views of Wakefield Beach. I struggle to sit up—this bed is too soft—and lean against the mahogany bedhead, bathing my face in the light of the rising sun. The Coral Sea's turquoise mingles with gold shards of reflected sunbeams. I wish I was in the water right now, swimming in those colours. There are a few things I need to wash off.

From here, perched on the cliff edge, in one direction I can see Wakefield River, north of the town, cutting through the land like a wound. Summer has always loved the river, although, as a breeding ground for saltwater crocs, it's not swimmable. She likes to look at it from the safety of the bridge that our father built across it—his first construction project.

In the other direction, a faultless beach sweeps north to south, wild and open to ocean waves. Halfway along the beach-front, one mansion, faux Victorian with a hint of Byzantium, dwarfs the other beachfront dwellings. It's the house we grew up in; at least, that was where we lived until Dad died.

My mother, Annabeth, must still be asleep in the spare room, so this is my chance to check out Summer's loot. If I were house-sitting, I wouldn't cram myself into the guest bedroom, but Annabeth revels in being unassuming. She tried to stop me sleeping here when I turned up late last night, but I couldn't resist.

I claw my way out of the heaped bedding and rub my bare feet into the thick carpet. March is still high summer in Wakefield, and as I pad around the room, the warm air kisses my naked body. This time yesterday, I was in the mountains in New Zealand, where winter was already frosting the morning air.

One wall of the walk-in wardrobe is lined with Summer's dresses, a rainbow of silk and lace. I'm surprised that her drawers are still full of lingerie, even though she and Adam plan to be overseas for a year. The lingerie is typical Summer stuff, overrun with roses, demurely styled, more suited to a pre-teen girl than a married woman of twenty-three. There are loads of it; she surely wouldn't notice if half of it disappeared—not that I would dream of stealing. I suppose she couldn't fit all her clothes on the yacht.

The yacht. *Bathsheba*. This is the nub of the thing. This is why I feel as though Summer and I have swapped places. Because Summer's on *Bathsheba*. And *Bathsheba*'s not mine, she never was mine, she never will be mine, but I feel that she ought to be. It feels as though Summer is sleeping in my bed, on my yacht.

Summer never loved *Bathsheba*, but now *Bathsheba* is her home. She and Adam have bought the yacht, bought her fair and square from Dad's estate, and now Summer and Adam own her as much as they own the house that I'm standing in right now.

What do I own? A shrinking bank account, a wedding ring I don't want anymore, a bunch of furniture I've left behind in New Zealand. A piano I'll probably never play again. It was a cheap instrument, anyway. Summer and Adam have a better one.

I pick up a bra and knicker set that's so innocent it's almost porno. Yellow gingham, it reeks of boarding school: hockey sticks and cold baths. The bra is a double D, and I wear a D, but it looks like it'll fit. I step into the panties. I want to see what Summer looks like in these.

As I'm fastening the bra, the phone rings in a distant part of the house. That'll wake Annabeth. I suppose I will have to face up to her and her questions about why I'm here. I pretended to be too tired last night.

I barely have time to think before Annabeth bursts in on me.

'Here she is,' my mother says into the handset as she minces across the bedroom in a frumpy nightie, her blonde hair looking frizzy and streaked with grey. My mother is at the age where she needs make-up and hair products to achieve the beauty she once woke up with; she's not looking her best right now. 'No, no, she was already awake. Love the gingham bra, Iris. Summer has one the same.' Her sleepy blue eyes peer at me myopically. She dangles the receiver in my face as though I won't be able to see it unless it's right under my nose.

I grab the phone and shoo Annabeth out of the room. 'Close the door behind you!' I call.

Who could be phoning me? Who even knows I'm back in Australia, let alone in my sister's house?

'Hello?' My voice is craven, as though I've been caught somewhere I shouldn't be.

'Iris! Thank goodness you're there.' It's Summer. Her voice breaks into jagged sobs. 'You have to help me. We're in trouble. You're the only one who can help.'

I can't quite focus, because I'm wondering whether Annabeth's comment about the bra gave the game away. Summer can be oddly territorial about her clothes. But my sister doesn't seem to have heard. She's saying something about Adam, something about how she needs me, Adam needs me. Adam wants her to say that it was his idea and he's praying I'll accept.

I gaze at a rack of Adam's white business shirts. Each one holds Adam's shape as though a row of invisible Adams is wearing them, here in the wardrobe with me. The shirts are so big in the chest, so long in the sleeve. I hold one to my face. It smells of cloves. I can see Adam in this pristine white, his skin glowing darkly.

'The poor little man, his pee-pee is swollen and red, and there's something seeping out. It's horrific. The foreskin is so stretched. He's crying all the time.'

What is she saying? I'm agog. We're twins, but we don't have *that* kind of relationship. I've never heard Summer describe

11

anyone's penis before, let alone her husband's. What the hell is wrong with him?

'The worst part is when he gets an erection. It's excruciating. Babies do get erections, you know. It's nothing sexual.'

Babies?

'Wait,' I say. 'Are you talking about *Tarquin*?'

'Who else could I be talking about?'

Silence.

Tarquin. The other thing that Summer took over when Helen died, along with Helen's house and Helen's husband. The baby.

Summer is Tarquin's mother now. Adam and Summer agreed that Tarquin deserved a normal family, so Tarquin calls Summer 'Mummy'. Or at least he will if the kid ever learns to speak.

'Summer, I know baby boys get erections,' I say. 'We have a younger brother, you know. I've seen these things.' Summer always assumes I know nothing about kids, explaining that they need a daily bath and a regular bedtime, or something equally fascinating, like I'm an idiot. The last thing I want to think about is Tarquin's pee-pee, especially if it's seeping.

'Trust me, you've never seen anything like this,' Summer says. 'It's becoming dangerous. The infection could spread. The doctors said he could lose his penis. He could *die*.' The word comes out with a sob. 'He needs surgery. An emergency circumcision. They can't fly him home. He's having the surgery today, here in Phuket. We're at the international hospital.'

Summer's voice is fast and fluttery. She's teetering on a tightrope between shouty hysteria and a flood of tears. Most of the time, Summer is the self-assured, gracious twin, while I'm nervous and gauche, but when the chips are down, I'm the one who keeps her head.

I step up to my role now. I hang Adam's shirt back on the rack and smooth it into place. No one could tell it's been touched. 'An international hospital sounds good,' I say.

'Yes,' she says. 'They've been so kind to us here.'

'That's good, and it's good that you've rung me,' I reply. I say 'good' like it's a mantra, calming Summer. 'Of course I can help. So you haven't told Annabeth yet?'

'I couldn't . . .' Summer's voice quavers again.

'I can tell her. She can fly up to Phuket today. I don't mind taking over the house-sitting for a few days.'

No response.

'For as long as you and Adam need it,' I add generously.

'No, no, Iris, we need you, not Mum.'

My head buzzes. Summer needs me. *Adam* needs me. But why? I'm no good with babies. Tarquin already has both his parents. The only parents he knows, anyway. What do they need me for?

I picture myself in Thailand, swanning around the Royal Phuket Marina with its flotilla of superyachts, drinking cocktails. Strong ones, not the virgin cocktails Dad bought us when we were kids. Surely not all those millionaire yachties want Thai girlfriends. Some of them must prefer blondes.

But what am I thinking? Tarquin is ill. It sounds like his penis is rotting off. There'll be no time for drinking and flirting. Surely.

'We're in a serious bind, Iris, and we can't tell just anybody about it. Only people we trust one hundred per cent.' Summer pauses.

'Well, obviously you can tell me,' I say.

'Of course,' says Summer. 'I'm just saying, you must keep this a secret. The thing is, our import permit for *Bathsheba* has expired. We've already checked her out of Thailand. We were ready to go, but the beaches are so beautiful here. We thought we could spend another couple of weeks in a quiet anchorage and no one would know. We never imagined Tarquin would get sick. It's terrible timing. If customs find *Bathsheba*'s still in Thailand, they'll seize her. The people here are lovely, but there's so much corruption.'

Summer makes it sound as though corruption is some affliction, like malaria, that the poor Thais suffer through no fault of their own. But I'm too keen to hear more to quibble with her.

'So what do you want me to do?'

'Oh, Twinnie, I don't know how to ask you such a huge favour. Adam's a good sailor, but he's barely been out of sight of land. You know how hard it is on the open sea. It's a long passage to the Seychelles, at least a fortnight, and the end of the season is near. The typhoons start in April, but we can't wait till April anyway. We need to get *Bathsheba* out of Thailand now. And you were always such a great sailor, Iris. We'll pay your plane fares, of course, and Adam says you can stand whichever watches you want.'

As Summer speaks, I step back into her bedroom and approach the bay window. The water glitters far below, swirling around sun-bleached rocks. I can't let myself believe Summer's words. They're too good to be true. I've melted through the glass, and I'm flying over the ocean, turning a joyous shade of aquamarine.

Adam's speaking in the background now. Has he been listening all along? 'Tell her I'll do all the night watches,' he says, in that deep voice flecked with the cadence of the Seychelles. His voice goes on more quietly. I hold the phone close to my ear and shut my eyes, straining to hear.

'Believe it or not, Iris *likes* sailing at night,' Summer says. When she speaks to Adam, her voice becomes playful, smooth, liquid. No wonder I can barely stand to be in the same room as my sister and her husband.

But it seems I wouldn't have to spend much time with the two of them. The plan seems to be that Summer will stay in Phuket with Tarquin and his festering genitalia, and I will leave behind my failed job, failed marriage and failed life, and sail across the Indian Ocean on the yacht I have loved since childhood. And who will go with me? My brother-in-law, the wealthy, handsome, charismatic Adam Romain.

ROSE CARLYLE

I imagine sailing into the Seychelles, a dream-country of coconut palms and halcyon beaches, but I'm not a mere tourist, because my husband is a local, so in a way it's a homecoming.

Well, not husband in my case. Brother-in-law. But still.

'Of course I want to help,' I say, 'but I have a lot of job interviews lined up.' This isn't true; I haven't started looking yet. I've been trying to figure out how to explain to prospective employers why I walked out on my last job. 'And I have a lot of bills.'

Summer's voice when it comes back is quieter. 'We'll cover everything,' she says. 'Plane fares, debts you need paid, anything you need. I'm sorry, Iris. I know things have been hard for you with Noah leaving. I know it isn't fair to ask. If I wasn't desperate. If *we* weren't desperate . . .'

It's not often that Summer's in need. All our life, she's been content with what she has, happy with her lot. As anyone would be who had Summer's lot. But I can't bear to stretch it out. She sounds truly unhappy—and in a moment, she might think of someone else to ask.

'I'll do it,' I say. 'I'll do it for you, Twinnie.'

Summer squeals down the phone.

In a few minutes, everything is planned. Adam has found a direct flight on his smartphone. I'll leave Wakefield this morning. I have an hour to pack and to tell our mother before I head to the airport. I'll be in Phuket by this evening. I'll be on *Bathsheba*.

Adam comes on the line. 'What's your date of birth? Oh, stupid me, of course I know that. What's your middle name? Same as Summer's?'

'No middle name.'

'Really, just Iris? OK, that's easy. Short and sweet. Hang on a second, hon—Iris—the website's confirming the booking.'

Did he almost call me honey? The thought has a deep effect on me. I feel it in my body. I flush with shame; I really should get out of Summer's underwear.

But now Adam's saying goodbye. In the background, Summer is asking about Tarquin's vaccinations, but Adam doesn't know the answers to her questions. He's always so vague, it makes me wonder how the hell he manages to run a travel agency. Summer has to handle all their life admin. He hands the phone back to her, and she asks me to email Tarquin's vaccination records to her. Then she hangs up.

Finding the records is easy. Summer has filed them all in the wardrobe. I'm struck by her extreme organisation. Her life is laid out here in writing; there's even a folder labelled 'Adam's favourite meals'. When I pull it off the shelf, a sex manual falls out. *The Millennial Kama Sutra*. It looks well worn.

I could browse all day, but I have to get moving. I have to dress, eat something, tell Annabeth the plan. My mother's barely got her head around my sudden appearance, and now I'm disappearing again. She'll freak out about Tarquin too. She treats the kid like he's her blood grandson.

First, I dart into the ensuite bathroom for one glimpse of Summer in her good-girl gingham. And that's when I see it. The one thing that Summer has changed about this house.

The two panes of glass must have cost a bomb, and it must have been quite an operation to hoist them up here. They seem larger than the door. They've been installed with great care. The angle is exact, the seam almost invisible. Even better than the one on the yacht.

It wouldn't bother me, it wouldn't gnaw at my insides, if Summer had genuinely wanted a double mirror. We are twins; I can't blame her for wanting the same things as I do. But Summer has never minded who she sees in the mirror. She's never been interested in the 'mirror twins' thing. I can see she has installed this mirror because it looks good. It fits into the space beautifully, and with the door to the bedroom open, it reflects the bay window and the ocean beyond.

Even the things Summer doesn't care about she gets first.

I stare diagonally into the double mirror. The girl in the mirror stares back. She's wearing Summer's yellow underwear, but she isn't Summer. It's her left cheek that's fuller, her left cheekbone that's higher.

The girl in the mirror is me.

CHAPTER 2

THE WILL

There was a moment when Summer was an only child. Annabeth's got a bohemian streak, so she refused to have an ultrasound during her pregnancy, even though Dad was desperate to know the baby's sex. And her belly wasn't very big. There was no clue that there were two babies.

So it was a girl. My mother held the rosy blonde infant in her arms and gave her the name she'd been saving up all her life: Summer Rose.

Then they realised I was coming. Dad doubtless felt his dashed hopes rise again—a second chance for a son. Annabeth just hoped that we would not be identical twins.

They were both disappointed. My father, ever logical, suggested Summer and Rose as names, but Annabeth couldn't take away the name with which she'd already blessed my sister.

Later that day, someone brought my mother a bunch of irises, and something about the spiky, unscented flowers must have appealed, because that's what my parents named me. Annabeth always told this story as if it meant something special, but I couldn't get past the idea that she had looked around the hospital room and named me after the first thing she laid eyes on, because she still wanted Summer to be Summer Rose.

Suitcase in hand, I hurry out of Summer and Adam's bedroom and down the floating staircase. I've organised for my Uncle Colton to drive me to the airport since Annabeth's eyesight is too poor these days. I won't let her come with me. After Summer's phone call, I've managed to fudge the truth, so she now has the impression that the reason I turned up in Australia was to go and help with *Bathsheba*. All the same, she's already asked me too many questions about Noah.

Uncle Colton is easier company, although as he gets older, his resemblance to Dad is becoming almost spooky. When I reach the bottom of the stairs, Colton is standing close by my mother's side in the spacious white living room, where everything is drenched in sunshine from the skylights that Adam has installed. The two of them are gazing at the larger-than-life framed photo of the newborn Tarquin on the living room wall. In the photo, Tarquin is skinny and sickly, with breathing tubes in his nose, and is held not by his dying mother but by a young neonatal nurse.

Standing together, my uncle and my mother both look as blond and well preserved as each other, and the ugly thought hits me that Annabeth might be attracted to this uncanny reincarnation of her husband. Then again, she probably can't see well enough to appreciate the similarity. She has macular degeneration, so everything in her world is low-res.

'So this is all Helen's stuff, the furniture, and the piano, of course?' Uncle Colton asks. Helen was a concert pianist, and her Steinway grand still has pride of place in Summer and Adam's living room. It's out of keeping with the decor, black and heavy where everything else is light.

'I guess nobody plays it?' he adds.

'I think Summer and Adam hope Tarquin will learn.' Annabeth heaves a sigh. 'It's funny that Summer has such a beautiful piano, when Iris is the one who plays.' *Funny* isn't quite the word I'd have used. I itch to open the lid and run my fingers over those immaculate keys, let sweet, warm music fill that airy space, but I'm running late.

On the way to the airport, Uncle Colton is his usual boring self. He drones on about what lovely girls Francine is raising and how well Virginia is doing in high school, but I'm only half-listening. The way he talks, anyone would think Francine was his wife rather than his brother's widow. One of the three wives my father left behind.

Alone in the departure lounge, having farewelled my uncle, I indulge in a bit of twin-spotting and glimpse several pairs. Most people don't notice twins, even identical ones, once they've grown out of the dress-alike phase. Few sets of twins are as alike as Summer and I, so a haircut and a change of clothes are all it takes to slip out of the public gaze.

But I never miss other twins. I can even spot fraternal twins, because it's not their looks that give them away.

A brother and sister, young teenagers, walk past, with the same deep, doleful eyes. They are out of sight in seconds, but I know. She's half a head taller, graceful and womanly, while he's still a skinny, sandy-haired boy. Most people will think she's a year or two older, but this doesn't bother the boy. They laugh about it together and look forward to the day when he'll tower over her. I can tell these things.

The way they're whispering as they walk—smiling, leaning their heads together—is the first clue, but the giveaway is that he's carrying her suitcase as well as his own. What teenage boy carries his sister's suitcase? A twin, that's who.

Next, a family settles into the seats opposite me. Mum, Dad and two girls who share a face. Mainland Chinese. I'm no good at guessing ethnicity, but you can always tell Chinese twins because their parents have that we-beat-the-one-child-policy smile. That smile seems to last the rest of their lives. If you ask me, they're barmy. I've been planning on a one-child policy since I was fourteen. I would be planning a no-child policy if it weren't for certain complications. If it weren't for my father's will.

The Chinese twins have started refusing to dress the same; their clothing is defiantly different. One is in a dress, the other jeans. One has short hair, even though it doesn't suit her. She took one for the team.

However different they look, though, they don't know how to stop behaving like twins. Their mother ferrets out a lunchbox and hands them a couple of hard-boiled eggs—Summer is like this too, always feeding Tarquin, apparently terrified that he might one day experience a hunger pang. The twins reach for the eggs with one movement. One twin peels her egg while the other waits, then the same twin peels the second egg. She eviscerates them both and hands the yolks to her sister, retaining the whites. Only now do the twins eat, as if responding to an unseen cue. Each pops the contents of her left hand into her mouth, then the right. They chew in unison.

I've met twins like this before, of course. Chloë and Zoë, my friends at law school in Melbourne, were this kind of twin. They shared clothes, friends, secrets. They could hardly credit that I had left my twin in a different city—Summer stayed in Wakefield and went to nursing school. Committing to four years apart from my twin seemed both the best and the worst decision of my life. I escaped constant comparisons by others, but my own comparisons after I left Wakefield were with social-media Summer, who was even more glamorous than the real girl.

All I needed to know to understand Chloë and Zoë's relationship was that each texted the other whenever she got a period. I prefer not to know when Summer's on the rag.

There's something nauseating about the way she wears white or pastel underwear every single day of the month, like a girl in a tampon commercial. And the thought of Summer's period always reminds me of the beauty pageant.

Was there a time when Summer and I were like Chloë and Zoë, like these egg-scoffing twins? I honestly can't remember. Summer would have been the twin who peeled the eggs and then let her sister eat both yolks. Everyone always knew she was the sweetheart. She was kind to the lost and the lame. Identical as we were, Summer was somehow more beautiful. She had inner beauty.

If there ever was such a time, it was my father's last act to destroy it. Since he died, Summer and I have not been like other twins. Dad taught me that there's not enough for two. There's only one life that we have to share.

———

Ridgeford Carmichael, known as Ridge—although I never had the balls to call him by his first name as I do Annabeth—was your typical Aussie self-made man, proud of all the things that people in other countries are ashamed of: his convict ancestry, his lack of education, his three wives, each younger, blonder and more fecund than the last.

When I was growing up, I knew that Carmichael Brothers was a construction firm, but Dad seemed to have a few other ventures going on, so I never figured out exactly where all his money came from. He was always embroiled in property investment, always wining and dining politicians, always travelling overseas. Dad was powerfully built, with rugged, sunburned features. Although he was more than a decade older than Annabeth, he didn't seem it; he was rowdy and vigorous till the day he died.

Dad grew up with no family of his own. His childhood was passed in foster care and a state home. All he seemed to know of his background was that some ancestor had been transported for stealing a beer glass from an English pub.

Perhaps that's why Dad was so dynastic. By the time he was twenty-two, he had found out that he had a younger brother and gained custody of Colton, who was twelve. Dad sent Colton to the best boarding school in Wakefield. Colton became his protégé, and then his business partner.

Dad put off having kids until he'd made his millions, and by that time his first wife, Margaret, was too old. After he divorced Margaret, Dad didn't repeat his mistake; Summer and I were conceived on our parents' honeymoon. When Annabeth called it quits after she produced our younger brother, Dad ran off with Francine, who was fresh out of Catholic school. But I still didn't realise the extent of his obsession with populating the world.

These are the facts of his life, but they don't capture what Dad was like. Perhaps all I need to say to describe my father is this: he didn't like nice people. I found this out the last time I saw him alive.

Our family was gathered at the dinner table in the big house on Beach Parade in early December, shortly after Summer and I had turned fourteen. Annabeth was telling a story about an encounter with a beggar. Earlier that day, she had taken Summer and me to Billabong to choose new beachwear for Christmas; numerous store-wrapped boxes were now sitting under our Christmas tree. On her way into the mall, Annabeth wished the beggar merry Christmas and held out a twenty. He, smelling like a rubbish bin, took the bill clean out of her hand and marched straight into a bottle shop.

'Right in front of me!' Annabeth exclaimed, smashing a generous portion of turkey cannelloni onto Dad's plate. He tilted the china, inspecting it for damage from the big silver serving spoon.

'So you were outside the bottle shop when you gave this bozo the cash?' Dad asked.

'I'm trying to raise our kids to be nice people, Ridge,' Annabeth said.

'Nice is dumb,' said Dad, and he turned to me and winked.

I lapped it up. Summer was the beauty in our family—even then I knew it—and Ben was the only boy, the heir. But I was the one Dad included in his special joke.

I surveyed my mother, my brother, my sister. Annabeth gave cash to a beggar outside a bottle shop. Ben, ten years old and small for his age, was so gentle that Dad had given up ever teaching him to hunt, even though he had great aim when firing at a tin can. And Summer, well, Summer was Summer.

But I was Iris, the unexpected twin, the surplus twin, and with that wink, Dad gave me a new place in our family. Not nice. Not dumb.

This is why I thought I would at least get my share of the family money—not that I expected Dad to die any time soon. Your average father might not have seen much in me, not compared with my angelic sister, but Dad always seemed to appreciate my cynical streak. Ridge hated the idea of his money being lost, and you have to have a fair amount of street smarts not to be bamboozled out of your fortune. It seemed that Dad thought I would be up to the task.

Annabeth and Dad were already divorced by then, which perhaps partly excuses his dinnertime pronouncements about her brainpower. Maybe it's weird that he still came for dinner sometimes, four years after leaving my mother, but he still owned the house on Beach Parade. Later, when I went to law school, I wondered how the hell Dad had managed to keep his property intact through two divorces. Maybe Annabeth was too nice for her own good. Or maybe the judges were afraid of Ridge Carmichael, the man who owned half of Wakefield. Whichever it was, when he died, Dad left his three wives and seven children not much more than comfortable. The bulk of his fortune, that's where it gets interesting.

For the first few years after the divorce, we stayed in the beach house. Dad moved in with his girlfriend, Francine, who lived in a penthouse in inner-city Wakefield. Francine had a two-year-old named Virginia. We assumed she was Francine's daughter from a previous relationship.

When Dad married Francine, they changed Virginia's surname to Carmichael. I still didn't question who her father might be, although my mother must have had her suspicions. But Annabeth wouldn't say a word against her ex-husband. She acted as if she had been lucky to be married to him in the first place, even though she was a very pretty, sweet-tempered woman—utterly wifely, a perfect match for a man like Ridge. The only way you could tell when something upset our mother was that she would do the housework with even more vigour than usual, slamming the vacuum cleaner into furniture, thumping pillows into place.

By the time Summer and I were fourteen, Francine had popped out three more babies: Vicky, Valerie and Vera Carmichael. Like Francine, the girls were all too blonde to be called blonde; their hair was white. The birth of Francine's fourth daughter tipped the balance of power. Now there were more of them than there were of us, and Francine started making noises about a house swap. It turned out that Ridge owned both properties. Nobody wants to live in an apartment with four kids, even if it is a multi-level penthouse with a rooftop garden and swimming pool, but I don't know whether Francine would have succeeded if Dad hadn't died.

After dinner that night, when I kissed Dad goodbye, I begged him to take me with him on his upcoming sailing holiday. Since the divorce, Dad had flown Summer and me and Ben up to Thailand every summer, but this year, he was taking Francine and their kids.

'I can help with the sailing, Dad,' I said. 'I'll even help with the babies.'

Dad laughed. 'Stay here and help your mother,' he said. 'Stop her from giving all my money away.'

Two weeks later, Dad had a heart attack on the pier at a beach in southern Phuket and was pronounced dead at the scene. Francine said his body had to be taken back to shore in a tuk-tuk because the ageing pier wasn't strong enough for an ambulance.

Francine and her children were back in Australia within two days. The live-aboard sailors of Phuket, a disparate bunch of hippies, old salts and dreamers from all over the world, had pulled together to help the young widow. They had organised the repatriation of Dad's body, fed and comforted the kids, and sailed *Bathsheba* back to the marina, hauling her out onto the hardstand, where she stood high and dry for the next nine years, because nobody in the family knew what to do with her.

I had met these people, these ragtag seamen, on our sailing holidays with Dad. He'd have a drink with them, but sometimes it seemed as if he only talked to them to collect stories about their stupidity: their amateur sailing, their dull lives, how the Thai tradesmen ripped them off. They were nice people, he'd say, like it was the worst thing you could say about anybody.

And now I understood. Nice is dumb.

At Dad's funeral, Annabeth wore black silk and Francine wore black satin. Francine, awash with pearls, led a cortège of ghost-pale daughters in matching white dresses, their dead-straight hair pulled back by long black ribbons. Annabeth—taller, but a much less imposing figure—was flanked by Summer and me in tailored linen and Ben in his first proper suit. Annabeth only had three children, but she had the boy. Francine was the newest, youngest wife, but Annabeth was still prettier. Besides, Annabeth had the beach house. Or so we thought.

Margaret didn't come to the funeral. I think she was the only wife who knew what Dad was really like. I was about to find out, before the service even started.

The funeral home was one of those one-stop shops that aims not to offend anyone and ends up being a soulless train station. When we arrived, a soft-spoken man with startlingly pink skin took Annabeth aside. He explained that Dad's casket would be rolled into the service on wheels. Health and safety regulations.

I don't know whether Dad could have mustered six loyal mates to carry him, anyway. There were hundreds of people arriving for the service, but they weren't Dad's bosom buddies. Apart from family, I didn't know any of them. They were smiling and chatting easily to each other. No one was crying.

The pink man asked my mother whether any of us would like to 'view the deceased before we close the casket for the ceremony'. He gestured down a quiet corridor, away from the room into which the crowd of cheerful mourners was pouring. He might not have figured out that Annabeth was an ex-wife. She looked forlorn enough to be the widow.

'My children are far too young for that,' Annabeth said. She steered us towards our relatives. Her parents were in a corner with my aunts and uncles and a few cousins. They looked hot, itchy and awkward in borrowed black clothes. January in Wakefield is a punishing time, and the air conditioning was showing its age.

I didn't mean to spy, but I needed to know that Dad was really dead, and I kind of wanted to see the coffin on wheels. It was easy to evade my grandparents and head down that corridor. I pushed open a tomb-like door and found myself alone with my father's dead body.

He had died in the tropics, and I guess he had been embalmed, but there was a faint odour in the room. I remembered a dog I had seen—and smelled—when I was a kid, lying dead in a gutter on a busy Thai street. I sure knew Dad was dead now.

Still, I crept forward until I saw him. The great Ridge Carmichael, reduced to a quiet, coffin-bound corpse. His body looked hollow, and his face was a horrible grey. Only his hair looked normal. He had recently turned sixty, but just a few strands of silver had pushed their way through the blond.

Sixty was old to be a father of small children, but it was young to die.

Tall vases bursting with white flowers stood sentinel around my father's coffin, emblems of love. And not any old flowers. Someone had chosen the varieties: roses and irises.

My eyes filled with tears. Someone had done this to honour me and my twin, Dad's firstborn children. None of his other kids had flower names.

I buried my nose in the nearest bouquet of irises and breathed deep. I knew they wouldn't have a fragrance, but it's a lifelong habit of mine to sniff my namesake flower. I've always wished they smelled as pretty as roses, and I guess a part of me believes that persistence should be enough to get what you want in this world.

As I was sniffing the odourless irises, being rewarded only with the smell of death, the door swooshed open behind me. I looked around. A cloth was draped over the trolley beneath the coffin, and it reached the floor. It was the only place to hide. I ducked under.

Just in time. I stiffened at the clack of stilettos. Mum always wore flat shoes. Who was this?

The intruder approached the casket and stood silent. I couldn't breathe.

Now the door opened again, and I heard a soft tread. 'Francine,' came my mother's voice. 'I apologise. They told me Ridge was alone.'

Francine and Annabeth had always been polite to each other. Too polite.

'No, I'm the one who should apologise,' said Francine. 'I agreed to allow you this time, but when it came to it, I couldn't bear them to put that . . . that *lid* on without seeing him again.'

'It was a small enough thing to ask,' said Annabeth. 'Ten minutes alone with the father of my children. You could have given me that. Soon you'll have everything that was mine.'

'What's that supposed to mean?'

'Do you think you could give me time to pack before you kick me out of my home?'

I was jammed against the wheels of the trolley. This space wasn't big enough to hide my body, and the toe of one shoe was sticking out from under the cloth. I curled up tighter, tucking my feet in with infinite slowness. My fingernails dug into the skin of my arms.

Francine's voice rose, her broad accent growing broader. 'You can't think I knew about the will. Of course I want the house, I've made no secret of that. Your children are nearly grown now, the girls anyway. You must see that you're the winner here, Annabeth. Your twins will be married and pregnant at eighteen—one of them, at least—and then you'll have everything. You've hit the jackpot. Virginia's only six. What hope does she have of beating them to the money? You can afford to give me the house. It's nothing compared with the millions coming your way. A hundred million, Annabeth.'

My body jerked, and I lost my balance and rocked back onto my heels with a thud. I froze, but the two women didn't seem to have heard. My mother was speaking now, in a voice I had never heard before—a cold, flat voice.

'How dare you,' she said. 'How dare you dream for one minute that I would prostitute my daughters for that money!

My children deserve better than this. Francine, I promise you, Summer and Iris will never *hear* of this will. If you want to pimp your daughter out in her teens, you're welcome to Ridge's money, every cent of it. We'll live on the crumbs he's left us with our dignity intact. My girls will marry and have children when they are ready, when they make their own free choice unsullied by Ridge's sick fantasies. No grandchild of mine will enter this world to win some filthy prize. To live out a dead man's dreams.'

Francine's shrill laugh made me shiver. 'Nice speech, Annabeth,' she said. 'How virtuous you sound. If you can keep silent, all power to you, but secrets this big have a way of getting out. I think my daughters deserve to know the truth. I trust them to do their best for their family . . . if your girls can keep their legs crossed long enough to give mine a chance. And now I'll leave you alone with the *father of your children.*'

'No,' said my mother. 'I've been here too long already.' Something in her voice—I could *hear* her eyes sweeping around the room—made me hold my breath, willing my body into a tighter ball.

And then both women were gone, and I was alone again with my father's body.

The room whirled around me. My father was dead, and my mother had become a different person, hard-edged and sour.

We had to give up the beach house. That was my first thought. Marriage, pregnancy, babies—at fourteen I didn't want to think about any of that. Annabeth had said she didn't want to tell us, so I would pretend not to know.

Summer didn't need to know.

I had always known Carmichael Brothers was a multi-million-dollar enterprise, and Uncle Colton was only the junior partner. Ridge owned the lion's share. Had owned.

Now I knew what his estate was worth. The beach house, the penthouse, what my mother described as 'crumbs', and a hundred million dollars.

As we chanted our way through the funeral service, Annabeth's and Francine's words spooled through my head, and I counted the years. Eighteen was the legal age for marriage, less than four years away for me and Summer, but Ben wouldn't be eighteen for eight years, and Virginia not for twelve. If Summer didn't know about the will, there was no way she would get married and have a baby in her teens. She wasn't that kind of girl. And Ben, well, Annabeth and Francine had treated Ben as out of the running. They hadn't mentioned him, hadn't questioned each other's silence. All the adults seemed to know that Ben wouldn't be fathering a child.

My father had known this, I realised. Dad's frustration, his suppressed rage at my little brother, was somehow connected with this mystery.

Introverted and scholarly even at the age of ten, Ben was not like the rest of us. Although he was usually more obedient than Summer and me. I sensed that he was waiting till he was old enough to forge his own path. It was as though he rejected Dad's values so completely that he couldn't be bothered arguing. He was just waiting Dad out.

I had heard Dad muttering about 'the Carmichael name dying out'. I couldn't imagine how this was related to Ben's rare acts of quiet rebellion, but this was the only part of the conversation that I didn't understand. What I knew for sure was that Ridge Carmichael, the grand patriarch, had not left his fortune to his son. And he hadn't split it seven ways. Like a medieval lord, he wanted it to stay together for as many generations as possible.

Dad had bequeathed his empire to the first of his seven children to marry and produce an heir.

———

Francine had been right about one thing. Secrets this big get out. Somehow or other, by the end of the funeral, Summer knew.

In the car on the way home, she whispered in my ear, 'I'm not going to let Dad rule my life. I don't care about his money. I'm not going to get married until I'm in love.'

And I thought, good for you, sister. Take your sweet time.

For me, the race was on.

CHAPTER 3

THE SWITCH

It's dark when I touch down at Phuket's international airport. I step from the static cool air of the plane into the swampy Thai night, and the tropical moisture presses on my skin.

I'm yawning as I cross the tarmac. It's been a long flight, and I haven't even adjusted to Queensland time. My body clock is still set for New Zealand. I have other adjustments to make too. I've come from the mountains to the tropics, from the lonely snow of alpine New Zealand to teeming touristy Thailand. I'm sweating in the humid heat.

And I'm still wearing my wedding ring. At least I've escaped having to explain things to Annabeth, and all the crying I would have had to endure. Summer won't pry. She knows all about me and Noah.

But that's all behind me now. My last day in New Zealand, I went to a beauty parlour and treated myself, as my symbolic way of leaving Noah behind. I scrolled through my Facebook page, looking for a photo of me at my best so I could show the beautician how I liked my hair to be styled and my eyebrows to be shaped, but I couldn't find one that looked right. In the end, I had to make do with an old photo of Summer that I happened to have in my wallet. Well, not that old. It was from her wedding day.

'Make me look like that,' I said to the girl.

'Gosh, I can hardly believe it's you,' the little cow said. 'Your eyebrows look so different. Weren't you a beautiful bride? And your husband looks like a movie star!'

Our eyebrows are the only way people can tell Summer and me apart. My eyebrows are thicker and lighter. Summer's are two neat dark lines, a surprising contrast to her golden hair, with an annoying sharp arch to them. But the beautician did a great job. She replicated them exactly.

Of course, I didn't think I'd be seeing Summer straight after the eyebrow-and-hair job. It's a little awkward as it looks like I've copied her, which is already something she seems to half-believe. I can tell, although she never mentions it.

I'm wrangling my suitcase in the arrivals lounge when a strong arm lifts it out of my hands, and I'm wrapped in a muscular embrace. Adam.

'Twinnie,' he murmurs. 'God, we're glad you're here!' He presses my face into his neck and holds me.

He smells sweet and musky, and his warmth catches me off guard. I've only met Adam a few times, on my visits home for family occasions such as his wedding to Summer, yet he always acts as though he knows me as well as he knows my sister, calling me by our twin nickname and including me in their in-jokes about the rest of our family. I hold my body still and remind myself that I'm his sister-in-law. Think *sister*. Friendly, not too friendly.

I look him in the eyes and frame a smile. 'Adam! Good to see you. I was expecting Summer.'

Adam's even taller than I remembered, and his voice is so deep it vibrates through me. His skin is tinted a beautiful red-gold; it's not much darker than mine and Summer's, but his black curls and radiant smile show that Africa has played a part in his heritage. Adam came to Australia as a teen-ager, the only child of globetrotting parents, and took to the country so zealously that his parents were persuaded to stay.

It's the kind of move only Summer could pull off, after her endless succession of interchangeable surfer-blond boyfriends, this out-of-the-blue marriage to a widower who already has a kid. Coming from the Seychelles, a country I had barely heard of, Adam's more glamorous and mysterious than a homegrown Australian husband could ever be. Of course, it helps that he runs a high-end travel agency and owns a clifftop mansion on Seacliff Crescent, one of Wakefield's most exclusive streets.

'One of us has to stay with Tarq all the time,' Adam says. 'The surgery went well, but he's got to fight off the sepsis.' His tone is solemn.

Damn. I should have opened with a concerned inquiry about 'Tarq'. Never mind; I'm sure I'll be hearing plenty about him. 'The poor little poppet,' I say with a frowny face.

'We need to get back to him,' Adam says. 'He hasn't woken up yet. I want to be there when he does. God, you're the image of Summer, Twinnie. I'll never learn to tell you two apart.' He hugs me again, a bear-like embrace. His face is in my hair. I swear he breathes in, like he wants to smell me.

Now he's striding towards the exit, and I struggle to keep up. Seems we're headed straight for the hospital. Am I facing an all-night bedside vigil? So much for cocktails at the marina.

The airport crowd is an even mix of Thai and *farang*, as they call us. I wonder as we sweep through the doors, do Adam and I look like husband and wife? It's always obvious that he and Summer are a couple, despite their contrasting looks, but perhaps it's marital bliss, radiating outwards, that marks them as belonging together.

What do Adam and I radiate? Awkwardness? Whenever I'm with him, it's hard not to think about how much Summer might have told Adam about me. The things he might know without being told. By being married to her, it's like he's seen me without my clothes.

Adam finds a taxi, opens the door for me and helps me into the back seat. 'Shove over,' he says with a smile as his thigh presses against mine.

I wriggle across the seat and wind down my window to breathe in the night. The driver sets off at a hectic pace. Typically, Adam has trouble remembering the name of the hospital.

As we head south, I try to update my mental map of Phuket after nearly ten years away. I'm looking forward to checking out my old haunts and dredging up some Thai phrases. But everything has changed. Narrow alleys of tuk-tuks and pedestrians have become multi-lane highways crammed with cars. My memories have been paved over. Even the smells are different. I remember night jasmine, not traffic fumes and sewage.

Adam has a lot to tell me, but his words are a jumble of hospital jargon and sentimentality. Unlike Summer, he skirts around any description of the infected body part that has brought me here. Through the haze of parental obsession, I glean a few useful facts. *Bathsheba* is in good shape, ready for sea and loaded with food and spare parts. Summer has stocked the yacht with enough provisions for at least two months. The SSB radio has broken down and the emergency beacon is obsolete, but Adam's bought a handheld satellite phone, which can download emails and weather forecasts, and make and receive voice calls. That's all we'll need for a safe passage.

'It's hard to schedule a convenient time to call, and the rate for live phone calls is outrageous,' says Adam, 'so we'll use email unless there's an emergency, if that's all right with you.' He actually seems to care whether I'm happy with his arrangements. As if there's anybody I need to talk to during the next few weeks. Or ever.

Adam seems to have come to grips with the essentials of yacht maintenance, and I soon feel comforted that *Bathsheba*'s not going to spring a catastrophic leak or lose her mast between here and Africa. I figure I can handle anything else that happens at sea.

'I gather it's all over with Noah?' Adam asks, leaning close. I nod.

'The man's insane,' says Adam, 'but his loss is some other lucky guy's gain. I guarantee you won't be the one looking back with regrets, Iris. Summer agrees with me. You're far too good for him.'

'Well, you *have* to think I'm pretty.'

I cringe at my flat joke, but Adam grins as though it's an everyday observation. 'Don't let my wife hear you say that,' he says. '*Pretty* is faint praise. I know you two are beauty queens.'

Beauty queens? Has Summer told Adam about the beauty pageant? Adam's open gaze reassures me that he can't know he's hitting a sore spot. Yet the compliment does seem to be an allusion to that day.

We pull up to a clean, modern building. Adam leads me through quiet, well-lit corridors to Tarquin's room, while I mentally rehearse my concerned-auntie routine.

It turns out I don't have to fake my reaction. The sight of my puny little—what is he—step-nephew, lying hooked up to machines, jolts me. Tarquin doesn't look any bigger than when I last saw him, at Summer's wedding, dressed in a ridiculous midget tuxedo. Back then he looked blooming and boisterous, barely a baby anymore, except that he still couldn't walk. He crawled all over the place, getting into everything and rolling on the ground until his white shirt was covered with grass stains. Now he lies sickly still. His reddish hair hangs limp against his forehead, and his little limbs look cold and vulnerable.

This is serious. Tarquin might be a brat, but my sister loves him. He's Adam's son. And here they are stuck in a foreign country, with an extravagant yacht at risk too. I'm glad I'm here to help. What if Tarquin dies while Adam and I are at sea? He'll be inconsolable.

I must look upset, because Adam gives my shoulder a brotherly squeeze. 'I know,' he says. 'It's a shock. This has been so hard for Summer.'

But where is Summer? Tarquin is alone in the stark room. He's asleep or unconscious, but if he had woken up, no one would have been here for him.

And now cool, soft arms envelop me, and the hospital smell gives way to the mingled aroma of apples and the beach.

Summer is here.

'Twinnie! I've missed you so much. How can I ever thank you for coming?' Her voice tinkles like silver. I turn and meet my sister's gaze. Her aqua eyes are steady and warm. She doesn't examine me—my haircut and eyebrows go unnoticed—she just stares into my soul. I wonder, not for the first time, whether there's anything I could ever do that wouldn't meet with her instant, free-flowing forgiveness. She's so trusting it kills me.

'I feel so bad,' she says. 'I swore not to leave Tarky alone for a second, but you guys took so long. I was busting for a pee, and I thought you would never get here!'

Adam looms towards us, and I step back before I get caught in the spousal embrace. He kisses Summer on the lips, a soulful, ardent kiss. Is that *tongue*, while his son's lying here in a coma? I can hardly bear to look. Then he lets go and gazes at his wife as though he's seeing her for the first time.

Summer truly is a thing of beauty. She's put on a kilo or two since I saw her in New Zealand a couple of months ago, but it's gone on in the right places. She's as curvy and golden as a peach and, as always, unconscious of her charm. She wears faded denim shorts and a cotton shirt that shows a glimpse of bronze midriff. Even in casual clothes, she looks like a girl in a catalogue; I feel overdressed in my red miniskirt and heels. Summer's legs are muscled, tanned, flawless. Mine might be skinnier, but they must look wobbly and pale.

Actually, there's one flaw. Summer leans over Tarquin's still body, and I glimpse the long red 'S' that snakes up her right inner thigh, disappearing into her shorts. I can never see my sister's scar without a guilty pang.

Adam picks up Tarquin's medical chart and settles into the bedside chair to read it. Uh-oh. Looks like we're here for the night. In fact, it's hard to imagine that the doting father will be able to tear himself away and set off across an ocean while his son-and-heir languishes at death's door.

Why have I come here? They didn't feed me enough on the plane, and hunger is putting an edge on everything. Is it gauche to ask for a bite of hot food and a comfortable place to lie down? Summer and Adam are whispering now, and all I can hear is *Tarq, Tarky, Tarquin*. Even if it weren't the world's most annoying name, you would hate it after you'd been in a room with this pair for five minutes. At least right now they have something real to worry about, instead of whether these organic rusks contain sugar or whether the moron needs yet another slathering of sunscreen.

It's hard to say which is more disgusting, their simmering chemistry or their shared obsession with the little tyke. Summer has entirely forgotten that Tarquin's not her own kid, although you would think the fact that he didn't come with a hundred-million-dollar sweetener would be a constant reminder. Then there is the fact that he doesn't look a bit like her. He takes after Adam, although his copper-coloured hair apparently comes from Helen, a mark of her Aboriginal heritage.

Summer never had a chance to get to know Helen, who was busy dying of something or other while Tarquin fought for his little life in neonatal intensive care. Adam wouldn't leave Helen's side, so the first glimpse he had of his baby was a photo of Tarquin in a nurse's arms that someone brought to Helen's ward. Months later, Adam had that photo blown up and hung on his living room wall.

Because the nurse in the photo is Summer. That's how she met Adam. She was nursing his baby while he watched his wife die. Afterwards, she was so sweet on the motherless little rat that Adam asked her to be Tarquin's godmother. They kept in touch after Tarquin was discharged from the neonatal unit, and then they started dating.

I don't know what I was hoping to find in Thailand. I thought we would be partying as the adults did back in the day. But reality has bitten. Summer's wrapped up in her own family. I slink towards the door. Maybe I can find a restaurant somewhere near the hospital. Or a bar.

'Sorry, Iris, we've kept you here far too long,' Summer says. 'I've got a meal and your bed ready on *Bathsheba*. Let's go.'

After one last lecherous kiss between her and Adam, she hefts my suitcase up, and we're out of there.

———

Outside the hospital are bustling streets, full of lights and shops, foot traffic and motor scooters. Heads turn as Summer and I walk past, naturally falling into step. We are one set of identical twins who still get noticed whenever we're together. Instant celebrity status. Summer is an it girl, a blonde bombshell. And I'm her mirror.

When I tell people about Summer's beauty, they always look at me funny. Is this my coy way of announcing that I think I'm a goddess? But it isn't. I am identical to Summer, but when I'm apart from her, I'm no one special. I don't turn heads. I'm just another reasonably pretty young woman who no doubt looks like she's trying too hard.

Summer doesn't have to try. Even in her nursing greens, hair tied back, face devoid of make-up, she's got it. Everywhere she goes, she's the sun in the morning sky. The first rose of spring. And I'm her shadow, her double, her ultimate accessory.

Summer finds a taxi. 'Yanui Beach,' she tells the driver. The name is familiar, but I can't think from where.

We zoom through the sparkling streets and I'm struck again by how much Phuket has changed. It's like seeing a beautiful woman ruined by age.

Summer catches my look. 'I know,' she says. 'The Phuket we loved is gone. Adam and I can't stand how crowded it is.' She squeezes my arm. 'But it feels good to have you here. It feels . . . right. Like we can let go of our memories of this place together.'

My heart has been beating too fast since I don't know when, and when she says this, it drops back into rhythm, slow and steady. Maybe my heartbeat is matching Summer's now that we're together. Something's changed since the last time I saw her, but I'm struggling to figure out what it is. She was as kind to me then, in the Southern Alps, as she is here. Summer is always kind, always blind to any kind of rivalry, but it's not grating on me anymore.

The taxi heads south, along a freeway that I don't remember.

'Yanui Beach,' I say to Summer. 'When did we go there?'

Summer shrugs. 'I don't remember,' she says. 'Everything's changed so much. Yanui is pretty, but it's jam-packed with restaurants. There are good points to the changes, though. Everyone speaks English now, and there are so many shops catering to Western tastes.'

Something in me preferred having to speak and eat Thai when in Thailand, but I let the comment pass. 'Why aren't you staying in a marina?' I ask.

Summer whispers her explanation, leaning so close that her breath tickles my ear. 'It's too risky to take *Bathsheba* into the marina when it's already checked out of customs.'

My dreams of cocktails and billionaires drift away in the steaming air. Oh well, that's not why I'm here. I'm here to sail. With Adam.

We leave the freeway and twist and turn through streets as busy as if it were bright day. Gangs of Western men with impressive beer bellies saunter past along the busy footpaths, drinks in hand. Thai girls loiter in the doorways to pubs— brothels?—wiggling in tinselly dresses.

'Are those girls legal?' I ask. 'They look twelve.'

'Most of them are older than they look,' says Summer, 'but it has been troubling us. In fact, we support a charity that helps get under-age girls out of the industry. Phuket's not all like this, though, Twinnie. There are unspoiled parts, and the yachting community is so lovely. We've made the best friends. It's hard to leave them.'

Summer makes 'the best friends' everywhere. She can leave them behind because she knows she'll make more wherever she goes. When she and Adam bought the yacht, she told me that they planned to spend six months sailing around the Seychelles, visiting Adam's extended family. Summer is unafraid of the deluge of in-laws.

At last we turn down a narrow street lit up with restaurants, and I glimpse perfect white sand. We're inches from the beach. Between ramshackle buildings, I see the black shining jewel that is the night ocean. The Andaman Sea. Through the open window, the eternal fresh smell of the wilderness wafts over me.

Summer pays the driver a sinful amount. 'That's almost the last of my baht,' she mutters, before disappearing into a shop for some last-minute supplies. I take off my red high heels and press my feet into the soft, crystalline sand. Even at night it's warm from the sun.

Yanui Beach. The name comes back to me. This is where Dad died. This is the place where I left my dreams. It's the last place I remember being happy, on our sailing holidays with Dad, after the divorce.

The last holiday, the Easter when we were thirteen, we sailed all the way to the Andaman Islands, spending two nights at sea. Dad made Summer and me take a watch together, sailing the boat through the black night so he could get some sleep. He said that he had taken on adult responsibilities at thirteen and that it had been the making of him. But Summer was so scared and useless that I sent her to bed and sailed *Bathsheba* on my own.

And it turned out Dad was right. I grew up that night. There were twenty tons of exquisite sailboat under my command, responding to my every move like a dance partner, and I tuned sails and hand-steered with an instinct I'd barely known I had. It was as though I'd been born to it. Sometimes when I played the piano, especially if no one else could hear me and I was just playing, not practising for an exam or concert, my hands felt like this—alive and natural, as though they knew things about life and living that I myself didn't know. At *Bathsheba*'s helm, my whole body stirred with that same sense of knowing, of being alive, of everything being right.

When Dad came on deck in the mauve dawn, *Bathsheba* was skimming through the milky waters of the Andaman Sea on a beam reach, eating up the miles. Dad had reefed the genoa before he went to bed, to keep things gentle, but I had unfurled it inch by inch, and now it was as full as a dream, and we were flying. Ahead, on the western horizon, a dark shape shimmered. South Andaman Island. Landfall.

Dad couldn't believe how many miles we'd made, and as the sun warmed the back of my neck, I basked in rare paternal praise. Summer, emerging sleepy-eyed from her quarter berth, accepted Dad's sarcastic rebuke as her due and congratulated me, while Ben stared at me as though I was some kind of sorceress.

'One day I'll take you across an ocean,' Dad said, and I was elated enough to reply, 'No, I'll take you!' Ben and Summer stiffened, and I thought I'd gone too far, but my father laughed, slapped me on my back, and said, 'Keep sailing, skipper, and I'll fry the bacon.'

I was on top of the world. Back then, there was no race to marry, no will that pitted us against our half-sisters, no need to have kids at all. Now I'm twenty-three, and for the first time in my life, I feel old. I can't believe I've let five years go by since I reached marriageable age and I still haven't produced the magic heir. An ugly halfwit could have done it by now, and here I am, brilliant and beautiful—well, perhaps not beautiful, but pretty enough—and still not pregnant. Even after Noah moved out, I took a few pregnancy tests in the hope he'd left me a small but significant parting gift, but no luck. Now my marriage is one hundred per cent over, and I have to wait twelve months before I can even get divorced. It's a disaster.

The one point of light, the one glimmer of hope, is that however dumb I've been these last five years, Summer's been dumber. Ever since she was fourteen, she has clung to the dopey idea that she's not going to let the will rule her life. She says she's happy with the money she and Adam have together. They are comfortable by most people's standards. Let's face it, they are wealthy. Just not Carmichael-fortune wealthy.

And Summer still says that Tarquin's 'enough for now' and that she's in no hurry to give Adam another baby.

Not even for a hundred million dollars.

———

Summer emerges from the shop and grabs my suitcase. She struggles with its weight.

'I'm sorry,' I say. 'I didn't realise we'd be at anchor. I would have packed lighter.'

'It's no problem,' says Summer.

I follow her down the beach. Restaurants have set out tables and chairs on the sand, and rows of *farang* are eating and drinking in the half-dark, but we glide past and leave them at the high-tide mark. The tide is a long way out, and down on the wet sand, in the darkness, we find the rarest thing in Asia: solitude.

The moon has not yet risen, but stars glimmer overhead. A *soi* dog slinks away from my sister as she trudges ahead of me towards a black shape at the water's edge.

'Do you recognise Solomon?' she asks.

Does she mean the dog? No—the looming shape ahead merges with my memory of the name.

Solomon, our dinghy. An antique rowing dory, crafted from New Zealand kauri, painted black to match *Bathsheba*. It waits for us in the shallows, quiet as an ambush.

It's not the most practical tender. There's no room to mount an outboard on its fine stern. I'm amazed Summer and Adam haven't replaced it with a motorised dinghy. Summer is no oarswoman.

My hand grips *Solomon*'s gunwale, and as the smooth timber warms my skin, I feel my childhood shimmering around me in the night. All the best moments, before Dad died. I learned to row in this dinghy, long before Summer or Ben could. And then we kids went everywhere in *Solomon*. We were free to explore beaches and coves, streams and caves. I was in charge.

And now *Solomon* belongs to Summer. I'm surprised to see my sister's dug the dinghy's anchor firmly into the sand against the rising tide. She was always useless at that sort of thing—but perhaps Adam did it.

'Can I row?' The words slip out of me.

'Of course,' Summer says. 'Twinnie, you're the skipper now! Adam and I know what a great sailor you are. I've told him how when we were teenagers you were always racing around the buoys with those blokes from the yacht club. We wouldn't dream of giving you orders. While you're here, *Bathsheba* is your ship.'

Two weeks or more of murmuring orders to Adam. I could get used to that.

Summer stows my suitcase in *Solomon* while I retrieve the anchor. We throw our shoes on top of the suitcase and push the dinghy into the calm water, cool and soft around our ankles.

'You get in now. Sit in the stern,' I say, holding the dinghy steady for her. Summer obeys. She's more agile than she used to be, but *Solomon* still shudders as she clambers to her seat.

I steer *Solomon* into deeper water, hitching up my skirt. Summer's right to put me in charge. I can't help but take control, the thousand habits that keep us safe at sea flooding back into my body like muscle memory. Take *Solomon* deep, don't let the bottom scrape the sand. Get everyone else in the dinghy first, keep the fine bow seaward. I could do this even if waves were crashing around us; I used to relish the challenge of launching a dinghy in surf, but the Andaman Sea is a millpond tonight. Still, good to keep up my seamanship. I push my feet against the seabed and alight in my rowing seat in one movement, grabbing the oars and pulling away from shore. I glance over my shoulder and see four or five anchor lights a few hundred metres away. No doubt the highest of these shines from *Bathsheba*'s masthead.

'Wait!' says Summer, but it's too late. We're in deep water already.

'What?'

'That's our last touch of land for two or three weeks,' she says. 'It feels like we should do something, say goodbye.'

'Our last touch of land?'

'We leave at first light,' she says.

My blood surges. No more tedious Tarquin, no more noisy traffic, no more sex tourists and child whores. I was excited to be coming to Phuket, but there's nothing for me here anymore. I'm ready to leave. Tomorrow, I'll be free. Tomorrow, it'll be me and the sweet blue ocean. Me and—

'We?' I say. 'What do you mean, we? Don't you mean Adam and me?'

'Oh, I can't believe Adam didn't tell you,' Summer says. 'There's been a last-minute change of plan. We didn't account for Thai bureaucracy. Seems they need a legal guardian to stay with Tarky to consent to any further medical procedures, and Adam is his only living guardian. So Adam has to stay.'

She has ripped away my reason for coming here, and I can't say a word.

Summer's face is in darkness, silhouetted against shoreside lights, but she must be able to see my expression. I turn to face the bow, as if trying to pick out *Bathsheba*'s form among the flock of anchored yachts.

'You're upset,' Summer says, 'but don't you see how much better this is? I mean, you and Adam barely know each other. What would you do out there for weeks on end?'

Adam's not coming. From the slump in my heart, I know it was he who lured me here. Two or three weeks alone with Adam, breathing his smell, gazing into his abyssal eyes, thrilling to his voice.

And yet it would have been agony. Brotherly jests, clumsy gallantry, me close to bursting with forbidden desire. It's not like he was going to dump Summer just because I sail better.

Summer said 'we', so she must mean that she and I will be sailing, but there's no way she is happy about this. Summer relies on Adam to keep her safe at sea. Sailing is hard physical work, and Summer, for all her grace, is a poor yachtswoman, slow and blundering.

I know what they want me to do. I assume a blank expression and turn back to Summer. I keep pushing the oars through the silky water.

'You want me to sail *Bathsheba* on my own, don't you?' I ask.

'You've always said that you wanted to,' says Summer.

She's right. I have always skited about my seamanship, and it is possible to sail *Bathsheba* single-handed. But a solo voyage means being on watch twenty-four hours a day, catching snatches of sleep where I dare. It means weeks of utter solitude, utter isolation.

Perhaps this is what I need. Leave my sister and her perfect life behind. Face my demons out there in the blue void.

No way. I regret my teenage bravado. If Summer thinks I'm keen on a solo voyage, I'm going to have to let her down. Being all alone out there would drive me crazy in half a day.

'I'm joking!' Summer cries. 'Do you think I would let you cross an ocean on your own when you're already having such a hard time? Besides, I love you, Iris. I want to be with you! Don't you see it's perfect? You've got me all to yourself all the way to Africa. Ooh, Twinnie! After we've lived apart for so long, it'll be such a bonding experience! I've never been so excited about anything in my life!'

She forgets where she is and lunges forward to hug me. *Solomon* lurches. I throw my body to starboard and press the oars down hard to stop both of us ending up in the sea.

CHAPTER 4

THE SURPRISE

I'm lying on a squab in *Bathsheba*'s cockpit, my arms pressed against the warm grain of the teak deck. My body rocks to the sweet rhythm of the tropical sea, and the lightest zephyr, the ghost of the night breeze, ruffles my bare limbs.

No blanket here. I've slept in my underwear. I sit up and take my first daytime look at Thailand. Yanui Beach is quiet at dawn, with a few dogs dotting the sand, a couple of hundred metres from the anchorage. Behind the beach, the land is heavily wooded. It's hard to connect this idyll with the bulging, jaded metropolis I glimpsed last night. The tables have been cleared from the beach, and the restaurants are hidden by foliage.

The other yachts anchored nearby are all ocean-going vessels. Each flies its flag from the stern, and from here I can pick out the Stars and Stripes and the Union Jack. One sloop flies the Australian flag, like *Bathsheba*. The crews of these boats must be sleeping below. I can imagine I'm the only person left alive in the world.

Summer keeps a fruit bowl in the pilot house, and I peel a banana and wander to the side deck to drop the skin overboard. At the splash, dark shapes flurry out from under the hull. Remoras. I remember these fish. They live under the hulls of yachts, pressed against the keel. They used to follow *Bathsheba* from one bay to the next, hitching a lift, living off scraps thrown overboard. They're like ghoulish ladies-in-waiting. Banana skin is not to their taste, though, and they take one sniff and dart back where they came from.

I stare down, absorbing the emerald warmth of the sea. We're anchored in deep water, but it's so clear I can make out hints of the ivory sand beneath. I slept in the best bed in the world. *Bathsheba*'s cockpit is the right length for my body, and the clink of her tall rigging, the creak of her timbers, the lap of wavelets, these sounds are my favourite lullaby.

Summer, true to her word, has treated me as skipper since I stepped on board. Last night, she presented me with Adam's sailing cap, which has 'Skipper' embroidered on it in gold thread. She has a set of these caps. Hers reads 'Crew' and is stupidly big on her head, and Tarquin's baby-sized cap reads 'Cabin Boy'. Summer carried my suitcase to *Bathsheba*'s stateroom, from which she had already removed her and Adam's things, squeezing herself back into the snug port quarter berth she and I shared as kids. The starboard quarter berth has been converted into a cosy nursery for Tarquin, or I should say restored to a nursery, since this is where Ben used to sleep when he was small enough to need bars on his cot.

To get below decks, I had to step over two childproof gates: one between the cockpit and the pilot house, and another between the pilot house and the ladder down to the saloon. The saloon occupies *Bathsheba*'s central space and comprises an open-plan galley, dining area and leather couch. Everything was as neat and nautical as ever, and starlight was streaming in from the round ports and the deck hatches that serve as skylights.

Bathsheba's layout is simple. From the saloon, doors lead aft to the quarter cabins, which are cramped and low, squashed under the pilot house. Another door leads forward to the stateroom, which spans the width of the yacht, with room for a plush, full-sized double bed and every convenience, even a TV bolted to the wall. The last door, of course, leads to the bathroom with its double mirror.

While I unpacked, Summer whipped up a spicy meal, *gang garee gai*; she remembered that I love Thai food. She poured me a glass of wine 'to celebrate our reunion'.

'I'm sorry it's not under better circumstances,' I said.

'But I'm so moved that you came for me,' she gushed. 'You're the best sister in the world. Let's make tonight special. Tarky's out of danger. He's in good hands, and the doctor said he could be discharged in a week or two. So let's focus on us.' She hesitated. 'I feel I didn't help things when I came to Queenstown.'

Only my sister could blame herself for the disintegration of my doomed marriage. She ought to have been exulting in having been proven right all along.

Summer has stuck to her plan of never telling a boyfriend about the will. Even though she's gifted, good-natured and gorgeous, she's been dumped more than once, and I've seen her sobbing her heart out over some worthless loser. Yet she never wavered. She didn't even tell Adam until after their wedding. What a honeymoon bonus for him.

I wish I had done the same with Noah. I didn't want the will to influence Noah's decision to marry me, but he was dithering, and I thought it might hurry things up a bit. Noah and I had been seeing each other in Melbourne for a few months, but then he accepted a junior partnership at a law firm in his home town in New Zealand. When I rang Summer to tell her about his planned departure, she announced that she and Adam had just got engaged.

Noah hadn't really broken up with me. Not completely. We were going to live in different countries and see other people for a while, that's all. I wanted him to take his time and be sure, but I thought he should be fully informed about the financial situation. Maybe he wouldn't even need to take this job with the fortune in our sights. We could elope, have a baby and be rolling in riches within a year.

The plan went well at first. The day after I told Noah about the fortune, we applied to be married on short notice. Within a fortnight, we were husband and wife, and I had moved to Queenstown with Noah and even wangled my way into a position at his firm. I didn't really want the job, but I didn't think it would be for long. I would be pregnant by the time I flew back to Wakefield for Summer's wedding. Things were looking good.

The first sign of trouble was when Noah didn't want to go to Summer's wedding a few months later. Something was wrong, but I didn't know what. Was he angry that I wasn't pregnant already? God knows we'd been trying. And Summer and Adam weren't rushing to have a baby. They were going to buy *Bathsheba* and sail around the world with Tarquin.

Lawyers have a stressful job, especially new partners, and I could overlook a few indiscretions. The trace of another woman's perfume, a purring voice in the background when Noah called to say I should go ahead and eat dinner on my own because he'd be working late again—these things don't matter in the big picture. Lori was his ex-girlfriend, a childhood sweetheart. Now they were back at the same firm, I could see how it could happen. I didn't care, did I?

But Noah and I weren't even having sex anymore.

Around this time, Summer came to visit. While she was in New Zealand, she tried to persuade Noah to give our marriage another go. I had a bad feeling about it all along. Once you've spent time with the nicer version of me, why would you stay? Summer did her best, but Noah moved out while I was dropping her at the airport.

I went on deluding myself that I could stay in Queenstown and keep working at his law firm. We were going to stay friends, Noah and I. And Lori. We're all adults. And if I was dignified and professional, or if he saw me dating some hot new guy, surely he would see what he was giving up and come running back to me. Maybe we wouldn't get back together permanently, but I only needed him around for a month or two. Hell, one night might do it. Doesn't everyone have sex with their ex a few times before they break up for good? It still seemed a better bet than trying to find a new husband, all the while hoping Summer would stay childless long enough for my divorce to come through.

Turns out that working for your ex alongside the woman he cheated with is one long exercise in humiliation, and sex with your ex isn't always a thing. Who knew. And when you do manage to snare a halfway decent-looking guy to dangle in front of your ex, he says, 'Good for you, Iris. I'm glad you're happy.' And the new guy says, 'You just wanted to show me off to your ex? Don't call me again.'

So that was New Zealand.

None of it seems to matter now that I'm here. I walk around *Bathsheba*'s deck, checking that everything is shipshape, and it feels as though I've dropped my problems overboard.

Dad and I used to dream about this passage, so I know what's ahead. A long glide westward across the Bay of

Bengal, then we'll dart south to cross the equator—squalls, doldrums—then a fast, wild ride across the western Indian Ocean, chased by the blustery southeast trades. Landfall in the Seychelles is about a fortnight away.

Time is of the essence. This late in the season, the easterly monsoon is weak, and in Thailand's long wind shadow, where we are now, it dies out each day by midday. The result is eerie stillness—hot, windless and rolly. One Easter holiday, we spent two hours in the middle of each day drifting and sweating on a painted ocean, like doomed ancient mariners. Dad refused to start the engine. He was what's known in yachting circles as a 'purist', which means someone too tight to motor, or to install a decent fuel tank, because he prefers to watch his crew wilt, even if his crew are his children. Especially if they're his children.

But apart from the over-reliance on her sails, *Bathsheba* is perfect. She's sixty feet long, but she's small for her length, as slender and light as a thoroughbred horse. Her mast is tall, and her Bermudan rig enables her to sail fast upwind. Summer and Adam have replaced the rigging here in Thailand, and it's flawless and new. It gleams in the morning light.

I'm most at home up here on deck. The stateroom has plenty of portholes and hatches for fresh air, but it's still claustrophobic on a warm night.

I fell asleep down there last night, shattered from my flight, while Summer was still plying me with food and wine. She was in a confessional mood, as if trying to set the scene for our transoceanic twin-bonding marathon. In fact, as I stretched out on the bed and let my eyes swim shut, I'm sure she started talking about her sex life.

'He likes to take things slow,' she was saying. 'I never feel rushed. He lights candles and gives me roses, and he knows just how to touch a woman. He gets so hard . . .'

Summer couldn't really be telling me this, could she? She's always been so prim. In my half-sleep, I struggled to make sense of what I heard.

'The sweet things he says when we make love,' Summer went on, 'even when he's thrusting so deep that it aches . . . And when he kisses me, it's like he's thirsty. He says it's like kissing the sun.'

I stand at *Bathsheba*'s bow and try to convince myself that I dreamed the conversation. Summer never talks like this. But I remember pulling a pillow over my ears, determined not to hear more. And then I surely did dream, because I felt firm lips pushing against my own, and I kissed back and opened my mouth wide, even though I knew I shouldn't be doing this, that this wasn't Noah, this wasn't my husband. He smelled so spicy-good, and his strong arms held me tight, pinning mine at my sides, but I didn't care, I wanted it. He pushed his tongue deep into my mouth, and with a tingle of surprise, I felt that his tongue was hard, impossibly hard, rock-hard.

It was too much to wake up in the stateroom, in Summer and Adam's sumptuous bed. The lights were out. Hours must have passed; Summer must have fallen asleep somewhere.

Desperate to shake off the dream, blushing in the dark, I stumbled up to the deck, where I threw myself on the nearest squab and fell asleep in the moonlight.

Now, I see Summer has already hoisted *Solomon* onto the davits at *Bathsheba*'s stern, and she's stowed the swimming ladder. There's no easy way to climb back on board, and I don't have time to waste on leisure, but this journey is going to be epic: I can't leave without some kind of ceremony. I climb the pulpit, high above the water, where I can look straight down at the black links of the anchor chain coiling into the deep. Unseen beneath me, buried in the seabed, *Bathsheba*'s big anchor is the only thing holding me to land. The ocean lures. The air sings. I raise my arms above my head. And I dive.

———

An hour later, we're sailing. My sister was roused either by the splash when I hit the water or my fist pounding on the hull once I resurfaced. She rushed up on deck and let the ladder down for me, beaming with admiring eyes.

'You're such a mermaid,' she said, extending an arm to help me over the stanchions and onto the side deck, where I stood with a salty puddle forming at my feet. 'You're so at home in the ocean. I feel so safe in your hands.'

We breakfasted on mango and passionfruit waffles, I checked the forecast, Summer made one last phone call to Adam, and we were off. Like Dad, I hoisted the mainsail before winching up the anchor, and *Bathsheba* drifted away from the continent of Asia silently, under sail.

Now I unfurl the new genoa while Summer helms. In her lubberly way, she points us straight downwind. With the wind directly behind us, each swell rocks *Bathsheba* from side to side, and the wind threatens to flick behind the mainsail. If that happens, we'll gybe: the mainsail and the boom will crash across the cockpit. On *Bathsheba*, the boom is at head height for anyone foolish enough to stand on the aft deck instead of safely within the cockpit. In an uncontrolled gybe, the boom could knock you unconscious, knock you overboard or kill you. Dad acknowledged that it was a design flaw, but he resisted having the boom raised, since the mainsail would have to be shortened, and that would slow us down.

I take the helm and alter course so that there's no risk of crash-gybing. The motion improves, and we speed up. We're on a broad reach, the best point of sail for *Bathsheba*. Summer, apologetic, tidies away the breakfast dishes and goes for a nap, aware there are nights ahead of little sleep.

The breeze sweeps across the stern from the northeast, and *Bathsheba* picks up her skirts and dances westward. I'm in charge, hand-steering, my eyes scanning the blue horizon. Flying fish skitter ahead of *Bathsheba*'s fine bow and leap in her wake. Behind me, the sun rises golden above Thailand, as the land fades to a low silhouette.

I fall into the rhythm, reacting to the gusts and lulls in the air, the crests and troughs in the water, as though I don't know where my body ends and *Bathsheba* begins. The tiller hums with the ocean's song. By midmorning, we're well out to sea. We've escaped Thailand's wind shadow, and nothing can stop us now.

My skin tingles with the warming sun. I'm alert, watching the compass, the weathervane, the sails, the water, but I barely need to think. My feet press into the timber; I've found my sea legs. I taste salt on my lips.

This is what I am born for. This is being alive.

———

Summer emerges in the noonday sun, balancing a platter of blueberries, camembert and caviar. It seems you can buy anything in Phuket these days.

'There isn't room in the fridge for everything,' she says, 'so you'll be doing me a favour by stuffing yourself with these. Let me flick on the autohelm so you can sit in the pilot house with me.'

I bite back the urge to criticise armchair sailing. Summer's right; it's absurd to hand-steer all the way across an ocean. Most sailors use their autohelm twenty-four hours a day and pass the long hours and days of a passage lolling in the pilot house, glancing around every few minutes to check for traffic. They might look at the electronic chart once an hour and scribble in the ship's log once a day. Only the rare sight of another ship or a change in wind or weather will force them out to the cockpit to handle the sails. Dad was an old-school sailor who trained us to use both paper and electronic charts, but even he was so fond of the autohelm that he nicknamed it Dave and liked to tell people that Dave was 'the best sailor on the boat'. But Dad insisted that we all learn to hand-steer, and for me, it's still my favourite way to sail, eking the best out of wind and wave, communing with sea and air.

Bathsheba, unusually for a yacht her size, has a tiller rather than a wheel, and when I take it in my hand or press it between my knees, steering by bending my legs to port or starboard in time with each rolling swell, it's like the ocean is breathing through my body. But this is a pastime for fresh mornings and clear nights, not long afternoons under the punishing Asian sun. Summer pushes a button, Dave wheezes to life, and I join my sister for a feast in the pilot house's welcome shade. Windows of reinforced glass give us wraparound views of sea and sky, and we naturally sit looking past each other, both of us scanning the surface with a sailor's instinct for the watch.

'It's hard to leave so many good mates behind in Thailand.' Summer sighs as I eat. 'But I know we'll make new friends wherever we go. It's hard to believe that I used to be not-so-keen on the yachting life. Another thing I have you to thank for, Iris. You opened my eyes to the magic of life on board, and now I can't imagine not living on *Bathsheba*. My life is paradise.'

The land has disappeared in our wake now, and *Bathsheba*, despite her swift motion, is poised in the exact centre of a circle of perfect blue. Summer seems remarkably at ease. Neither of us suffers from seasickness, but she always used to be frightened of the open sea.

'But you can't afford to live on board forever, can you?' I ask. 'Adam has to go back to work sometime?'

Summer gave up nursing when she married Adam, taking over the care of Tarquin. They could afford it, and they can afford a very long holiday, leaving the travel agency in Adam's parents' hands, but their money won't last forever.

Summer jerks her eyes away. 'This . . . this is what I was trying to explain last night,' she says. 'It didn't seem fair to set off on a serious passage like this without telling you all the facts, but I didn't realise how tired you were. You fell asleep in the middle of our conversation.'

By now I'd almost convinced myself that Summer's porno talk last night was a jet-lag-induced nightmare, but her coy blush tells me not only that it was real, but that she's about to start up again.

'The thing is,' she says, 'I know I've had a lot of boyfriends, maybe even more than you, but I wasn't getting out of it what everybody probably assumed. It's not that I'm frigid, more what you might call slow to warm up. To be honest, most of my boyfriends, I didn't even sleep with them. I could tell it wasn't going to happen, if you know what I mean.'

Prissy little Summer. It's like I already knew this. Nobody can be as virtuous as Summer has always seemed without really being a bit of a prude.

Now it feels as though she's undressing in front of me, but who am I to interrupt? I push another mouthful of blueberries between my lips and close them. I'm a bit grossed out, but I have to find out where this is going.

'Even when I first married Adam . . . Don't get me wrong, we were in love, but things still didn't . . . move quickly. He was very patient. He's a lovely man.'

There's nothing I can say at this point. I can't agree. This is a side to Adam's loveliness that I can know nothing about.

'It was when we came to the tropics that everything changed,' she continues. She shifts in her seat, pulling her sarong away from the backs of her thighs, where it clings to her skin. 'The warm nights, the ocean, the way Adam smells, even when he sweats, they set me on fire. We weren't expecting it, but suddenly we were so hungry for each other, it's like we went crazy. We'd have to rush back to the boat and put Tarquin in his crib. We could hardly wait for him to fall asleep, we could hardly keep quiet.'

Summer breaks off. She's staring past me out the pilot house window, with an expression so intent, so focused, that I feel as if a great ship is bearing down on us on a collision course, but for some reason my sister won't warn me, and I can't bring myself to look. I can't take my eyes off her face, off her little rosebud mouth, even though I have a feeling it's about to pronounce my doom.

That's when she says it.

'So, there was this one time, about two weeks ago, and you know I don't drink much, but Adam had bought this bottle of rosé bubbles because, you know, he loves to buy me anything to do with roses. So we're in this little bay off the coast, sitting on the foredeck where it's a little cooler, where there's a little breeze and a little bit of swell from the south, and *Bathsheba*'s rocking a little.'

Every time she says 'little', Summer presses her finger against her thigh. Her sarong has fallen open, and I can see the long scar, the elongated S, leading upwards. It still looks like a fresh wound after all these years; Summer has mentioned that it reopened recently, as coral cuts tend to do. I wonder if it will ever fade, if it will ever heal properly.

'And Tarquin was asleep, thank goodness, because I start thinking about Adam, about his body, and it's like my pussy takes over my brain.'

I've never heard Summer say *pussy* before. It's like she's purring; the word breathes across the space between us, tickling the air.

'My whole body was throbbing. I could feel my blood rushing to my skin, rushing to my breasts, and there was a sort of pulsing deep down inside. Now I understand why people go mad for sex, Iris. I had to have him, right then, right there on the foredeck. There was a bunch of hooligans partying on the next boat, not far away, and the sun was still high, it was daytime, but I didn't care. I ripped off all my clothes and pushed him onto the deck and climbed onto him.

His big, hard—God, it felt good. We made love right there, bruising ourselves on the deck, and we were so noisy, I swear half Phuket heard us, and I didn't care, I didn't care if I died.'

And now she looks me in the eye. 'I guess you've figured out what I'm trying to say.'

So this isn't the whole story. There's more. It's going to get worse.

'I want you to know that we didn't plan this,' Summer says. 'Adam's good about contraception, but I jumped him. We didn't have any condoms on board. I had them on my shopping list for the next day. I want you to know it was only that one time, and it was an accident. Because I never wanted to do this, Iris—I never wanted it to be this way between us.'

I've been so distracted by Summer's pretty story, so caught up in the dream, so busy imagining Adam's hardness rising up from the foredeck like a samson post, that only now do I hear what she's saying. And she looks so sorry, so nice-is-dumbly sorry for ruining my life, that I make it easy for her. I say what she can't bring herself to tell me.

'Congratulations. You're pregnant.'

CHAPTER 5

THE PAGEANT

When we found out about the will, I thought that Summer's and my rivalry would be intense. We were competing for a hundred million dollars. No one else was in the running. Even if there hadn't been some secret concerning Ben, he was four years younger. We would have four years to marry and reproduce before he reached eighteen.

Ben came out in his early teens, and no one was surprised. I realised the adults had known for a long time. Ben didn't prance around in sparkly hotpants or try to pash the other boys at school, but somehow, the adults all knew. Ridge Carmichael had fathered seven children, but he hadn't produced a heterosexual son.

The Carmichael name was going to die out. It must have driven my father crazy.

I guess Dad thought we would all be adults when he passed away, so he never imagined his daughters would be racing to be teen brides. He didn't want us to make the mistake he had made, which had led to him divorcing Margaret—the mistake of leaving the business of having children until too late. We girls wouldn't have the option of trying again with a younger wife.

The day after Dad's funeral I snuck into my mother's bedroom and nabbed a copy of the will. Locked in the bathroom, I hurriedly photographed each page with my phone to read later in private. The rules were laid out in plain English. My father was progressive in his own way, an equal-opportunity testator. The grandchild didn't have to be a boy. But it had to be given the Carmichael name, and it had to be first.

Technically, the money stayed in trust until this precious grandchild came of age, but the parents of the heir were the trustees and had wide powers to use the money however they liked. They could spend it on themselves or their other children, but they couldn't share it with the rest of us. My father had no interest in compensating losers. It was winner takes all.

Summer and I might have put off marriage until our thirties if it weren't for Francine and our four half-sisters. They were little girls when Dad died, but they were Francine's only hope.

Within days of Dad's funeral, Annabeth and Francine were communicating through lawyers. Plush envelopes were delivered to the beach house by signature courier. Annabeth would scuttle off to read them in her bedroom and emerge red-faced and silent. She would have long conversations on the phone—I was never sure with whom, despite a campaign of eavesdropping—weeping over Francine's lack of compassion and her own need for 'time to grieve'. *She* had been married to Dad for the longest.

None of it made any difference. Boxes sprouted in our living room while our Christmas tree still stood, brown as brushwood, in a forlorn corner. My mother's tears gave way to anger. Books were banged into boxes; pots and pans were crashed into crates. But she was careful with the crystal and the glassware. She didn't break anything.

Annabeth seemed to be packing that whole summer, making sure that 'the homewrecker', as she began to call Francine, wouldn't get her hands on any of our jewellery or china. That was when I figured out who Virginia's father was.

'The child has to be conceived and born in wedlock,' Annabeth moaned into the phone one day, as she knelt over a box half-packed with champagne flutes. 'No, it can't be legitimised retrospectively. There must be at least nine months between the wedding and the birth, or medical evidence proving the baby was premature. Yet Virginia's not excluded. Now if that isn't hypocrisy, I don't know what is. Vicky too. Vicky was born only six months after their wedding.'

Her listener must have said something soothing, because my mother's tone changed. 'Yes, yes, I know, plenty of time,' she mumbled. 'She's six. No, of course I wouldn't want the child punished for Ridge's sins, but honestly, *Virginia*, what a name to give a bastard! Might as well have named the child Adultery!'

A similar conversation took place the next day, and the next. The hot weather wore on, Ben and Summer squabbled and whinged, and Annabeth began to look for any excuse to get us out of her hair. She sent us to the beach every morning with strict instructions not to come back for two hours, but we seldom managed half so long. We would forget to bring water or run out of food; one time we forgot sunscreen, and fair-skinned Ben was so badly burned that he couldn't go back outside for a week.

Annabeth was so desperate to be alone that she forced me to gatecrash Summer's annual end-of-holiday sleepover at her best friend's house. With her soft, bovine eyes and brunette ringlets, Letitia Buckingham was exactly the sort of sweet fool Summer doted on. She and Summer had been friends since kindergarten, but I couldn't stand her.

Not content with running the PTA, Letitia's mother had set up the Wakefield Beach Committee, an organisation that specialised in ruining Wakefield Beach with unbeachy events, crowding it with unbeachy people in unbeachy clothes. So far that summer, she had staged a fashion parade and a talent quest. Mr Buckingham had laid down boardwalks over the sand so his wife could strut around in the high heels that seemed glued to her feet. I kept as far away from these events as possible, swimming at the far end of the beach where nobody would spot me.

The day after the sleepover, Mrs Buckingham was running the inaugural Wakefield Beach Junior Beauty Pageant, for girls under sixteen so that Letitia could take part. Three sashes, gold, silver and bronze, waited by the front door of the Buckinghams' house, along with a gold tiara. Mrs Buckingham had them on display as if she'd won them herself.

I pictured Mrs Buckingham wearing the tiara. Her first name was Celia, and I relished the contrast between this name—classical, ethereal—and Mrs Buckingham's great slab of a face, her body as square and slow as a bus. She was easily ten years older than Annabeth, and they would have had nothing in common if their daughters weren't thick as thieves. Annabeth, still slender and tragi-beautiful, was the sort of woman you'd expect to be running a beauty pageant, not a middle-aged monstrosity like Celia Buckingham.

Celia was drinking a cappuccino in her vast kitchen, watching us girls eat breakfast and droning on about the weather forecast (windy), which presented a problem for all those floaty ball gowns and delicate coiffures. I suggested relocating to Wakefield Mall 'and leaving the beach for people who like being outdoors'. Celia glared at me.

Annabeth had told us we were not to come home till afternoon, but that didn't mean I had to hang with the Buckinghams all day. I would head for my usual spot at the far end of the beach. I didn't need company; it'd be me and the ocean.

But when I tried to make my escape, I learned there were other plans for me. 'Your mother has paid your entry fee,'

Celia announced, standing at her front door, impassable as a rhinoceros.

I dragged out every excuse from a bad case of stage fright to 'beauty pageants exploit women', but Celia steamrolled over my words. Even Summer betrayed me, refusing to join my rebellion. 'Let's go and have fun,' she said. 'Do it for Mum. You know how hard this move is for her.'

At the beach, marquees flapped in the breeze, like a flock of giant gulls about to take flight. For now, though, the elements seemed to be held in check. I caught glimpses of sparkling ocean, free and wild, but the marquees obscured it, which was no doubt how Celia Buckingham liked things to be.

There was a long line of girls waiting to register for the pageant. They fell silent as Summer, Letitia and I walked past, the insiders who didn't need to queue. Most of them were about our age, maybe a year older. Pretty, but not that pretty.

I couldn't resist a smirk at the battle Celia must have been fighting. Letitia, lithe and bronze, would have had this contest in the bag if it weren't for her house guests.

Now Summer and Letitia were filling out the registration forms. I read mine. 'What's this about tasteful swimwear?' I asked. Like there was anything tasteful about a beauty pageant for under-age girls.

'No bikinis,' said Celia.

There was already a flock of perverts settling into the sand around the catwalk, so it was a relief to learn that none of them were going to see any bare teen torsos. But Summer and I had only brought bikinis. We had to go home and fetch one-piece togs. Summer phoned Annabeth as we walked along Beach Parade, since we'd been ordered not to turn up unannounced.

I was surprised to hear Summer trying to get out of the pageant. 'I'll help you pack, Mum, I promise this time,' she said. 'I'm sorry we've been . . . not the most helpful . . .'

I could half-hear what Annabeth was saying. Of course we should do the pageant. We were the prettiest girls in Queensland.

It was a glittering hot morning, and Summer's hair was molten gold, rippling over her tanned shoulders and down to her waist. She was wearing skimpy white shorts, and her legs had just enough muscle and grace to rescue them from being called skinny.

It was a recent transformation. I don't know whether Summer had noticed, but I had seen the way boys looked at her. And men. Neither of us had our period yet, but Summer looked like a woman. Her bra was a size bigger than mine, and her hips flared more, although we still fit the same clothes.

'That's the problem, Mum,' she said, blinking back tears. Summer cried a lot these days—she was all tender-hearted over lost puppies and that sort of crap. 'We can't both win, can we? And it will be so horrible for whichever one of us comes second.'

She hastily added, 'Not that I'm assuming anything. There were some very pretty girls back there.'

Annabeth's laugh resounded through the phone, so jubilant, exulting in Summer's modesty. Why did I never think of lines like this? I was dreading the same thing as Summer. We were twins, after all; it was scary how often we had the same thoughts, although it would never have occurred to me to pretend that my concern was unselfish, that I was worried about hurting my sister's feelings.

But that was the thing. Summer wasn't pretending.

'Of course they won't split you girls up!' Annabeth exclaimed when we got home. 'Even I can't tell you apart these days. You two are going to share that crown!'

Nice is dumb. Annabeth really believed this. And perhaps Summer believed it too, because she was about to do the nicest, dumbest thing of her life.

———

Living at the beach as we did, Summer and I owned a lot of bikinis. The only one-piece swimming costumes we had were our school swimsuits, which were modest, white and, of course, identical. Summer was going through a long phase of refusing to dress alike, even at home, so I was surprised she didn't complain.

Back at the beach, we pranced along the catwalk in our evening wear, supplied by the low-rent clothing chain that was sponsoring the event, with about thirty other hopefuls.

I tried not to look at the crowd, which included a disconcerting number of lobster-red old men.

Then we changed into swimwear. Lining up to return to the stage, I surveyed our rivals. The scrawny no-hoper twelve-year-olds whose mums were using the pageant as day care. The girls who were pretty, but too shy and backward to carry it off. The ugly dreamers.

The one thing I was enjoying was Celia's losing battle to eradicate sex from a beauty contest. She'd tried so hard, choosing a middle-aged woman, one of her friends, as a judge, and insisting on demure evening wear (below the knee) and swimwear. But it was no use. One girl was sent off the stage because her swimsuit was G-string style, but not before she attracted a round of wolf-whistles. Celia made an announcement, reminding the crowd that we were 'schoolgirls, not models'. It just made the show seem kinkier.

Ten finalists were announced: me, Summer, Letitia and seven wannabes. Celia called us back on stage and we circled until our feet ached. Was the judge still choosing between us? Someone ought to have told her that if two girls shared first place, she didn't have to choose a second place. She could place Letitia third and be done with it.

The stage was high, and I was hot and hungry and fearful that sweat patches were appearing at my armpits and crotch. And the longer we circled, the more another possibility entered my mind.

I couldn't shake the idea. Why was the judge finding this so hard? The answer was obvious. She was trying to choose between me and Summer.

Of course we weren't going to share the prize. There was one golden sash, one gold crown.

Summer didn't care who won, and you could see it. Her movements were liquid, her heart-shaped face was innocent of make-up, her smile was wholesome.

Summer was going to win. It wasn't the bigger bosom or the new, fertile curve to her hips and thighs. It was the thing Summer had that I would never have. Inner beauty. Like the bullshit they talk on the TV pageants. True beauty comes from within.

Somebody didn't want little girls crying on stage, so we were set free to sit in the audience. They were going to announce the winners any minute.

Annabeth and Ben turned up as we were finding some-where to sit. My mother wore her brittle public smile. And then Ben gave me a look, a brotherly look, a look of pity and friendship, and I saw something. Despite all the crap, I did care about the result. I didn't want to smile and clap while Summer shone in her golden tiara. This was going to suck.

I formed a desperate plan. Up on the dunes were the old public changing rooms and toilet. Celia Buckingham was ploughing her way onto the stage. Annabeth was deep in conversation with another mother.

'I'm busting,' I told Ben, and I made a dash for the loo.

From the changing rooms, I couldn't hear the actual announcements, but I could hear the tone of Celia's foghorn voice, punctuated by rounds of applause. This was fantastic. I was missing it. For the sake of realism, I sat in the stall with my white one-piece round my ankles, pretending to pee. Five more minutes and it would all be over. I could collect my loser's sash later.

I heard the clatter of running feet, a hammering on the stall. 'Darling!' Annabeth panted. 'You've won! You're the winner!' Despite her earlier confidence, she sounded surprised. Amazed.

I pulled my togs up and dashed out of the stall, forgetting to flush. I didn't think anything except that I was sharing the prize with my sister. Annabeth had been right after all. Nice is dumb doesn't always mean nice is wrong. That was fine. I was happy with first equal. I was walking on air. Running on air.

But as I approached the stage, I almost fell flat on my face. I saw that they'd announced the prize winners in reverse order, starting with third.

Summer was already up there wearing a sash, and it wasn't gold.

It wasn't silver.

Letitia was wearing the silver sash. She was smiling, her dark eyes agleam. Even in my transports of delight, I registered this, because I couldn't help being the bitch, even in my moment of triumph. Letitia's moist eyes told me she had thought *she* would win. Was she insane?

But even more insane was the fact that she had beaten Summer.

And so had I.

Summer's sash was bronze.

Not only had the judge decided I was the more beautiful twin, she'd placed another girl between us. Like she wanted the whole beach to know that it wasn't hard to choose.

Summer's eyes were dry. She was watching me, smiling with genuine love, that sunny, straight gaze. Her poise was a strange kind of victory. I could never have done what she was doing right now.

I mounted the steps to the catwalk slowly. I pulled my shoulders back. I paused midway to my place to find Ben in the audience and give him a wave, but he and Annabeth both had their eyes fixed on Summer.

I took my place between the vanquished. The judge stepped forward with my gold sash and tiara. That glittering tiara. It was magnificent.

Celia was still narrating for the audience, like they needed subtitles. Words like 'charming' and 'delightful' swirled around me in a happy cloud. Beneath me were admiring faces, clapping hands.

I was Miss Wakefield Beach. I was a beauty queen.

As the crown was placed on my head, I swung my arm in a wide, graceful arc. The beauty pageant wave. What made them choose me? Was Summer actually fat? But everybody said they couldn't tell us apart.

I forgot all my objections to beauty pageants. I was the most beautiful girl in Wakefield.

I was prettier than Summer.

'Ladies and gentlemen,' Celia continued, 'I present to you Miss Wakefield Beach: Summer Carmichael.'

That was the kind of sister I had. When I was hiding in the toilets, they announced that third place went to Iris Carmichael, and Summer went on stage and took the humiliation for me. She knew she had won, and she let me wear the sash, let me take the crown. And she was such a nice person that she thought I would love it up there, soaking up the glory meant for her, revelling in the adulation, the darling of the crowd.

Nice is dumb.

———

We nearly got away with it. It wasn't until we were about to go home, still in our swimsuits and sashes, me in my tiara, that Ben said, 'There's blood running down your leg, Iris.' He was looking at Summer, of course.

Had the scar on Summer's leg opened up, as it did from time to time? No, it wasn't that. It was her period, seeping out from her white togs. But it didn't matter where the blood came from. What mattered was that as soon as Ben said it, everybody—Annabeth, Letitia, Celia, a bunch of trailing girls—looked at Summer's thigh. Everybody saw the scar, long and red and unmistakable beneath the smear of blood. S for Summer.

Everybody knew which twin was which now. And everybody was staring at me. The ugly twin in her undeserved crown.

'Summer, darling,' came my mother's trembling voice, 'what a beautiful thing you did for your sister.'

I couldn't speak. I ripped off my sash and crashed my crown onto my sister's head. And then I took off running for the one thing I had wanted all day. The ocean.

CHAPTER 6

THE PLOT

I stare at Summer's pregnant belly. It's all over. The dream is dead.

My eyes fill with tears, and I fake a so-happy-I'm-crying vibe. Maybe Summer buys it. When you're nice, you think other people are nice too.

It's not even the money. Losing one hundred million dollars I never had doesn't feel real to me yet. What I think of is the pageant.

Letitia Buckingham cried when she came second to Summer, and I thought she was deluded. What a fool to dream of beating my sister. And yet, here I am nine years later being a bigger fool. Even though my sister is married—married to a man who loves being a dad—and even though my own marriage has fallen apart, I still believed that things would work out for me, and that the money would end up in my hands.

It seems like it ought to be mine.

I throw my arms around my sister. She smells and feels different already, as though she's softening and blurring around the new life growing inside her. There's a delicacy about her, an over-ripeness, an odour that's fruity and almost fungal. Fertility is one step away from decay.

When Adam kissed her at the hospital back in Thailand, I almost sensed the secret between them. He gazed at her as if she'd done something miraculous. She kind of has.

Noah asked me, on our wedding night, whether I was afraid of childbirth, and I heard in his voice that he wanted the pregnancy over with. He didn't want to watch me swell up and burst. I have a feeling Adam feels differently. He finds this new, full-figured Summer hotter than ever. Her breasts are already swelling; her belly is rounder.

'It's early days,' says Summer. 'Adam said I was doing everything Helen did when she was pregnant, reacting to smells and tastes, so I took one of those super-sensitive tests before I was even overdue. In fact my period was only due'— she counts—'three or four days from now. But I already knew it would be positive. I just knew.'

'I'm so happy for you, Twinnie,' I say. My guts twist and coil.

If only it was just the money, but it's not. Even without the inheritance, Summer's life is beyond perfect. She's married to the love of her life. She's on a year-long holiday on a luxurious yacht. And she's about to have what I realise she's always wanted. A baby.

'I'm happy for you too, Twinnie,' Summer murmurs. What nonsense is this? She catches my confused look.

'Adam and I will provide for you now,' she says. 'The money's safe from Francine. We can't share the inheritance with you, but we can give you our own money—Adam's money, I should say. We'll make sure you never go without. Adam's very generous, as I'm sure you'll find out.'

'Thank you.' I just about choke on the words. I feel like an old-age pensioner being promised grocery money. 'Why would you be worried about Francine, though? Virginia's only fifteen.'

'Let's not spoil the moment by talking about our step-mother,' says Summer. 'I'll fill you in on her some other time. Oh, Twinnie! I wish I could clone my life! I wish you had an Adam and a *Bathsheba* and a baby too! But you will one day, I know it! You'll have everything I've got! I'm first, that's all! Anyway, we need to make a plan. There's lots to sort out.'

For a moment I think she wants to involve me in the minutiae of her pregnancy, her birth plan and that sort of crap. There's nothing I want to talk about less. Fortunately she's being more pragmatic than that. She's talking about the voyage.

One of us has to be on watch every minute, day and night, for the next two weeks or more. Summer's been so obsequious since I stepped on board that I was thinking I could take my pick of watches, enjoying the starlit evenings and the rosy dawns, and leaving the hot noon and the graveyard shifts to my grateful sister. But now I'm at sea with a pregnant woman.

Summer is going to want her beauty sleep. All the hard parts will be my job.

———

From the age of fourteen, I played along with Summer's sweet dream, pretending that the will wasn't going to stop me marrying for love. Like Summer, I wasn't going to tell any of my boyfriends about the money.

In truth, from the day of Dad's funeral, I had a plan. The day I turned eighteen, I would marry someone. Anyone. I would go hell for leather at this baby-making lark.

My eighteenth birthday was looming, and I was about to propose to my boyfriend at the time (Kash—the name suited him perfectly) when I realised my mistake.

I wasn't that excited about my future. The money was going to be fantastic, obviously, but I was going to be married to Kash, whom I had chosen for his likely willingness to go along with the scheme, but who otherwise didn't inspire me as a life companion. I couldn't care less that I wouldn't have the fairytale wedding Summer was fond of imagining for herself, but the shameful rush to the registry office, the pregnancy wreaking havoc on my body: what teenage girl wants that?

A couple of weeks before my birthday, I asked Kash, as though it was a whimsical, off-the-wall question, how much money he would have to be offered to marry me and have a baby.

'Fifty bucks,' he said. 'As long as we're only married on paper, and I wouldn't have to, like, see the kid.'

I started thinking. Did I need to rush into this? Summer wasn't seeing anyone. My plan had assumed that Summer was like me, that she might also elope as soon as she turned eighteen to get the money.

But Summer would never do this. I knew it in my heart. No furtive scramble to the altar for her. She would be open and true. She would get married when she fell in love, and she would do everything the proper way. Announcement, engagement party, big wedding. These things take time.

I had time. I had eight years before Virginia turned eighteen. The odds were that I would find someone better than Kash. Worst-case scenario, I'd marry whomever I was dating when Summer announced her engagement. Best-case scenario, I'd actually fall in love before then.

In hindsight, Kash would have made a better husband than Noah. The irony is not lost on me.

After hours of boring reverse-negotiation (Who can be the sweetest sweetie-pie?), Summer and I settle on a watch schedule. Summer claims to enjoy sailing through the heat of the day and doesn't mind staying up late, watching darkness fall. It's getting up in the pitch black that she struggles with, being wrenched from sleep. So she'll keep watch from noon till late afternoon, then I'll take over while she prepares dinner—we both know she's the better cook. We'll eat early, while it's still light, and she'll take the sunset-to-midnight watch while I get a few hours' sleep. Then she'll wake me, and I'll stand watch till dawn. From dawn till noon is flexi-time; we'll see which of us is more tired.

'So I'm making a pregnant woman stay up till midnight every night for a fortnight,' I say. 'That hardly makes me sister of the year.'

'You have to sleep sometime.' Summer beams. 'I'll be fine. You're almost as obliging as Adam.'

We fall into a routine of day and night, wake and sleep, sun and starlight, and *Bathsheba* flies across the Bay of Bengal. It's as if Dad is still on the boat; we instinctively follow his old rules. We never leave the cockpit without clipping our harnesses to the jackstays that run the length of the deck, and as an added precaution, before stepping onto the deck, we call the other to come and watch. Most of the time, though, the sails can be handled from within the cockpit.

If something needs to be done on the foredeck during Summer's watch, I generally do it for her. In fact, I don't think she leaves the pilot house during her watches. She's not fond of handling the sails. That's fine with me. All I need is for her to be a pair of eyes so I can get some sleep.

During the first week of our passage, I discover changes to the yacht, improvements that Adam has made. I thought *Bathsheba* was perfect, but I have to admit that the bigger fridge allows for luxury dining to a standard I didn't think possible at sea. Night after night, Summer serves up fresh Thai cuisine as if she's a specialty chef on an ocean liner.

Adam has also installed an extra water tank, so instead of stewing in our own sweat until we reach port, Summer and I can shower every day—a quick, cold shower, but that's all you need in the tropics.

Summer showers at noon using the cockpit's open-air shower, a simple handheld showerhead, taking advantage of the privacy offered by an ocean passage. In the cockpit, I'm treated to a daily striptease, and there's no more schoolgirl underwear. It's all whorish bras and lacy G-strings in white and pink and scarlet.

'Adam bought me this,' she coos, dropping a sinfully tiny piece of satin studded with diamantes onto the cockpit floor. As the cold water runs over her warm skin, she shows off her lush body, her all-over tan, to the sun. She rubs wild rose shower gel over her full breasts and her almost-flat belly, and it froths in her irritatingly neat line of pubic hair. Her nipples are already swelling with pregnancy, darkening from pink to ruby red.

Her fresh underthings, always matching, always Victoria's Secret or Agent Provocateur, are waiting for her, hung over the tiller. Now I know why she left the prim stuff back in Wakefield. Her tastes have changed.

I used to be the lingerie queen, poring over catalogues, trying on the kinkiest numbers in the most luxurious stores. But I racked up too many debts, and my collection has suffered. The whites have faded to dishwater grey, the cups are sagging, and half the time I can't even match the bra to the knickers.

One thing Adam hasn't changed on this boat is the under-sized fuel tank. Fortunately, the autohelm and fridge run on solar panels, so we don't need fuel, as long as there's enough wind to keep us sailing.

I can't help but admire Adam. If Dad had shown as much consideration for Annabeth's comfort as Adam has for Summer's, maybe my mother wouldn't have wanted to get off the boat. Maybe Dad could have left Carmichael Brothers in Colton's hands, as he talked of doing, and we could all have made it to Africa back when we were still a family. Before Francine.

There's even a washing machine and a dryer, installed one over the other in a cupboard beside the bathroom. There's not enough water or power to use them at sea, but Summer has already piled her used underthings into the hamper, ready to be laundered as soon as we get to port.

'Adam installed it as a surprise,' Summer tells me when I first pull open the oak door and find the gleaming white-goods cleverly concealed behind it. She whispers in my ear, as though *Bathsheba* is listening, 'Don't tell anyone, but it's my favourite thing on the boat.'

My favourite thing is still the double mirror. Living on Summer's yacht, amid Summer's things, eating Summer's cooking, hearing about Adam and Tarquin and the baby, I almost feel I'm disappearing, dissolving in the heat. I keep an excited-auntie smile hovering on my face, ready to employ should Summer pop into view while I'm on watch in the cockpit, or resting below in the stateroom, or walking from one place to the other—this is what life is reduced to on an ocean passage. But in the bathroom, I can be me. No smile. The girl in the mirror is miserable, but at least she's real.

And I'm still a better sailor than Summer. Every day we use the sat phone to download a weather forecast and an email from Adam—Tarquin's improving slowly—but Summer's really only interested in the latter. She keeps watch OK, but I still reef down each night after dinner for her so that *Bathsheba* is manageable in the darkness, and then I shake the reefs out when she wakes me at midnight to begin my watch. The monsoon wind continues strong and steady from the starboard quarter, and each night I relish the moment when, as Summer turns in for the night, I shake the sails out, and *Bathsheba*, given free rein, breaks from a constrained canter into her tireless westward gallop.

Africa awaits.

———

Despite everything, I'm happy at *Bathsheba*'s helm. I can forget about Noah and his new girlfriend, Lori. I can forget about Summer and Adam. I can forget about the baby.

All around me is the peaceful night ocean. We haven't seen a single boat, a single sign of human life, in a week. Above me, the mast sways among the wheeling Indian stars. In the silent dark, fantasies fill my deprived senses. One night, all night, we seem to be sailing downhill, as though the ocean has tilted, and I can't shift the sense that we're going some-where I've been before, many years ago—some deep ancestral home that lurks beyond the limits of my earliest memories. Another night I surely doze on watch, because I can smell Adam, I can taste him, in the cockpit with me, encircling me in his manly arms, pressing against my mouth with that strange, hard tongue. Another night I convince myself that Summer and Adam have given me *Bathsheba*, modest compensation for their monstrous betrayal. I'm sailing around the world's oceans, rounding the Horn, steering *Bathsheba* through sleet and snow into the uncharted south, keeping watch for icebergs.

My dreams are exposed in the sober light of day, a mad-woman's folly. Summer and Adam love *Bathsheba* now; they will never give her to me. Adam will do all the hard jobs on board, and Summer will make *Bathsheba* a home, mothering Tarquin and the baby, feeding Adam, making love every night. They'll never leave the tropics. Their life will be perpetual summer.

On a passage with a crew of two, you don't see much of each other. One of you is always on watch, the other sleeping. But Summer and I sit together each evening in the cockpit after dinner, and Summer talks.

I never thought of us as drifting apart. If the will had driven a wedge between us, Summer was blissfully unaware. She was never unfriendly, not even when I eloped with Noah, stealing a march on her wedding, but now she's more than friendly. She's loving, but she was loving in Queenstown. It's something more than that. She's celebrating me. Despite the mess I've made of my life, Summer shows no pity or condescension. She treats me like a queen.

All the same, her talk is a little too much. She doesn't mean to pain me, but every topic of conversation advertises how fabulous it is to be Summer. I've always thought that raising a dead woman's kid would be tedious, but it has its benefits. Adam is so grateful to Summer for loving Tarquin that he does everything he can to make life easy for her, always arranging babysitters and nannies to ease the load, or taking Tarquin out himself to give her 'me time'.

And Tarquin is the least attractive part of Summer's life. Everything else is even better. A travel agent makes a great husband. They've only lived on *Bathsheba* a short time, but Adam has taken them to all my favourite places, Thailand's hidden jewels: the cave-islands of Phang Nga Bay; the coral gardens of the Surins; Paradise Beach, where elephants come to bathe. While *Bathsheba*'s rigging was being replaced, Adam flew Summer up to Burma for a 'second honeymoon', leaving Tarquin with a nanny. They hadn't even been married a year.

The most sickening part is that Adam's such a romantic. I wouldn't mind if Summer was sharing pervy stories about kinky sex on night beaches, but there's more to it than that. Adam is deeply in love. I guess the dead wife taught him that life is fleeting, so now he piles on the candlelit dinners, the spontaneous gifts—jewellery, perfume, white lingerie—the slow seductions, each as fresh and unassuming as a first date.

'He still looks shy when he kisses me,' she says, 'and yet his kisses are so *masterful*. He does things no other man would dare to do, but they're amazing. I can't even begin to describe what he does. Let's just say he loves to give me pleasure. His control is extraordinary He drives me wild.'

Tonight, though, things are different. I have to interrupt Summer's chatter because the wind is changing. *Bathsheba* is sluggish, as though finally tired out, and her sails flap.

'We've outrun the monsoon,' I tell Summer. 'This wind is only going to get lighter, and soon it'll change and we'll be beating into it. We need to cross the equator now.'

Summer tries not to look surprised. She fetches the paper chart from the pilot house and spreads it across the cockpit seat, weighing it down with her dinner plate. 'Adam drew a course,' she says. 'Where are we now?'

'This isn't a straight east-to-west passage,' I say, leaning over the chart dismissively, but Adam's pencilled line is in fact similar to my own passage plan. Not bad for a novice. About halfway across the Indian Ocean, the line zigzags south for about three hundred miles before resuming a westward course.

But it's not surprising that we've made the same plan; this is the only logical route. In the northern hemisphere, the monsoon has taken us as far as it can, but luckily for us, as it dies, the southeast trades spring into life in the southern hemisphere. They'll be strengthening as March turns to April. Wind and waves will be more boisterous than here in the north, and we'll bounce all the way to Africa.

The problem is getting to the trade winds. The equatorial zone is only three hundred miles north to south, but it's a hard three hundred miles, where the wind comes in crazy squalls between long windless stretches, and the swells roll in all directions at once. Paradoxically, yachts lurch and wallow more without wind to steady their sails, and our family's previous equator crossing, back in Indonesia, is the only time I remember being seasick. Most sailors motor straight across the zone, and I plan to do the same, although it will use up most of *Bathsheba*'s fuel.

'I wish we could stop somewhere for a while,' says Summer. 'I feel more tired each day.'

I feel the same. But we're a long way from civilisation. The Maldives, the nearest country on the chart, would be a long slog upwind from here. They're already far behind us.

'I'm tired too,' I say. My skin prickles at the thought that Summer is overexerting herself in early pregnancy. What if she were to miscarry? It would be awful for her, and it's not like it would help me. She would be pregnant again in no time. But what was it she said about Francine?

It's strange being a twin. Neither of us has mentioned our stepmother since the day Summer told me she was pregnant, over a week ago, but Summer's next words are 'I still need to tell you about Francine.'

While I set *Bathsheba* on her new southerly course, Summer takes our dishes and the chart below decks and comes back with her iPad.

'You're friends with Virginia on Facebook, right?' she asks. 'So what was the last update you saw from her?'

My half-sister's Facebook posts are an endless series of boring schoolgirl memes, but I can't remember seeing any news from her in a while. 'I guess she's gone off Facebook,' I suggest.

This comment earns Summer's tinkling laugh. 'No,' she says. 'She's put us on restricted. It looks like we're still friends, but we can't see her posts. Francine's done the same, and the younger girls. I've looked them all up, and all I can see is their profile pics. We're not getting any of their news.'

'I don't see how you can know that for sure,' I say. 'If you can't see their posts, how do you know they're posting?'

'Because of Adam,' Summer replies, flourishing the iPad. 'Adam doesn't really use Facebook. He doesn't even have a profile pic. So I guess when Francine told Virginia to put us all on restricted, she forgot about Adam. She couldn't have known that I occasionally check Facebook when I'm using Adam's iPad, which is logged into his account.'

'What do you mean by "us all"?'

'You, me, probably Ben and Mum,' says Summer. 'We're all on restricted so we don't know what's going on.'

'And you think Francine told our half-sisters to do this?'

'That's my theory.'

'So what's going on?' I ask. 'Uncle Colton said the girls are all well, and Virginia's doing great at school . . .'

'Well, I'm sorry to have to say this, but Adam reckons Uncle Colton's in on it,' says Summer. 'Tell me, have you never wondered why our uncle, a wealthy, handsome man like our father, hasn't married and has no children of his own?'

I remember Uncle Colton standing beside my mother when he came to drive me to the airport, and how good they looked together, both well-groomed, trim and fit. What's it like for him to spend time with his dead brother's beautiful ex-wife? For Annabeth to spend time with her dead ex-husband's brother? Is it awkward? Or better than awkward?

But Summer's next question is a surprise. 'And what about Francine? Not a single boyfriend since Dad died. Why not? She's attractive, still in her thirties, affluent enough—although she'd be much better off if Virginia were to inherit the money, and you know some people always want more money. So has she really been single all these years?'

My mother fades out of my mental picture, and Francine's face takes her place beside Colton. Younger, blonder and more ruthless. Dad chose Francine over Annabeth, so why wouldn't Colton too?

It seems out of character for Summer to imagine love—or whatever it is, some secret sexual thing—between our stepmother and our uncle. 'Do you really think he's fucking Francine?' I ask.

'Steady on, Iris! No, I don't think anything of the sort. It was Adam's idea. I don't like to speculate. But I'll tell you what isn't speculation . . .' She taps away on the iPad.

'Summer, I hate to break it to you, but you can't check Facebook in the middle of the Indian Ocean.'

'I know,' she says, 'but Adam took screenshots. Here!' She thrusts the screen in my face.

It's Virginia's Facebook page. My half-sister is looking a hell of a lot older and prettier than last time I saw her, at Summer's wedding late last year. In her profile pic, her skin-tight dress reveals her new curves. She's lost the albino look. Her brows and lashes are darker, and her hair is curled. It makes her look a lot more like us.

'There are more screenshots,' says Summer, flicking her hand across the screen. There's a new, steely tone in her voice, and she darts her eyes at the screen and away again, as though she can hardly bear to look at our half-sister.

In the next screenshot, a group of young people pose on a windswept beach. The sand is jet black, and a great rock rises behind them, like a lion looking out to sea.

'This photo isn't from Virginia's page,' says Summer. 'This is Jake, an old schoolfriend of Adam's.' She points to a smiling face in the foreground.

'I know that beach,' I say. 'That's Lion Rock at Piha Beach in New Zealand.'

'That's right,' says Summer. 'Take a good look.'

I don't recognise anyone in the foreground, but in the background, a platinum blonde in a multicoloured bikini looks familiar. I point to her. 'Do you think that's Virginia?'

'I'm certain,' says Summer. 'I gave her that rainbow bikini. Now, have a squiz at this.'

It's another beach photo, a close-up of a teenage boy, as chalky blond as Virginia. The caption reads, 'Richie turns sixteen', and the name 'Richard Bishop' is tagged. His face takes up most of the frame, but I can see that he is seated with a girl standing behind him. A female torso is visible, bare except for a scrap of rainbow fabric, and slender arms encircle his shoulders in an embrace that looks both intimate and uncomfortable. The girl's face is out of shot, but I can see snow-white hair.

'See, Richard lives in New Zealand.' Summer scrolls through the screenshots and points to the words.

'Richard Bishop. That name rings a bell.' I hunt through my brain for the memory.

'Bishop is Francine's maiden name. Richard is her brother's stepson. His real dad was never in the picture, so he has his stepfather's surname.'

I'm beginning to understand Summer's hostility. 'Yuck,' I say. 'That means he and Virginia are practically cousins. And they're dating?'

'I don't know if *dating* is the word,' says Summer. 'Gross as it is, I wish they were *dating*, but look at her posture. Look at her arms. They should be resting on his shoulders, but instead they're hovering an inch above his body. She's trying not to touch him. You can see that she's not into him. So tell me, what would be the point in dating a relative who you don't even like?'

I take the iPad from Summer and look again at the close-up of Richard. It's as though the girl's face has been deliberately cropped out. I zoom in on the arm hovering above Richard's shoulder, on the left hand. She's wearing a fat diamond ring.

'They're engaged,' I say. 'Francine's jacked it up with her brother, and they'll marry as soon as Virginia's eighteen. They're keeping it secret from us so we don't hurry up. I don't know what we can do, though. They're not truly related, and even if they were actual cousins, it isn't against the law to marry your cousin.'

'Damn,' says Summer. 'I was hoping you would say it was illegal. Or at least that it was possible to object to the wedding. Isn't that why the priest asks whether anyone has a reason why these two shouldn't be wed?'

'No,' I say. 'You have to have a *lawful* reason why they shouldn't be wed. Like that one of them is already married, or that the marriage is incestuous—but even real first cousins don't count as incest. Not in Australia, and not in New Zealand either, I'm afraid. But the marriage law is different there.'

The back of my neck prickles. I've been thinking that fifteen is awfully early to be getting engaged. Now I remember something else about New Zealand's marriage laws.

'So it's kind of lucky that I'm pregnant,' says Summer. 'Otherwise, look what Francine was capable of. She was going to marry Virginia off on her eighteenth birthday.'

'It's worse than that, Summer,' I say. 'Don't you see? New Zealand is the key. New Zealand is their trump card. All along we thought there was plenty of time, but Francine was hatching her plan, and Uncle Colton too, maybe. The point is, the legal age of marriage in New Zealand is different from Australia. With your parents' permission—and I reckon *that* won't be a problem—you can marry in New Zealand at sixteen. When is Virginia's birthday?'

Summer sits up straight. Her eyes are round. 'May! Virginia's sixteen on the first of May!'

It's almost April already. No doubt the wedding is one month away.

Nice is dumb. I can't believe that Summer and Adam worked out Francine's evil plot before I did, and yet they didn't think to check the legal marriage age in New Zealand. So Summer is risking a one-hundred-million-dollar pregnancy on an ocean voyage. If Summer miscarries, there won't be time to conceive again before Virginia's wedding. Everyone knows teenagers are crazy-fertile. Virginia will be pregnant before the cake is cut.

CHAPTER 7

THE ZONE

'What are you doing crossing an ocean in your condition?' are my next words to Summer. 'A lot is riding on this pregnancy!' I set the iPad down on the cockpit seat and take an honest look at my pregnant sister. Despite the soft glow of the setting sun, she looks frazzled. Her lips are chapped; there are rings under her eyes.

'Don't be so Victorian,' Summer replies. 'It's healthy to be active during pregnancy. And plenty of women miscarry even though they sit quietly at home. I could have stayed in Thailand and lost the baby and *Bathsheba*! Besides, I refuse to live a life dictated by the whims of a wicked stepmother. Even if I had known the legal age for marriage in New Zealand, it wouldn't have changed anything. I mean, I don't care that Francine's trying to trick us out of the money. I care what she's doing to her own daughter. As if the marriage wasn't bad enough, Virginia has to go to bed with the boy and make a baby! It's child trafficking!'

This is very high-minded of Summer. Somehow, I think Virginia's happy to be trafficked for that sort of money. She's already scored herself a ring that looks almost as big as Summer's princess-cut diamond.

I feel as if my head is in a vice. It's more than the thought of two sisters pregnant, which somehow makes me feel unsexed. There's also something masculine about being skipper. I haven't worn Adam's 'Skipper' cap much, although Summer wears her big 'Crew' cap all the time, even when she's in the pilot house.

I've taken charge of the boat, but not of the crew. A skipper should always set rules, especially when people are doing solo watches. And I remember Summer merrily pointing the boat straight downwind the day we left Thailand. The girl is no sailor.

'I should have said this before,' I say. 'I know you mostly do, but now I want it to be a rule that you stay in the pilot house on your watches. We don't want you slipping over in your condition. Call me if anything needs doing.'

I can't believe I've let her stay up till midnight each night so I can get a few hours' sleep at a normal hour. If Virginia gets the money, there'll be no scraps for me. Not *Bathsheba*, not any yacht, not even grocery money.

'From now on I'm only sleeping during the day,' I say. 'I'll keep watch all night. You need your rest.'

Forty-eight hours later, we're still in the zone. We've only made two hundred miles, which is my fault. My stubborn attempts to sail on my watches have resulted in lots of swearing, a little seasickness, and zero progress. *Bathsheba* has lolled drunkenly in the windless washing-machine water while her sails flapped uselessly. Those few times when the wind did strike, with pounding warm rain, she would heel so violently, it was as though a giant hand had pressed her sailcloth flat against the sea.

Summer has motored all the way through her watches, with the sails safely furled, making better progress. Even so, we've somehow drifted forty miles back east. I'm surprised, because the charts don't show any strong currents here, but I try not to let it get to me. The key is to get south to the trade winds. Then we'll make up lost ground fast enough. Summer is relying on me, and so is her unborn child.

During the long nights awake, fruitlessly trying to sail, I can't stop thinking about Virginia. I've never had much time for my half-siblings—when you have a twin you don't need more sisters, and in any case, all four of them are pale reflections of Summer.

Virginia is nice enough, but she's boring. I don't even know what her hobbies are, apart from incest and stealing other people's fortunes.

But I feel protective of her, a feeling at odds with my new protectiveness towards Summer. Virginia's still a kid. Why didn't Summer and Adam speak out about this engagement? If they, or I, don't intervene, Virginia's going to end up married to a relative and pregnant for no reason whatsoever.

'Of course I want to stop the wedding,' Summer says when I broach the topic in the cockpit at dinnertime. The afternoon of abortive sailing has killed her culinary zeal. The pasta puttanesca has an odd, canned flavour, and Summer barely touches hers, though I wolf mine down. 'Too many things were happening at once,' she says. 'I'd just done the pregnancy test, we'd checked the boat out of Thailand, and Tarquin had pus all over his nappy—'

'Stop,' I say, choking on an olive. 'I get the picture.'

'Remember, we didn't realise the wedding was imminent. And there's still plenty of time to tell Virginia before the first of May. But you see . . .' Summer closes her eyes and places a graceful hand on her little belly. 'It's hard to describe. I feel so protective of this budding life. It feels wrong to reveal her existence to my enemies, to people who wish me harm, when she's so new, so vulnerable.'

She. Summer can't know her baby's sex yet, but she imagines a daughter. It's not surprising when she already has Tarquin, but the thought tears at my insides.

I suppose it is because this baby will be 'the Carmichael heir' that I've always imagined it would be a boy. When Noah and I were trying to conceive, I assumed our baby would be male. I never imagined myself having a daughter. I never allowed myself to.

I stare at Summer's tanned abdomen, half-revealed by the gold sarong she's taken to wearing every day now. Perhaps she's bursting out of her other clothes already.

Legally, Summer's baby is my niece, but genetically, she'll be as much my daughter as she is Summer's. I'll experience the glory and magic of laying eyes on my offspring, my genetic legacy, for the first time, not with my own baby but with Summer's. I'll hold her in my arms, smell her and feel her weight, but however much Summer lets me hold the baby, I'll have to hand her back.

Somehow, it feels as if Summer has stolen from me.

'You look like the walking dead, Iris,' says Summer. 'You can't keep staying up all night. I haven't been getting to sleep before midnight anyway. Go and get some rest.'

I argue, but Summer is insistent. 'I'm young and healthy, and I'm a night owl these days. All I'm going to do is sit here and keep watch while Dave sails the boat.' She pats the autohelm control. 'I promise to call you if anything needs to be done. In fact, I keep meaning to tell you this, or did you already know? If you want to check on me, you can watch me on TV.' She gestures towards the stateroom.

'What are you talking about?' I ask.

'So you don't know? I thought Dad might have told you. There's a camera mounted on the pilot house right above the compass, and it's wired to the stateroom TV. You remember how the TV never worked? That's because Dad didn't want us to know how to turn it on. He kept a remote control hidden in that locked drawer above the bed, the drawer I'm keeping my wedding ring in while we sail, you know. Those times when we thought Dad was trusting us to stand watch on our own? He could check on us without getting out of bed.'

'So have you been watching me?'

Summer laughs. 'Of course not. I'm not even sure if it still works. I've been sleeping in the quarter berth, remember?'

I'm relieved. My time on the helm, especially at night, when I let my thoughts wander, is my most private time. I've spent more time than I would like to admit thinking about Adam. Perhaps my fantasies could be read on my face or in the movement of my body. If anyone could read me, it would be my twin.

But I also feel betrayed. Not by Summer; she's clearly telling the truth. By Dad. The night of my first solo watch, I revelled in the responsibility and the solitude. And he was spying on me.

I'm still uneasy about Summer staying up so late, but I'm exhausted, and in the end, sleep wins out over common sense. I start the engine, furl our flapping sails, check *Bathsheba*'s course and roll into bed. God help me, I leave my dumb, pregnant sister up there on her own.

'Wake me at midnight,' I say, as I always do, and she says, 'Of course.'

I wake in the stateroom, face down on the bed as usual, sunshine kissing my neck. It's bold day. *Bathsheba* is thrumming with engine noise. I look up. The angle of the morning sun through the portholes tells me that we're still pointing south.

But something has changed. I've slid to the edge of the bed. I struggle to my feet and stand on a sloping floor. *Bathsheba* is no longer wallowing in the doldrums. She's heeled over to starboard.

I peer through the ports. The confused seas of the zone have given way to neat rows of rolling southeast swells.

We've found the trade winds! The new energy in the air zings through my body. Like millennia of mariners before me, I'm thrilled at our escape from what felt like a windless death. Through the skylight, I see that Summer has hoisted the main, but she's done a lousy job. The sail is flapping, and only the engine is powering us forward.

She should have woken me. I could have got us sailing properly, turned us westward, killed the engine. Now we've wasted time and fuel.

I can't even remember coming down for a morning nap. The last thing I recall is going to bed at sunset after the pasta puttanesca, not even bothering with the dishes, feeling groggy and thick with sleep. Before I turned in, I realised we would cross the equator on Summer's watch, and I went back up the ladder to remind her that it was traditional to throw a party and tip buckets of seawater over the crew when crossing the line. Some people celebrate with a jump in the ocean.

'I'm too pregnant for that sort of shit,' Summer said.

I didn't argue with her. She must have been exhausted to swear like that.

'Don't bother waking me for the crossing, then,' I said. I should have been excited about returning to the southern hemisphere, *home*, but I needed my bed. 'I'll try to sleep through till midnight. Unless you need me, of course.'

'Night-night, Twinnie,' said Summer.

But I can't remember her waking me at midnight. Here I am and it's day. Has my tired, pregnant sister kept watch all night?

A chill lurches through my body. The engine drones on, and *Bathsheba*, who always feels alive to me, is a cold, hard, dead thing, a mass of metal and timber lashed together, thrusting its way south through endless ocean. I stumble out through the saloon, up through the pilot house.

The cockpit is empty.

I scan the foredeck, my face screwing into a scowl, ready to bawl her out for going up there on her own. Right after our big safety talk. But the scowl drops away half-formed, because she's not there.

She's nowhere.

Jagged shards of ice are stabbing at the back of my neck. It's like something, some monstrous thing, is pulling me, pulling my head around. *You know where you have to look.*

So I look. I peer at the ocean behind me, as far as I can see, between the twin mounds of *Bathsheba*'s widening wake. The water is leaden, an unbroken poisonous grey.

'Summer!' I call. And then louder and louder. 'Summer! SUMMER!'

The bathroom. Of course! A rush of relief. I almost skip down to the saloon. I rattle at the bathroom door, but it swings open at my touch. My ghostly face stares back at me from the double mirror. No Summer.

No Summer in the quarter berth. No Summer in Tarquin's cage-like crib. No Summer anywhere down below.

'Summer! SUMMER!' I'm screaming her name.

I run back up on deck. Careless of the boom, of my lack of life jacket or harness, I jump onto the cabin top, desperate to see further. I turn and turn and turn, ducking under the mainsail to see all around. I peer at every inch of ocean. Nothing.

What am I thinking? If Summer is out there, we're sailing away from her right now. I rush to the pilot house and press the red button. *Alter course to port ten degrees.* The autohelm strains the tiller sideways. *Bathsheba* swerves into the oncoming swell. I push again, again, as fast as I can, but I don't forget to count. Eighteen times and *Bathsheba* is on a reciprocal course. Due north.

I run to the mast. There are folding rungs on each side of it that climbers can pull down as they ascend. I saw Dad do it once. He was berthed in a marina, with Annabeth doggedly hanging on to the other end of a safety line, but watching him still made me sick to my stomach.

No time for safety lines now. I bang the first few rungs down and start to climb, but the sail flaps in my face, obscuring my view. I must go higher.

Summer, Summer, where are you?

My palms are slick with sweat, my bare soles too, slippery as oil. I glance between my feet. *Bathsheba*'s deck, now matchbox-small, seesaws below me. If I fall, I die. I'll hit the deck and be killed instantly, or miss and land in the ocean, and watch *Bathsheba* sail blithely away.

Is this what happened to Summer?

I can't think it. I can't stop climbing. Delay might mean life or death for Summer. I reach up to knock down the next rung, and my hand slips on the sharp metal. I should climb down, find some gloves or shoes to protect my hands and feet from these nightmarish prongs, but I don't have time. I have to get up. I have to find her.

One step. Another. My skin is clammy and cold. The mast is an endless ladder. And now I'm here, at the top. The masthead is a mess of pulleys, the LED light, the windvane, a bunch of paraphernalia bolted on. Everything jolts and bounces. The head of the sail slams from side to side. The sea's motion is magnified by height, and the wind's stronger up here. I cling to a random mass of ropes, and now they're stained red. I've cut my hand open on something but I don't know what—I didn't feel it.

I look and look and look. Summer, her gold sarong, her yellow hair, her big white cap. I scan the ocean all the way to the horizon. I'm in front of the mast, facing aft. I twist my body around to see towards the bow. I feel as though I can see forever. Sea and sky are grey. I strain for a speck of colour. Anything that could be Summer.

The sun comes out, painting everything blue, and the great oceanic swells roll on far beneath me, line after line after line. These waves have not stopped in millions of years. They will not stop for me. The mast sways like a tree in a storm and my belly is a nest of coiling snakes. Vomit pours out of my mouth and floats in suspended time before it splatters over both water and deck below. But still I look.

There is nothing. Nothing. Only blue and blue and blue.

The ocean has swallowed Summer whole.

A movement behind me. A flap. I turn. A white seabird is level with my eyes. As majestic as an albatross. Its head feathers glow a golden yellow like a crown. It's a gannet, a bird of the south. I recognise it from home. It meets my gaze and peels off in a wide arc towards the horizon. Soon it's a speck, a dark spot against the bright sun.

I'm in the southern hemisphere and I'm alone. My heart clamours like a living creature, racing and fighting, straining in my right breast. Without Summer it has no rhythm. It seems to know the truth already.

I'm no longer a twin. Summer is dead.

CHAPTER 8

THE SEARCH

Yet I keep searching. I'm methodical, unwearying, whole-hearted. I've never done anything so passionately. I search so hard it nearly kills me.

I can't remember climbing down the mast. It seems like seconds later that I'm in the pilot house, refining *Bathsheba*'s course. Plan, look up, look around, plan more. I smear the logbook with blood as I calculate drift due to current and alter *Bathsheba*'s course slightly east. As time goes by, Summer will have drifted further. I must imagine a living sister, floating alive in tropical waters. I draw a search radius on the chart.

The empty phone cradle in the pilot house is a sickening, unreal sight. Worse is when I look in the chart table drawer, the only other place the sat phone could realistically be. I check everywhere Summer might have left it, turning lockers inside out, creating chaos. Nothing.

No sat phone.

How far away is help, even if I do find the phone? The nearest countries are the Maldives, the Seychelles, Madagascar, Somalia. Hardly the world's richest countries. Do they have search-and-rescue planes? Do they have search-and-rescue anything?

'Mayday, mayday, mayday.' My voice trembles as I speak into the VHF radio, but I remember what to say. *Bathsheba*'s call sign. Man overboard. Our latitude and longitude, course and speed. I read the numbers off the GPS.

It's hopeless, though. I need the SSB radio, but as Adam said, it's broken. I can't get a peep out of it. The VHF is for use within sight of land or another ship, and we haven't seen either since Thailand. I keep it switched on, but of course no one replies.

I try to set off the emergency beacon, even though Adam said it was obsolete, but it's dead. I can't even turn it on.

Bathsheba is faster under sail than motor, so I turn off the engine and unfurl the genoa. The silence is gruesome. I know for certain that I am alone on board. Still, I write a list of essential tasks, including 'search inside boat'.

Summer's harness, with its inflatable life jacket, lies on the pilot house floor. I whimper when I see it.

I must make unbearable calculations. I must make sure I search the area where Summer is most likely to be. Don't think about her not being on the surface. Don't think, *Summer's body*. I must cover maximum ground in the time Summer can stay alive. I can't think *sharks*. I can't think *exhaustion*, although I know that without her life jacket, Summer will have to tread water to keep afloat. But I force myself to think about hypothermia. The equator is sweltering hot, but even here, seawater will suck Summer's body heat away.

Certain macabre conversations come to mind from years ago. Drunken sailors clinking cocktails in the marina, thrilling themselves with the horror of the words 'man overboard', careless of the kids eavesdropping on their third-hand stories. But I'm grateful. I'm grateful to these morbid drunkards because they told me how long Summer can last. A man was found alive once, *once*, after twenty-eight hours, but it was in a strait, not the open ocean, and the water in the area was exceptionally warm. Even so, it was considered a miracle.

Life comes in pieces. Memories, colours—the white sail glimpsed through the skylight, the golden-headed gannet—flash through my brain with hallucinatory sharpness. My emotions are ridiculous. I feel a strange pleasure that I'm left-handed, since the injury to my right hand won't slow me down as much as it might have. I'm proud *Bathsheba* is sailing so fast. I'm nailing this rescue.

But my heart knows the truth. Men overboard are found in movies, but the reality is different. Even if someone sees you go over, it can be hard to get you back. When I woke this morning, it had been nearly twelve hours since I saw Summer. Unwoken by her, my weary body had called in overdue sleep, slumbering so deeply that Summer's decision to hoist the mainsail, and the noise and change in motion that would normally have had me springing onto the deck, failed to rouse me. Now I have no idea when she did it. No idea where she went over. No idea how.

———

By noon, I'm back in the zone.

This gives me a clue as to when Summer raised the sail. The wind boundary, where the southeast trades give way to the equatorial tumult, doesn't move much in a day, so if it took me six hours to get back to the zone, it stands to reason that we left it six hours before I woke. Midnight or maybe a little earlier, since we're moving faster now.

I have to think hard. Summer would have raised the sail after she left the zone.

Wait. She can't have fallen after midnight. That was when she was meant to wake me. There's no way Summer would have sailed on through my watch.

I've narrowed down the window of time. Maybe forty minutes before midnight, ten minutes after. With insane elation, I redraw my search radius. Allowing for the uncertain rate of drift of a body—*a swimmer*—I have a search radius of five nautical miles.

I must do the geometry. Area of a circle. Pi times the radius squared. Thank God I know this stuff.

I have a search area of seventy-eight square miles.

My sister has been in the water for twelve hours. She has twelve more hours to live, sixteen at most, and the sun sets in six hours. I don't know how much fuel is in *Bathsheba*'s tank, but searching under sail at the edge of the zone is complicated. I can't make *Bathsheba* sail straight upwind, and the sails obscure my view.

Stay alive, Summer. Stay alive.

I set the yacht on course and shove the autohelm remote control into the pocket of my shorts. I pack the VHF radio and a water bottle into a backpack, along with some chocolate, although I can't imagine ever eating again. I furl the sails and start the engine. I clip on my harness with its carabiners. I put on my skipper's cap, and sling sunglasses and binoculars around my neck.

I climb the mast again.

No fear this time. Death seems a small thing. At the top, I clip myself to the masthead so my arms are free. I can steer *Bathsheba* from up here, using the remote control.

Nothing to do now but look.

And think.

Nine years of my life melt away. The hundred million has distracted me for nine years, but it's forgotten now. All I can think about is Summer, my twin, the better half of my soul.

I love Summer. I'll never love anyone, man or woman, as I love her. It's not her beauty or her kindness or her blessed life. I love her because she's my sister, and I'd kill for her, I'd die for her, if I could.

I have to find her.

———

The sun has burned its way across the sky. It's sinking towards a bed of clouds, and the sea's colours are softening.

I'm still at the masthead. My water bottle is empty. I tried to eat the chocolate, but it was ashes in my mouth. My limbs barely respond to my brain's signals to move. I've tried all possible postures, shifting my weight from one leg to the other, to my arms, letting myself droop in the safety harness. They're all excruciating.

I hate the ocean. I hate the colour blue. I hate the sun. But I don't want it to set. I will it to stay high and bright in the sky.

I've always been here at the masthead. I will always be here. The clink of the rigging is the clink of the chains of dead men. The sails are shrouds.

But still I stare at the sea. Summer. Her shining hair. I can see it in my mind, but it's not here.

I don't need the sunglasses anymore. The sea is mauve, lavender, indigo. It gleams rose-gold. The sky is soft as a dove.

And now I'm staring into blackness.

Climbing down is death. It's not only that my arms and legs are cadaver-stiff, that my skin throbs with sunburn, that my wounded hand is searing, that my throat is parched from crying, from screaming for my sister. What's worse is that when I touch the deck, when I crumple in a heap at the foot of the mast, I have to face the fact that it's over.

I've lost Summer.

———

There's a voice in my head telling me to go on. It's a cold, hateful voice, and it tells me things I don't want to know.

You have to get sleep, it says. *Don't lie there and mope on the deck. You can't search in the dark. Go and lie in a soft bed. You need to be refreshed. The search starts again at dawn.*

Maybe Summer stayed warm somehow. Maybe she was wearing warm clothes when she fell. Maybe something fell in with her and she could pull herself partly out of the water, although I've already checked, and nothing is missing except the sat phone. *Solomon* is still hoisted on the davits. The life raft is still lashed to the foredeck.

Maybe the water here is warmer than I thought. Maybe Summer is especially good at keeping herself warm.

You must keep searching.

I obey the voice. I drag myself to the pilot house and turn on the navigation lights. The needle of the fuel gauge hovers on empty, but the engine runs on. I shut it off. *You have to save fuel for tomorrow.*

I hate tomorrow. I stumble down to the saloon as *Bathsheba*, drifting with wind and current now, begins to wallow in the disturbed seas.

Not here, says the voice as I lurch towards the couch. *Sleep in the nice big bed. Get your rest.*

I must trust that, if we do cross paths with another vessel overnight, the helmsman will spot *Bathsheba*'s dim nav lights and steer clear of her. Dad taught us that not keeping watch was unforgivable, a sacrilege, but I have no choice. I have to sleep. In any case, we haven't seen a ship since Thailand. I've called on the VHF all day. And right now, we're in the middle of the world's emptiest ocean, days from the shipping lanes. Nobody's coming.

In the stateroom, I flick on the light. I glimpse my dark reflection in the TV screen.

The TV. Blood rushes to my head. I feel as if I've been struck across the chest. The CCTV! What did Summer say? Is it a live feed, or does it record? She wasn't even sure if it worked.

The remote. She said the remote was in the locked drawer with her wedding ring. Dad would never tell us where he kept the key, and Summer didn't say either. I pull out my sailor's knife and jab at the desk drawer. It's eighteen hours since Summer disappeared. Don't those tapes wipe every twenty-four hours? I don't know much about the technology when Dad installed it all those years ago. Did they use discs?

Jab, jab. I'm stabbing at the drawer like an assassin. It moves a little, and I grab the handle and wrench it. The drawer hits the floor, its contents scattering. I snatch Summer's wedding band and engagement ring as they roll away. I push them onto my bloodied right hand for safekeeping.

The remote. I scramble at the remote, point it at the TV, jam my finger against the 'on' button. Nothing.

Batteries. The batteries are flat. I rip them out and they clatter to the floor. I run to the pilot house. Under the chart table, there's a colony of batteries of all sizes.

Here they are, two new-looking double A batteries. I rush back to the stateroom, fumbling them into place as I go. This time the TV screen flickers.

I scroll through channels. Nothing but static.

And now blackness. But there's a time and date at the bottom of the screen. Seven p.m., twenty-ninth of March. A live feed.

How do I rewind? I press all the buttons on the remote. How do I make this work? The system must have a brain somewhere.

I pull the TV out from the wall. Plugged in behind it is an old laptop. I run my finger over the trackpad and the screen lights up. Inside an application called 'Home CCTV' I find the same live feed that is playing on the TV screen, and, in another window, seven files, each with a different date. I click on the most recent one, dated yesterday.

I start watching at eleven p.m., twenty-eighth March. I cue forward in short bursts. All is dark.

At fifteen minutes to midnight, the cockpit light comes on, and Summer appears.

'Yes!' I shout. She looks so familiar and so very alive that I sink onto the bed with a sigh, as if everything is OK, as if I've found her. Then I remember what I'm about to witness. My sister's death.

———

Hope is a demon. It toys with you, it flirts, and then when you start to trust it, it vanishes. It dies. First Summer died, and now hope dies too.

Summer stands in the cockpit in her little shorts and that big cap, frowning. She's not worried about something, though. This is the look Summer wears when she's pleased with herself. She's planning a surprise.

The camera is level with the boat, not the horizon, so it's hard to tell which way the boat heels as Summer hoists the main. The sea behind the cockpit appears to rise on the right and sink on the left of the screen. Since the camera's pointing aft, that means the sea on the port side rose, or rather, the boat heeled to port.

Summer must have met a westerly wind as we came out of the zone. Why didn't I tell her what to expect? Did she realise this was the wrong direction for the trades? This must have been a fluke, a local wind. It was never going to last.

But Summer doesn't know this. She trims the sail and sits, looking as if sailing's some new miracle that she has invented.

A few minutes go by. Summer jumps up and runs towards the camera. Her face looms large and then disappears out of view. She's gone into the pilot house.

She reappears holding the sat phone to her ear.

She faces the bow. Her face is right in front of the camera now, huge on the screen. Her eyes are swivelled towards the phone. She presses it closer against her cheek. Her expression is pure bliss. It must be Adam.

Why would he call? Has something happened to Tarquin?

Summer jumps onto the cockpit seat, standing tall so the phone is high. She's speaking into it. I can tell she's shouting. It must be a bad line.

Now there's a wobble. Summer's body jerks as if the boat has jolted her. I can guess what's happening, but Summer doesn't know.

The wind is shifting. She feels something is wrong, and she reacts in the worst possible way. She thinks the strange motion is caused by something ahead. She stands up on the aft deck to get a better look. She's wearing no harness, no life jacket.

Thwack.

The footage is silent, but I hear the crash that kills her like an explosion in my skull. The wind flicks behind the mainsail.

Bathsheba crash-gybes, and the boom smashes into Summer's head. Her ragdoll body flies into the ocean.

———

She was killed instantly. She must have been. I say the words aloud to convince myself, but I know there's a chance she wasn't. She might have only been knocked unconscious.

She still wouldn't have suffered. With no life jacket, she would drown before she could wake up.

But I still search. I search the whole next day. All day the same thought haunts me. Not only is there no chance of finding Summer alive, but there's been no chance for a long time. I'm looking for a body, and I don't even know whether bodies float at sea. I'm not searching because I have hope. I'm searching because the only alternative is not to search.

I search inside the yacht, even though I know Summer can't be on board. I know every inch of *Bathsheba*, and I search everywhere, just for something to do. Back in the zone, when the wind fails, I haul the sails down and let *Bathsheba* come to a halt, and then, naked, holding a snorkelling mask, I jump into the turquoise void and swim right under the hull, as though my sister's corpse might be trapped between keel and rudder. It would have terrified me once, the risk that *Bathsheba* might pick up speed while I was under here—a yacht can outpace a swimmer in the lightest wind, even with her sails down— but now it doesn't seem to matter.

Let *Bathsheba* float away. Let me join Summer. It's quiet down here under the boat. The water is mild and clean, and blood and sweat wash away into the blue.

But there's nothing here. Even the remoras are gone. *Bathsheba*'s black hull stands in the immense clarity of the ocean. I can see forever into the deep. It's so clear that my flailing feet seem to be dropping through sky, and I imagine my sister's body on an endless journey down. I open my mouth and let water flood in, rich and salty. It would be so easy to fall.

The silence is a creature about to pounce. I am the only person in the world.

I swim to the other side of the hull. The sea's surface seen from below is like a mirror. And I have come through the mirror into Summer's world, the world of the deep. Beyond, high above me, the sun is a yellow blur.

I surface and clutch at the swimming ladder, desperate for air. Cool water has washed reason back into my brain. Against my closed eyelids, the sun burns a bloody pink, a shock after days of unending blue.

I'm a young woman, and life is long. I want to hear music again. I want to feel piano keys moving lightly beneath my fingertips. I want to stand in the desert or in the snow. I want to make love to someone.

I don't want to die here.

I climb back on board.

Still the madness grips me. The sun burns hotter each day in the merciless sky. *Bathsheba*'s out of fuel, so I have to search under sail. Water is running low, but still I can't point the bow towards Africa. Perhaps I'm overdue already. How many days have I been searching? Adam will be waiting in Thailand for news. Tarquin too, a baby who's already lost one mother. I must not think about them.

I comb *Bathsheba* again and come up with a few cans of Coke and two bottles of wine. They give me a couple more days to search.

I could pour all the water down the drain, all the Coke, all the wine. The thought sets my head buzzing. What if I do it in a moment of despair? Condemn myself to a slow, fatal agony?

I could open the through-hulls and let *Bathsheba* fill with water. Tie myself to the bed so I stay inside her. We would disappear without trace.

I could lie on the foredeck until the sun burns me to the point of no return.

I could beat south to Antarctica.

I fantasise about rain.

I sleep in Summer's quarter berth. The gold sarong that I had imagined she was wearing lies discarded on her bunk, still smelling of apples and white beaches. I press my face into it and then tie it around my waist. With my fingernail, I scratch a long curve down my left inner thigh, a mark to match Summer's scar.

We were eight or nine years old when it happened. We were anchored in paradise, an uninhabited coral island, but Dad was in a bad mood. He ordered us kids to go to shore 'and stay there till the bats are flying'. As always, I took the oars.

We had to row over the reef to get to shore, but I thought I knew where the pass was. Next thing my body was crashing into water. I surfaced in darkness, inside *Solomon*'s upturned hull. I took a deep breath and swam out, and I came up in a sea of blood. Summer was screaming.

I righted the dinghy, pushed Ben back on board, and sent him back to *Bathsheba* to get help. Despite Ben's gentle demeanour, I knew I could rely on him. He was small for the oars, but I had taught him how to row, how to 'put your back into it' when you needed to push hard against wind or waves. Once I saw he was making progress, I turned to Summer and pulled her to shore. On the beach, I wrapped a wet towel around her leg, trying to stop the bleeding.

Later, everybody said I'd done well, but I knew the truth. Coral cuts never heal. Summer was scarred for life, and it was my fault. I should have borne the scar.

I will make myself into Summer. I will bring her back to life. All I need to do to resurrect my sister is make her scar.

I stand in the cockpit, where *Bathsheba*'s motion is gentlest. I pull out my sailing knife, and it hovers above my thigh. My hand still aches where I tore it open climbing the mast. I don't want another wound. I don't want more pain. But I have to do this. I have to bring Summer back.

The knife kisses my skin, but I can't push hard enough. Something's wrong.

Before the knife draws blood, I stop. What am I thinking? I'm about to make a bad mistake.

I'm so used to picturing Summer standing in front of me. I can almost see her now. I'm her mirror and she's mine. I was about to make a scar that mirrored hers.

I don't want to be her mirror anymore. I want to be Summer, the perfect twin, the one who is the right way round, but I'm confused. I can't get it straight in my mind.

My head throbs. Is my memory of Summer fading already? I can see her in front of me, but I can't step into her body and see her scar from her perspective. I can't remember which thigh is scarred. I know it curves back at the top and towards her knee at the bottom, and I know it's an S shape. S for Summer.

I check what I've drawn with my fingernail. It's not an S, it's backwards, a curvy Z. I've drawn it on the wrong leg.

I can't get this wrong. I take a pen and draw the S up the inside of my right thigh, starting at the bottom. I know precisely where it ends. Right at the line of her underwear.

Adam must love that scar. Summer said he was blind to her flaws, but surely he wouldn't see it as a flaw. It's part of Summer, part of the sweet, soft body he loves, but he's never going to see it again.

I grip my knife and draw the S again. This time in blood.

CHAPTER 9

THE SACRIFICE

In the end, I do it for Summer. I have to leave her behind for her sake. I have to stay alive and reach land so that Adam will know what happened to her. That death was swift. That she didn't suffer.

I turn west with a plodding slowness, but *Bathsheba* doesn't catch my mood. She skips and dances across the ocean. It's easy sailing from here. Less than a week.

No more hand-steering for me, though. I've lost all pleasure in staring at the ocean and the sky. I hate them. I sit in the pilot house and barely look for ships for days, until it occurs to me that if we collide with a fishing boat, I might kill more people.

I've already killed too many people.

I can't think about the baby, but nightmares come. The child rotting inside her mother's dead womb. The only thing left behind as Summer's limbs drop away, as her body dissolves around it. Carrion for sea creatures.

———

I write lists. The people I have to tell. The people whose hearts I have to break.

Adam.

Tarquin.

Annabeth.

Ben.

My brother's in New York studying economics in a posthumous attempt to win Dad's approval. He'll come as fast as he can to comfort me. The others will be too torn apart by grief to think about what I've been through.

There'll be more people to tell. Summer's friends. Letitia Buckingham is still her best friend, and she has former work colleagues whom I don't know at all.

I'll have to tell Francine and Colton and my four half-sisters.

The thought of my stepmother's fake grief, her secret joy, is the final straw.

———

I've been rationing water since I realised I was short, but the wind is light, and I'm not making much ground. I count it out, count miles, calculate, ration. I can't believe how blasé Summer was, showering every day, letting me shower. We should have been much more conservative with water from the start. Now, I have to seriously cut back, for safety's sake.

My skin is hot all the time. My head pounds. I cry without tears now and lick my lips with a rasping tongue. The sea is a cool, alluring blue, tantalisingly drinkable. Even the sky looks wet, as if I could drink the dew from it.

The sun is a torment. I promised myself I would save the wine for last, but one hot afternoon, I open a bottle and drink it to the dregs. The next day I finish the other bottle. To reduce my need for fluid, I sleep all day and wake at dusk. I hardly pee anymore.

I lose touch with the sun. I rise with the moon, now full in the evening sky. I talk to the moon. I talk to *Bathsheba*.

Bathsheba seemed dead when I lost Summer, but she comes back to life now, as if she is trying to save me. I've abdicated as skipper, given up, lain down to die, but she keeps sailing, keeps me safe inside her. The mothership. She is my third mother, my black mother, after golden Annabeth and white Francine. When I sleep, I float in her gentle womb.

When we were kids, Dad told us that Bathsheba was the wife of King David, the mother of King Solomon. Summer loved Bible stories. She would explain to everyone that this was why our autohelm was called Dave, and our dinghy *Solomon*.

Then we overheard Dad telling some other yachties the real story. He was entertaining them with drinks in the cockpit while we kids eavesdropped from the saloon. We heard him say that when David met Bathsheba, she was another man's wife, and David raped her.

Summer rushed into the cockpit. She was crying. 'You have to change her name!' she screamed. 'And you've named our autohelm after a rapist! I'm never touching it again!'

Our guests tittered awkwardly. Dad told Summer she was being absurd, but she didn't stop. In the end, he sent her to bed without dinner.

I was happy. Summer was so rarely in trouble. And I liked Bathsheba's story. From rape victim to the mother of kings.

I relive Summer's rage. I stand in the cockpit, where she stood shouting at Dad, and I shout and swear as if he's here with me. As if I'm Summer.

All of Summer's failings come back to me, few as they were. Her fleeting moments of anger or thoughtlessness. You're not supposed to think ill of the dead, but I can't help it.

When our parents told us the story behind my name, the flower chosen at random, Ben said it was lucky there were no petunias in the room. Summer took up the joke and found that it offered endless variations. 'Hi, Tulip,' she'd say. 'How's it going, Begonia?'

It went on for months. Summer found names even uglier than Iris. *Hydrangea. Chrysanthemum. Gladiolus.* She never used my real name anymore, and other kids at school joined in. I tried to laugh along, to whack some names back at her. *Autumn. Winter.* Nothing worked.

Ben was the one who stopped it. 'Can't you see she hates it?' he said to Summer. 'It's bad enough that your organs are in the right place and you have the best name. You don't have to tease her as well.'

When Summer realised how mean she'd been, she cried. I ended up comforting her.

I don't want to be thinking about these things. I want to remember Summer in her perfection. Even her faults were so forgivable.

———

We sail over the Seychelles Bank beneath a bloody moon, and the waves bang and crash against the hull. Shallow water makes the sea uneasy. Landfall looms.

I zoom out on the chart until I can see the whole Indian Ocean, the vast stretches of Asia and Africa and the Middle East. I know I have to stay on this course. I must make landfall tomorrow. I'm low on water. Yet my hand hovers over the button to alter course.

I could just keep sailing. West to Madagascar. North to Somalia, where pirates roam. South to the Southern Ocean and its monster waves. Anywhere.

Tomorrow I have to break the news. Adam has already lost a wife. How will I find the right words to tell him? When Helen died, at least her baby was saved.

———

There are notes all over the pilot house table in my handwriting. *Fuller left cheek, higher left cheekbone.* No one ever notices these differences. No one can tell us apart. *Thicker eyebrows.* But I've had them shaped. *Skinnier.* But I would be skinnier after a long sea voyage.

Left-handed. My left-handedness is the outward sign of my organ reversal, but it's not a physical sign, only a behaviour. I can't write very well with my right hand, but at the moment, it's wrapped in a bandage. No one would expect me to be able to write with it.

Heart and other organs reversed. Does Adam know this?

Sailing. Playing the piano. These are the things I'm better at than Summer. But it's easy to fake being bad at sailing. Perhaps it's harder to fake being a bad pianist. Safer to keep away from pianos.

Cooking and children. The things Summer is better at. They're not rocket science. I could do them if I had to. As for nursing, Summer gave that up already.

The differences between Summer and me that I can't hide from the world are her scar and her pregnancy, and I just gave myself the scar.

———

I don't know when the idea first comes. Perhaps in the heat of noon. I wake in *Bathsheba*'s black womb, dreaming of Summer.

I could escape. Jobless, homeless, loveless no more. *Bathsheba* would be mine. Adam would be mine. The money would be mine.

The baby would be mine.

But there is no baby.

Perhaps the idea was always with me. Was it with me when I wrote the notes that are scattered all over the chart table? Was it with me when I climbed the mast?

Was the idea with me when I left my own life behind to step aboard Summer's yacht with Summer's husband? Was the idea with me when I crouched beneath my father's corpse, learning that he had chosen not to split his fortune?

When I mutilated my leg, I wasn't thinking about this. I had no plans. The act felt symbolic. A meaningful way to honour Summer, like a tattoo.

You can't lie to Adam. OK, he can't tell us apart, and he's so inattentive that he wouldn't notice a few slip ups. And I know Summer's life very well now, even her sex life. She talked openly on this trip. I heard so much about Adam that he invaded my dreams.

Not long after I watched the CCTV footage, I grew afraid that it would be lost before anyone else could see it. Only seven days of footage was there—it must auto-delete after that. I saved the file onto a disc, ejected the disc and put it in a drawer. Now, I find a spot where the fabric has ripped away from the lining of my suitcase, and I tuck the disc inside.

I can't deny the temptation. I would no longer be the woman who couldn't keep her husband, even with the Carmichael fortune as bait. I would no longer be out of work, out of a home. Annabeth would never have to know that Noah left me. He could play the part of heartbroken husband if he wanted.

I rummage through my life as if it's a bag of goodies, looking for something that I want to keep. I don't find anything. There's not even anyone to mourn me. My mother has always been closer to Summer. The person I love most in the world, perhaps the only person I love in the world now, is my brother, but what difference would it make to Ben whether he lost one sister or the other?

———

I'm not going to do it. I would never lie to Adam. But I worry about the awkwardness of turning up in the Seychelles on someone else's boat, with a convenient story about the owner falling overboard. Even with the disc, things could get lost in translation. I don't want to end up in an African prison.

And my passport. I can't believe I never checked out of Thailand. It seemed like a minor detail at the time. Summer and the boat were checked out, but I wasn't. Now it feels ominous. Seychellois immigration will surely be unimpressed. I spent so long circling in the zone, searching for Summer, that I'm overdue, which will add to the suspicion. In the middle of it all, I will have to phone Adam in Thailand and break the news.

———

I can pretend to be Summer to the Seychellois authorities, get through customs and immigration, catch a plane to Thailand and tell Adam in person. Iris Carmichael isn't on the crew list. No one in the Seychelles need ever know that someone fell overboard.

Except, Adam is Seychellois. It's a tiny country, and Adam has a big family. In his grief, he'll rush home. He'll find out that nobody in the Seychelles knew of Summer's disappearance. What will he think of me? I'll seem like a crazy woman.

Perhaps I could tell the authorities that Iris fell overboard. As Summer, I wouldn't come under the same suspicion, because I'm the yacht owner with all my papers in order, married to a Seychellois citizen, entitled to citizenship myself. They'd investigate the disappearance, so it wouldn't look suspicious, but they'd let me leave the country to reunite with my husband. And then I could tell Adam the truth.

But what if the news spreads? Wealthy Australian girls don't fall off yachts every day. It'll make the newspaper. The news might reach Thailand.

I can't be Iris to Adam and Summer to everybody else. He won't be able to hide his shock and grief.

Perhaps I could break it to Adam slowly. First I tell him that I'm Summer, but I've lost the baby. Iris fell overboard, and I lost the baby from the strain. That would kind of prepare him for the worse news to come. It would give me the chance to wait for the right moment to tell him the truth.

I couldn't keep up the charade for more than a few days. Even though I know Summer so well, even though I know her most intimate secrets, I couldn't be Summer for the rest of my life. I can impersonate Summer, but that doesn't mean I want to.

I think about a version of Summer who didn't die. She has *Bathsheba* and Adam and Tarquin, while I have nothing. Even if she weren't pregnant already, if she were still alive, she might still have time to get pregnant, to beat Virginia to the money. And even without the money, she has Adam and his money and his love.

I would be doing everyone a favour. It would be a kindness to Adam, to Tarquin, to Annabeth. A kindness to Summer.

So far she's dead only to me. In the eyes of the rest of the world, Summer lives on.

I wrap myself in her sarong, lie in her bed, breathe in her apple scent, imagine Adam's arms around me. Every night, every morning, for the rest of my life. Crossing oceans on *Bathsheba*. Making love on the foredeck, naked in the golden sun. Raising our baby together, the Carmichael heir.

If I tell the truth, what will happen? There's no life for me back in Wakefield. I'll have to fly back to my mother, who's living in Summer's house. But that won't work. Where will Adam and Tarquin be? They'll want their house back. Adam won't keep sailing without Summer, and he won't want me in his home. He won't be able to stand the sight of me, the living image of his lost love.

They won't want *Bathsheba*. She's the place where Summer died. Perhaps Adam will give her to me after all, and I can set off and sail around the world on my own.

The years stretch out ahead of me. The rest of my life circling the world's oceans, searching for Summer. Or I could be Summer, and no one will search for her at all. No one will search for Iris. No one will miss her. It would be a favour to them all.

But I can't do it. It's too great a sacrifice. My life might be empty, but it's my life. It's who I am.

Francine will triumph. There's nothing I can do about it.

———

I think about artificial insemination. When Noah left, I thought I was pregnant. I had tender breasts and all the other signs, but then I got my period, and obviously, there was no more sex after that.

If only I had kept a single sample of Noah's sperm. To think how much of it we collected in condoms and threw away before we were married. The baby would have been born late, but babies are early or late sometimes, aren't they? It isn't an exact science.

Noah would have been delighted. What child is unwanted when it's born with a hundred-million-dollar cheque in its mouth?

If I could get Adam on his own. Summer's dead, but you have to pretend I'm Summer. I don't want anything from you except a sperm sample. I'll split the money with you.

It's impossible. He'd be a wreck. Adam's a straight-up guy; he's not going to be a good actor. And, like Noah, he's inexplicably uninterested in the money. He and Summer got pregnant *by accident*.

Maybe he'd do it to thwart Francine. Or maybe not.

I'm not going to do this. It's too hard.

I drop my engagement and wedding rings overboard anyway. They vanish in *Bathsheba*'s turbulent green wake. I don't know why I kept them so long, and the dull little emerald that Noah thought matched my eyes always looked tawdry beside Summer's diamond. I shift her rose-gold rings from my right hand to my left. I don't want to lose them.

It's like passing through a mirror.

———

On my last night at sea I sail into a lightning storm. The wind stops as if someone closed a door, and the sea is still. The sails hang lifeless, but the black sky is shattered by a thousand spears of light.

I'm meant to put the electronics in the oven to protect them from lightning strike, but the sat phone is gone, and I don't care about anything else. Certainly not the iPad, with its screenshots of slutty Virginia. Let it fry. Let it all fry.

I stand on the foredeck in the blackness, one foot on the samson post, right where Summer and Adam made the baby. I'm tall, and it's the furthest from the mast I can get. Bring it on.

The air crackles and bursts into stars. My ears ring with the thunder. But nothing touches me. I am the albatross around my own neck. I'm too condemned even to die.

———

With *Bathsheba*'s fuel tank empty, there's no way out of the lightning storm. After watching it for hours, I sleep in the cockpit and wake cold. It's still dark, but stars are fading from the sky. Air rushes lightly over my skin. I force myself to my feet and hoist the sails.

First light sees us racing towards Port Victoria under a wild hot sky. The wind freshens, and *Bathsheba* is overpowered, but I can't bear to shorten sail. She bucks and shrieks, but I push on. My lips are dry; my throat throbs. My skin is so hot, it feels flaky, as if it might turn to powder and blow away.

The island of Mahé is steep and rugged on the horizon, and as I approach, its silhouette resolves into hills clad in dense bush. I long to climb them. Land. Soon I will stand on stable ground.

The waves grow lumpy and tumultuous. The sea behind me builds into a rage. The sky is concrete now, the water doomsday dull, yet it does not rain. My body is arid. My body is a desert.

I urge *Bathsheba* forward. I can see the islet, Sainte Anne, now, with the taller peaks of Mahé behind. Between them are shelter, calm waters, the port.

As I race towards Sainte Anne, the sea growls and roars. *Bathsheba* skids and careers like a race car. We have never sailed so fast, but I feel as though we will never get there. My thirst is a force driving us on.

And now Sainte Anne is to port, and we turn and leave the turmoil behind. We're here. The harbour is flat, and the town waits calm and pleasant and ordinary, off to starboard, nestled between sea and hill. Civilisation. People.

But *Bathsheba* races onwards. I should have dropped the sails already—to wait so long and now be short of time! I leap from one side of the cockpit to the other, cranking winches, swearing, sweating, tripping on lines. I drop the main, and now I can't control the yacht. With only the genoa flying, she's unbalanced. I push the tiller hard to starboard, but I can't bring her up into the wind. I'm going to hit the island. I'm going to crash into the Seychelles.

I must drop anchor fast. No time to choose where. The depth alarm screams. We're about to touch the bottom. I can't let the anchor out slowly; I pull out the brake and let it clatter into the water along with fifty metres of chain. It sounds like a catastrophe. I realise I'm wet. I'm soaked, and the deck is streaming with water. I didn't even feel the rain. I suck it off my arm, but it's salty and foul on my skin.

But the anchor's holding, dug in by the squally wind. I snatch the genoa sheet and winch for dear life, furling the sail before we can blow off the anchor, as a voice comes on the VHF. A human voice at last. Deeply accented English.

'Yacht *Bathsheba*, Yacht *Bathsheba*, this is the Port Authority. You have anchored in a restricted area. Please move your vessel.'

I press the transmit button. 'I can't move,' I sob. 'I'm out of fuel. I'm out of water. Please, please help me. My sister's lost. My sister's lost at sea.'

———

A motorboat appears from the inner harbour and heads towards me. A long orange launch. Men in military uniforms stand on the foredeck. A dozen or more. Are they policemen? I duck below decks. What will I say to them? Are they here to question me?

I haven't showered since I lost Summer. I stink, and my clothes hang loose on me. In the double mirror, a strange face greets me. She's deeply tanned, her skin peeling and ruby-brown. She's gaunt, red-eyed and savage. Sodden hair clings to her face and neck, and her sarong is dirty and torn. Her right hand and right leg are bandaged.

I tear the bandage off my leg. The wound beneath is already healing to a red line.

The girl in the mirror isn't Summer or Iris. She's unrecognisable. Her eyes are hostile, barbaric.

I'll at least wash off some of this smell. I grab a rag and jam the faucet up, but of course, nothing comes out.

Now there's an angry banging on the hull. Deep voices, boots stomping. They're coming aboard. I can't greet them like this. I yank open the bathroom cupboard and grab a bottle of Summer's perfume. I spray my body. The smell of Summer. Apples and the beach.

A deep voice is calling, a strange accent. 'Captain! Captain! This is the police.'

I race to the cockpit. I'm going to tell them the truth.

I step out into the sunshine, and I'm swept off my feet. Strong arms embrace me, the sweet smell of cloves. Hot tears fall on my face.

'Summer, Summer, Summer,' he says. 'Thank God you're safe. You're so late. I died waiting for you. I'm never letting you out of my sight again!'

I cling to him, and a dam bursts deep inside me. I cry and cry. I split in two with crying.

'Adam,' I sob. 'Darling, it's worse than you think. I've lost my sister.'

In the end, I do it for Summer.

'I've lost Iris,' I say. 'Iris is dead.'

PART II
SUMMER

CHAPTER 10

THE POLICE

'm Summer. I'm Summer. I'm Summer.

I'm the beauty queen, the wife, the mother, the firstborn. I melt into my husband's arms, and a rushing red warmth rises through my body, tingly and electric. My skin seems to melt; I almost dissolve into Adam. We're wrapped in each other, covering each other in joyful tears.

Nobody has to grieve. The perfect family is safe and well.

No matter what happens afterwards, it will all be worth it for this, this moment, now. I am the good twin and I am loved. Adam holds me so tightly my feet lift off the ground.

The policeman can barely wait for Adam to set me down before his questions begin. Who am I? What is my business in the Seychelles?

'My name is Summer Rose Romain,' I say. 'I'm married to a Seychellois citizen. This is our yacht.'

The policeman glares at me from across the cockpit. I clutch Adam's warm hand. For a big man, the officer has a fine jaw, high cheekbones, a face that reveals the skeleton beneath. The sun reflects off his police badge and shines in my eyes. He swaggers around, burly and brusque.

'Are you a citizen?' His voice booms. 'Do you speak Creole?'

Adam pulls me gently down into the cockpit seat beside him and squeezes my hand. He replies for me, a burst of noise. Am I expected to understand this? Has Adam taught me any Creole?

There are a hundred, a thousand things I'm meant to know. I can't do this.

I never dreamed Adam would be here. What is he doing in the Seychelles?

'Summer? Summer!'

I jerk my head up. I must learn to answer to my name!

My husband shakes his head, his eyes wide. 'This is hopeless,' he says. 'I can barely recognise my wife. Think what she's been through. She was all alone out there. You saw she can't sail. Her sister is the sailor. *Was* the sailor.' His voice cracks.

The policeman puts his hand on Adam's shoulder and speaks again in Creole, but his voice is quieter. They whisper

back and forth, as though there's some chance I'll understand. Is there? Creole sounds like French. Iris took French
at school, and phrases pop out now from the sea of sound.

Dans la mer. In the sea. *Bonne femme.* Good woman.

I don't think I've learned any Creole. I'm not supposed to
know these words.

Handcuffs jangle from the inspector's belt. He lights a
cigarette, inhales, and flicks the ash onto the teak floor.

Who is the 'good woman'? Me or the one who is *dans la mer*?

'I know this is hard, baby.' Adam draws me closer, laying
a protective arm across my lap. 'But can you tell us where
Iris fell? Where should we search?'

I don't have to fake my response. Sobs break out of me,
and I can barely speak through the heaving of my chest. 'It
was a week ago—more—it was a thousand miles away!' I cry.
'I woke up and she was gone! I searched. I searched for days
and days. I searched till I ran out of fuel. I searched till I was
running out of water.'

The police inspector has more questions. He fires them at
me in English and Creole. Adam translates. The other men
march up and down the deck in the hot sun. *Bathsheba* wobbles
under the heavy tread of their boots. A knot of them are
smoking at the bow, taking turns to glare at me between puffs.

I'm only telling one lie, but that's the only part the inspector
doesn't question. Everything else comes under scrutiny. I must
seem like a fraud with a poorly concocted story. There's so
much I don't know. What day of the week did my sister

disappear? I don't even know what day it is today. The inspector makes a big deal of the fact that I was asleep at the time, as if I should have stayed awake across the entire Indian Ocean. Me, a pregnant woman.

'Let's check the ship's log,' Adam says. He moves towards the pilot house.

'Yes!' I shout. Too enthusiastic. I know the log backs up my story. I took care last night to throw away my crazy notes, even the paper beneath them, in case the indent of my pen showed through. I flung the 'Skipper' cap overboard too, in order to keep my options open, even though I was determined not to pull this stunt. But now I have to double-check that there are no stray pieces of paper lying around the pilot house. Did I throw everything overboard that I needed to? I stand up to look, and my legs buckle. Adam rushes back and takes me in his arms. My face presses into his collar, his soft cotton shirt. I close my eyes and inhale.

'My wife is pregnant, sir,' he says. 'She's been through an ordeal. Iris is her twin. Their bond is incredible. We can't imagine what she's going through. She must feel like her soul has been torn out.'

He continues in Creole, but the police inspector cuts through. 'I am a twin.'

Adam stops short. I start. I feel that this man can see right through me. He's not going to fall for this incredible bond bullshit.

'Take your wife into the shade,' he says. 'We don't want our witness collapsing. Get her some water.'

'There's no water,' I say. 'There's not a drop left.' I let my legs wobble as Adam helps me step over the child-gate into the pilot house. What can it mean that I'm 'our witness'?

The inspector pushes his way down to the saloon and I see him moving the faucet up and down, turning it from side to side, to no avail. He lurches into the bathroom, no doubt to try the tap in there.

Now he pounds back up to the deck, brushing past us, shouting orders in Creole, his face a deep, angry frown. The men on the foredeck stomp aft to where the launch is tethered. *Bathsheba* lists under their assembled weight.

'We will take you to shore, Mrs Romain,' the inspector barks.

I stand. This is it. He's seen something in the bathroom, and he knows.

'Wait,' says Adam. He speaks to the inspector in Creole.

I can't tell what's going on. I haven't even caught the policeman's name, and I can't imagine why he had to bring ten or twelve men to the boat. Are they the regular customs team or are they onto me? I can't read the vibe between him and Adam. They seem to be engaged in some sort of staring competition, but I can't tell if it's going to end in smiles or blows.

The inspector blinks first. He comes back towards us and holds out his hand. 'Mrs Romain,' he says, 'you have searched for your sister until you ran out of water. It is a miracle that you have survived. You must take care of yourself and your baby. The *interrogation*'—he says the word the French way—'can wait. First we will take you to the hospital.'

'No!' I cry. I'm not letting a doctor anywhere near me till I've told Adam the truth about the baby. Everybody— Adam, the inspector, the men on the side deck—turns and stares. 'Please, I just need water and food. I've barely eaten since it happened, but I don't want anything to delay your investigation. Please take the ship's log to shore. It records our position when she disappeared.'

I'm already learning. Don't say names. Say 'she'. Be vague, like you can't bear to think about it. Like you can't remember. Let them see you stumble.

The men climb down into the launch one by one. While we wait in the hot sunshine, the inspector opens the log. He turns page after page filled with Iris's neat, backwards-slanted handwriting, the purplish ink smudged by her left hand. Her last entry is at six p.m. on the twenty-eighth of March. It's precise and impersonal, the latitude and longitude noted to three decimal places. *Motoring due south to cross equatorial zone. Wind changeable. Making 6 knots. Confused seas, squally weather.*

The next page is covered with the scribblings of a madwoman. GPS coordinates are scrawled at all angles, illegible, covered in dried blood. A crude chart of the area lays out a search grid covered with arrows. No one would recognise this mess as the handwriting of either twin.

The inspector snaps the book shut and ushers me to the side deck. It's a big step down to the launch, but even with my weakness and thirst, I could skip down in an instant. But I lean against Adam's firm shoulder, and he and the inspector take an arm each and lift me down, like a little doll, into the brawny arms of the troops. I'm in a sea of men, all panting to hold me up as the launch bobs and bumps against *Bathsheba*'s side.

Something surges inside me like an ocean swell. I can do this. I can be Summer. The things I don't know, they're details. Adam is familiar in my arms, like we've been married for years.

I've got Summer's essence. I've been practising for this all my life. I *am* Summer. And every man in sight is falling over himself to help me.

The madness that engulfed me on *Bathsheba* will be my best friend. Summer can't remember things, Summer seems different, Summer gets confused. Of course she does. Out there on the ocean, she lost her soul.

There's no one to compare me with anymore. No one with fuller breasts, a sweeter smile, virtue spilling out of her every pore. Twins grow less alike as they age, but that won't happen now. Summer and Iris are back how they started. They're one person again. One girl. And her name is Summer Rose.

I step from the police launch onto land, and this time the dizziness is real. The concrete pier is solid, but I want it to sway. I ought to be glad that I've made it to land, but my body craves *Bathsheba*'s rhythm. Ahead of me is a grassy area, iridescent green. Rich soil shows moist between the blades. I stumble towards it, escorted by Adam and the inspector, like a celebrity or a prisoner. I sink onto the softness and press my face against the green. I can barely stop myself from sucking at the wet soil.

My chest heaves with sobs, but I'm too dry for tears. I can hear the men behind me, their sorrowful murmurings, as if they're watching a kitten die. And now Adam is holding something to my lips. A bottle.

I drink and drink. And when I am full to bursting, I pour the water over my head. My face, my neck, my body are instantly cool and fresh. My hair and sarong cling to my skin.

My thirst quenched, I take in my surroundings for the first time. We are on a street, a tropical street crowded with colourfully dressed people. Everyone is staring. I look around, half-expecting to see my twin standing beside me.

An older woman steps forward, her face alive with concern. 'Excuse me, sir, madam, I'm from the yacht club,' she says, her eyes darting between me and Adam, who is lifting me back to my feet. 'We heard your radio transmission. We wish to offer our deepest sympathies. The yacht club is open to you both. There are showers and food, a place to lie down. You are our guests.'

'Thank you,' says Adam.

'I can't,' I say. 'I have to help the police.'

'Summer, you're going to be no use to anyone if you don't look after yourself,' Adam says. 'Inspector Barbé has the log. Let him investigate. You need food and rest. For the baby.'

I steal a glance at Inspector Barbé, expecting him to object, but he nods his assent. 'Take your time, Mrs Romain,' he says. 'We will handle the search now.'

I'm almost carried along the street. People swirl around me, and I can see they're Adam's people, the Seychellois. They have his open face, his strong build. Everything is fuzzy with heat. Coconut palms loom above me. We pass street stalls, and a warm meaty aroma pervades the fragrant air. 'Food,' I say. 'Food.'

'It's all right, there's food at the yacht club,' the man holding my shoulders says, and I start—it's not Adam anymore. Where did he go? This man is dressed the same, feels the same, smells the same. His voice has the same deep cadence. But his eyes are a light gold, startling after Adam's pools of dark brown.

'Don't worry, Adam's run ahead,' says the man. 'I'm Daniel. I'm taking you there now. You'll be back with Adam in a moment. He's organising someone to refuel the boat and take it to the marina. The yachties are helping you, they're taking a fuel tank out by dinghy.'

A man and a woman in tattered clothes brush past us, grey-haired, skin like dark leather. The man holds a diesel carry-can, and the woman's bright blue eyes meet mine. Her gaze is wise, sorrowful and kind, and I know they're the yachties helping me—the poor young pregnant wife who lost her sister at sea.

I know the type: penniless yachties, always the first to lend a hand. I remember what Dad would have said. Nice is dumb.

'Are you a yachtie?' I ask Daniel.

'No, I'm Adam's cousin, remember? We talked on the phone after your wedding.'

I stumble and lean harder on his arm. That way he won't expect an answer.

We walk through a boatyard and enter a covered deck area overlooking the water where groups of people are seated for lunch. It's noisy and casual; I can hear a mix of languages. This must be the yacht club. I'm ushered to a table. Food and drink appear from nowhere. A glass of milk of all things. It flows down my throat like nectar. I stuff some hot chips in my mouth. Daniel orders more milk.

People circle us, whispering. Everyone's keeping their distance. Is it delicacy, or are they too harrowed by my story to look me in the face? Even Daniel keeps his eyes downcast.

This is going to be so much easier than I thought. I won Inspector Barbé over with my empty water tanks, and no one wants to question a pregnant woman. If anything gets awkward, I can cry or act crazy. I barely need to act.

'. . . all his family are here,' Daniel is saying. 'He tried to keep your pregnancy a secret, but he was under so much stress.

He was in a bad state after that phone call. He tried to call you to tell you about Tarquin, and then after that *nothing* for twelve days. The yacht was nearly a week overdue, Summer.'

Tarquin.

Adam was calling me about Tarquin.

The fucking changeling. I've forgotten to ask about my stepson, no, my_ *son*. Jesus, I can't even remember how old the brat is. And where the hell is he?

I've messed up big time. I should have been crying out for Tarquin the moment I got here. *Where's my little boy? I need my little boy!*

But that's not even the worst of it. Twelve bloody days, and I didn't think to wonder what Adam was saying to me on that sat phone call. Or what I said to him.

My lips were moving, but you can't read lips off grainy CCTV footage. Even if I could somehow get back to the yacht and play that disc—it's still hidden in my suitcase lining—*Iris's* suitcase lining—it wouldn't help.

Did Adam hear the *thwack* that killed my sister? The boom crashing into her skull? He must have heard a loud noise, maybe a splash, and then the line would have cut, and he wouldn't have been able to call back. And now he's going to find out that the phone is missing. How am I going to explain all this? He thinks he was talking to me, Summer, the twin who survived.

One thing is certain: I can never let Adam see that footage.

What did he say to me on that call? Something about Tarquin? They were only going to make phone calls in emergencies. What has happened to Tarquin?

A crash. I've dropped the milk on the floor. My hands are shaking. Daniel catches me as I reach to pick up the broken glass.

'Leave it,' he says. 'Don't eat or drink anymore for now. Your body needs time to recover. You need to rest.'

I almost blurt out something about him being no expert, when a voice behind me says, 'Doctor Romain, your car is here.'

Doctor Romain. Jesus, the last thing I need near me is a freaking doctor. Can he diagnose a fake pregnancy from across the table? Somehow, I find myself being led out of the yacht club. I've barely noticed where I was, but I glance around as I'm leaving. The diners at the other tables avert their eyes.

The yacht club has no walls; a set of white pillars hold up the roof, like something from ancient Rome. On the nearest pillar, level with my eyes, is an algal stain. A watermark. I look around and see a similar stain on every pillar at the same height. I press my hand into it, and the plaster crumbles.

I'm standing underwater in this building, up to my eyes in the sea. I'm drowning, but I can't move. 'Is this really here?' I ask. 'Did the sea come into this building? Up to here?'

I turn and look behind. The waters of the harbour reach almost to the edge of the yacht club. From here I can see the concrete pier and, beyond it, *Bathsheba*'s mast bobbing in the open harbour. But how could the sea have come so high? Am I hallucinating?

'The tsunami,' Adam says. No, not Adam, Daniel. 'Back in 2004.'

I'm straining for breath. The air turns ocean-green, and I'm stuck, anchored by my feet. Daniel takes me by the shoulders and steers me outside—a flash of sunshine—and then into his car. I'm on a leather seat in the back of an air-conditioned sedan. Daniel sits beside me, and his driver pulls out onto the road.

I can't ask Daniel what happened here, how many people died. I'm torn into madness by the loss of one person. How many friends did Daniel lose? What did the people here live through?

I've heard about the tsunami before, of course; nobody could spend time in Phuket and not hear, but it was something that had happened to other people. The sea takes its toll.

I thought I was exempt, but now Iris Carmichael is lost at sea. Somehow, I'm still here, but it's only a matter of time. Collapsing into Doctor Romain's steady arms, I feel I can see the future. The sea will claim its dead.

I walk a fine line between delicate and sick. Too distraught to be questioned, but not mad enough to be hospitalised. Would it cross the line to ask where Tarquin is? To have forgotten every word of the phone call?

The sedan glides along a modern road, through succulent forest. Women bounce along the footpath in tube tops and miniskirts. They look free and happy, comfortable in their beautiful clothes. If I were Seychelloise, I could get out of the car and disappear into the crowd.

No, I don't need to escape. I can do this. Adam and I haven't been married long, and he's never been able to tell me apart from my twin.

I need to get back to Adam. Why did he leave me with his cousin? I can't understand how I didn't notice the switch.

And where is Daniel taking me? Please not a hospital. I can't ask. Alone with a doctor, I'm history. I can feel Daniel pressing his fingers into me, confusion appearing on his chiselled features as he palpates my empty womb.

I'll pull him onto the examination table, on top of me, my hand snaking into his pants. *Doctor, give me a baby. I'll split the cash with you.* He must have a lot of Adam's DNA. No one would ever know.

'Adam's waiting for us at La Belle Romance,' says Daniel. He's reading something on his phone. 'He's leaving your son with my mother for the night. Tarquin's desperate to see you, Adam says, but he thinks it's not a good idea. Not until'— Daniel smiles uncomfortably—'you're more like yourself.'

I frame a sad-but-compliant expression. Like I'm desperate to see Tarquin, but too tired to argue. Doctor knows best.

If I never see the kid again, it will be too soon.

———

I've heard Adam and Summer talk about La Belle Romance.
A big part of Adam's business involves booking wealthy
Australians into his grandparents' hotel. Romain Travel
attracts a lot of honeymooners, and older couples celebrating
anniversaries. Yet I have always pictured a rundown building,
rustic, cramped.

Daniel's driver takes us over the steep hills of Mahé's interior
and down towards the opposite coast, and now the car turns
into a boulevard lined with flourishing frangipani and verti-
ginous palms. The dangling coconuts are a weird doubled
shape, as though each one tried and failed to split in two.

We pull up in front of a palace. The parapets and colon-
nades hail from a bygone era, yet the building is impeccably
maintained, and the white walls glisten in the afternoon sun.
The surroundings are Arcadian; manicured grounds sweep
down to a postcard of a beach. Are those actual peacocks
prowling amid the sculpted herbage?

'You're rich,' I blurt out, then feel my face grow hot.

Daniel smiles. 'We would be, if my grandparents hadn't
had eight children,' he says. 'There are sixteen grandchildren
now, so we each own a sliver of this place, but yes, it keeps
the wolf from the door. Speaking of which, wait here, let me
get your door for you.'

He jumps out of the car, and I'm alone with my image
of sixteen Adams and Daniels who each own a slice of this
paradise.

My door swings open, but it's not Daniel—it's Adam. His voice is gentle and sweet, but he's not talking to me.

'Look who's here, matey,' he coos. 'Mummy's back.'

I guess we turned up sooner than expected. Standing beside Adam on the green lawn is one of the many heirs to this fortune. He stands as still as a statue, and he stares at me as if I am a ghost.

Tarquin.

My son.

CHAPTER 11

THE DISC

'Tarquin! Tarky!' I tumble out of the car, my mouth stumbling over the unfamiliar nickname. Isn't *he* supposed to run into *my* arms? But he stands his ground and even—am I imagining this?—shrinks back as I scoop him into a decent impression of a loving embrace.

I've barely seen Tarquin since the wedding. In Thailand he was unconscious, and he didn't seem to have grown any bigger. All this time, I've been thinking he was a baby, a formless puddle of baby fat rolling around in a onesie. But this is a boy, a fully formed human. A stranger.

What do I say? How do I talk to him? 'Goochie goochie goo' or 'How are you, young man?' I can't speak in case I get it wrong, so I stay silent, covering my confusion with tears. I cling to the kid, willing him to hug me back, trembling lest he come out with some bombshell like, 'Hello, Aunty Iris.' He wriggles in my arms.

Adam is talking in a sing-song voice. 'Look, it's Mummy. Tarky missed Mummy, didn't he?'

I take my cue from Adam. 'Hello, Tarky,' I say, an octave higher than my usual tone. 'Mummy missed you too.'

Tarquin says nothing. Adam continues to speak for him. 'Tarky is happy now.'

Thank God. It seems that the brat still hasn't learned to speak. I remain on edge, in case his silence is mere bashfulness, but when he starts babbling, 'Orby-borby-borby,' it's the most welcome sound. Adam's lack of attention to the noise shows me that he doesn't expect his son to say anything meaningful. Tarquin isn't as grown up as he looks; it's just that they've cut off his curls, and he's walking on his own two feet at last. Aside from that, he's still a baby.

Fortunately, Tarquin is soon packed off with some relative. I have nothing to fear from a mute, as long as I can keep emoting like a long-lost mother every time I see him.

I'm introduced to a bevy of in-laws. I can't believe how many I have: grandparents, aunts and uncles, cousins with their wives and children. Luckily, Adam's an only child, and apart from his parents, who are in Australia, I haven't met any of his family before. In any case, Adam fends off any difficult questions, explaining that his dear wife is in shock.

I pass through a glittering lobby of polished marble and ascend a sweeping staircase. The luxury at La Belle Romance goes beyond extravagant and into the realms of disconcerting. They install us in the Diamond Suite, which must be the hotel's finest. I goddamn hope so, anyway. The word *magnifique* was coined to describe the chandelier in here.

Daniel changes the dressing on my wounded hand, I take a long shower, and soon I am languishing on a purple chaise longue while manservants bring me platters of fruit. Adam hovers like an anxious nurse, and Daniel lurks behind him. The doctor is adamant that I shouldn't overeat, but eventually he relents and lets me scoff a chunk of spicy lamb.

'I thought you said your wife was vegetarian?' he asks Adam.

'I said she had vegetarian leanings . . .' Adam replies, before I have a chance to freak out—Summer had dipped in and out of vegetarianism so many times, I'd stopped paying attention. Did she eat meat on the boat? Surely she did? She definitely cooked a few meat dishes.

'But you know how it is with pregnancy,' Adam continues, shrugging. 'She got hungry.'

Pregnancy. It's too late to tell Adam I've had a miscarriage. Why have I let the moment go by? I guess because that was what saved me from the police inspector. That and the empty water tanks were what tipped him from suspicion to sympathy. If I hadn't been poor pregnant Mrs Romain, he would have dragged me off to the police cells. Perhaps he still will, but at least I'll have time to get my story sorted first.

Never mind. I can have a miscarriage later.

Adam is so fond and attentive that chills run up and down my body as he kneels by the chaise longue, leaning close to me, brushing a stray hair from my face, squeezing my hand. But he's being so platonic, so *respectful* of my grief. And the doctor is circling like an oceanic predator, staring at me with his golden eyes. Am I behaving like a pregnant woman?

'Could you hear me when I called you on the sat phone?' Adam asks, pressing his cheek against mine, so close that I can't see his face. 'Was that before or after you lost Iris?'

My brain is spinning around inside my skull. What am I meant to say? How can he not know whether or not Iris had fallen overboard when he phoned me? Is this a trick question?

Hold on. There's a gift in his words. A great big escape clause.

'No,' I say slowly. 'No, I couldn't hear you when you called me on the sat phone.' I wrap my arms around his head, keeping his cheek pressed against mine. There's a hint of stubble, a little roughness in his smooth skin. 'Couldn't you hear me either?'

'Nothing,' says Adam. 'Just a whooshing sound. Then the phone went dead. I tried to call back, but I couldn't get through.'

'Yes,' I say. 'That's right. The phone went dead. Then I went to bed, and I—she—she said she would keep the phone with her in case you rang back. Afterwards, I couldn't find it. She must have been holding it when . . . when . . .'

'Don't think about it now,' Adam says, rocking back on his heels and taking my hands. 'It's too much for you.'

I let a tear leak down my cheek. I've explained away the call and the disappearance of the phone. It ties up beautifully.

I might as well push on and find out more. 'It's all so confusing,' I say. 'Why were you phoning? I thought the sat phone was only for emergencies.'

'I know,' Adam says, 'but I wanted to tell you the good news that we would be waiting for you here. And I couldn't last one more day without hearing my wife's beautiful voice.'

I remember Summer's blissful excitement, her impulsive leap onto the aft deck. Her desperation to hear her husband. So it was Adam's love, Adam's need for Summer, that struck the fatal blow.

I shove more pineapple in my mouth. I've finessed my way through a tough conversation, but what about the disc? The disc doesn't fit with the story I've just told.

I didn't chuck the disc overboard with my emerald ring and my notes in case I had to show it to the police. Without Adam, I thought the police might doubt my story. The footage was evidence that my sister did fall overboard, that it was an accident.

But Adam's presence changes things. My little insurance policy has become a problem. Perhaps I could have explained away the 'Crew' cap, even though Adam might wonder why Iris was wearing it. But I can't explain the fact that the girl who is on the sat phone goes overboard, now that I've claimed that I took the call myself.

Dammit, if only I had known that he couldn't hear anything, I could have claimed that Iris took the call, and then I could have shown him the footage. Too late now. The disc could ruin everything. It has to go.

Adam's phone rings. 'Hi, Adam here.' His voice is strained, metallic. 'I'm afraid you need to prepare yourself . . .' He walks out of the room, but through the open door I hear a wailing, long and keening. The woman through the phone is my mother.

I feel like my blood is draining out of me. My mother! Why didn't I foresee that she might phone Adam?

I have mucked everything up. I should jump off this chaise longue and run after Adam, who's hightailing it down a hallway to save me from the clamour. I'll shout to my mother that it's not true. She's not dead.

But I stay where I am. It is true. Annabeth has lost a daughter. If it matters to her which one, if mothers do have favourites even when they pretend not to, then I'm doing her a favour.

I was only going to pull this prank for a few days to get out of the Seychelles, but how can I undo it now? Annabeth was never meant to hear this news.

Adam comes back into the room with a harrowed expression.

'I'm sorry you had to tell her,' I say. 'I should have phoned Mum sooner. I'll phone my brother myself.'

'No,' he says, 'your mum's phoning him. She said she wanted to.'

I think of my brother's voice, the steady ordinariness of it. I want him here. I need him. Ben is my only sibling now. Francine's girls, raised to hate us, don't count. Ben will be here in a few days. He'll come as soon as he can, I know he will. I have to hold out till then.

Ben won't recognise me, not the way I look at the moment. Or if he does, will it matter to him? What's one sister over another? He's quiet, timid. He won't speak up.

In the early evening, I ask Adam to take me back to *Bathsheba*, but he resists.

'My grandparents have given us this suite for as long as we like,' he says. 'I thought you would never want to see that boat again.'

I have to give a reason. I can't say that I don't like being surrounded by his family. I can't say I miss being at sea.

'It's the last place I was with my sister,' I say, 'the last place she was alive.'

Adam looks doubtful, but I keep asking, and at last he agrees to drive me back. Tarquin will spend the night with relations. Daniel lends us his car.

In the car, I'm alone with Adam for the first time. Daniel's driver is apparently busy elsewhere. Now is the time to come clean. *Honey, I lost the baby.* It would be so easy to say, but what next? *Let's conceive another baby right away.* But this baby was an accident, and my body has been through an ordeal. What if he wants to wait?

The words won't come. And Adam doesn't stop talking all the way to the marina, where *Bathsheba* is waiting for us. He tells me how he nearly died when *Bathsheba* was overdue, how he panicked when he saw me on deck, struggling to handle the yacht on my own. How his heart overflowed when he found me safe and held me in his arms again. 'I'm going to get you through this, Summer, like you got me through losing Helen.'

Everything he says is *I love you, I love you, I love you.*

We park at Eden Island Marina and walk past a line of open-air restaurants, their neon signs glowing in the dusk. French, Turkish, Brazilian, Chinese. Spicy aromas waft through the evening air.

'Where do you want to eat?' asks Adam.

I can't think about food. I need to be alone on the boat. I need to get rid of the disc. But I can't tell Adam to go and dine without me. This is our big reunion.

Apart from when he needs the bathroom, Adam has no reason to leave me alone all evening. And I can't get the disc while he's in the bathroom. My injured hand is clumsy. There won't be time, and he might hear something. On a boat you can feel the motion when someone moves a suitcase around.

Now we see the supermarket, the stalls outside stacked with papayas and limes. 'Oh, fresh food,' I say. 'Can't we eat on board? I want to be alone with you.'

'I'll cook you dinner, beautiful,' Adam says. 'Let's grab some steak and veggies, maybe some apple juice?'

Steak sounds great. No need to keep up the vegetarianism, obviously. 'Would you mind doing the shopping?' I ask. 'I'll meet you on the boat.'

'I think we should stick together,' says Adam. 'You might find it hard being back there on your own.'

'No, no, I'll be fine,' I say. 'If anything, I'm landsick. I need the boat's motion.'

Such an un-Summer-ish thing to say, but it works.

'OK,' says Adam.

'See you soon, babe,' I say casually.

I force myself to walk slowly until he is out of sight. Then I scurry along the floating dock towards *Bathsheba*. Her mast is dead ahead, but I've come down the wrong walkway. Damn! I'm close, but I can't leap over three metres of water, so I have to double back almost all the way to the supermarket to get to the right pontoon.

I finally reach the yacht and rush to the stateroom, where I drag Iris's suitcase out of a locker and unzip it with fluttery hands. I slide my hand inside the lining, feeling for the disc. Nothing. Is it gone? Could the police have searched the boat and found it already? Just as I'm about to give up, my fingers close around the cold, thin plastic. I yank it out with a suppressed cry of joy and shove the suitcase back in the locker.

Night is falling as I climb up to the cockpit. This must be the right thing to do. I've sorted things with the police, or

Adam did—who cares—so it's time for the disc to go for a swim. It's annoying that it's going to be in the shallow marina instead of the bottomless ocean, but seabed is seabed. No one goes digging around down there.

The marina is quiet, but it's still light, and there are lots of other boats around. Anyone could be inside another boat, looking out. Dropping things overboard in a marina is taboo, so it's the sort of thing that another sailor would notice and remember. Someone might mention it in front of Adam.

I'll wait. Men are never quick in the supermarket. Any minute now, the hasty tropical night will cloak me in privacy. I'll let it get a little darker.

———

The sky is charcoal, and the disc has a dull sheen as it drops into the wet black void between *Bathsheba*'s hull and the floating pontoon. It slips into nothingness.

Footsteps. I look up. Adam is striding along the pontoon towards me.

Did he see me? His face is screwed into a ball of fury, or perhaps fear—I can't read his expressions yet. He's holding his phone.

'Bad news,' he says. 'That was Barbé.'

He climbs on board and flicks on the torch on his phone. Bending low, he shines it around the sides of the cockpit.

Under the cockpit seat, half-covered by the squabs, is a series of red splashes. Blood.

That wound I cut into my leg, that ritual for Summer. I was standing right here. I can't believe I sailed all the way across the ocean and didn't take a moment to clean up the blood.

Adam shines the torch in my face, and my lower lip trembles. 'That's blood, isn't it?' he asks.

'Did he see it?' I ask. 'Why did he phone *you* about it?'

'Who, Barbé? No, he doesn't know about it. At least I think he doesn't,' Adam says. 'I saw it when he was questioning you, but none of the policemen seemed to notice it. Thank God they didn't sit down. They would have been staring right at it. Then, what with having to tell your mum the news and deal with Tarq, I forgot about it. Obviously it's from the wound on your hand or maybe fish blood or something—did you catch a fish? But we don't want them getting any ideas. I've been thinking, Summer, don't tell the police anything about Iris, the weird shit, I mean—the dressing alike, the copycat haircuts. I don't mean to scare you, but the police here are not like in Australia.'

He brushes his hand over my face, pushing back the hair from my eyes. I can't understand what he means by 'weird shit'. I got a haircut similar to Summer's back in New Zealand, and OK, it wasn't the first time I had given a hairdresser a photo of Summer to copy, but only for the sake of conveni-ence. As for the clothes, I did occasionally take advantage of

Summer's habit of posting photos of her new outfits online complete with price tags, but only in order to pick up bargains. I never intended to *copy* her.

I can hardly argue with Adam. I have to focus on the here and now. What is he trying to tell me about the police? I had begun to think Inspector Barbé's hostility towards me was all in my guilty head—despite his myriad questions, he treated me kindly—but maybe not.

'So, what's the bad news?' I ask.

'I don't know how to tell you this,' Adam says.

His eyes are black pools, inscrutable. I lean in towards him, tilt my lips up towards his face. Love me, Adam. Protect me.

'This is a small country,' says Adam. 'They don't have a proper coastguard, the police force is basic, and it's been twelve days, Summer.'

'Yes,' I say.

'I'm just going to come out and say this. There's not going to be a search. They don't have the resources.'

Is he serious? Of course there's not going to be a search. My sister died twelve days ago, over a thousand miles away. Her body is at the bottom of the sea.

I can't be bothered acting shocked or surprised. 'Adam, I know,' I say. 'I searched for her beyond the point of reason. I know she's gone.'

Adam gives my shoulder a sympathetic squeeze. 'So, you woke to find her missing,' he says. 'Any clues as to how she fell?'

I have to feign ignorance. 'All I know is that she was there when I went to bed, and when I woke up, she was gone. I don't really want to imagine the details.'

'I hoped there might be a way of getting some answers,' says Adam, 'but it was a dead end. I didn't want to get your hopes up, so I came back to the yacht while you were with Daniel to check the CCTV that your dad installed. Unfortunately, it's an old system that only keeps the last week of footage, so it was too late.'

'It's OK,' I say. 'I've had time to come to terms with the thought that I'll never know exactly what happened. Maybe it's better this way.'

'I understand,' says Adam. 'No point driving yourself mad wondering. Knowing what caused Iris to fall wouldn't change anything.'

Adam holds me close for a long time. His neck is just the right height for my face to nestle into. Then he settles me in the pilot house with a glass of apple juice, as though I'm an invalid, and fetches a bucket of soapy water—it seems the yachties have replenished our tanks. He washes the cockpit clean of blood. Every last trace.

He didn't even ask his wife where the blood came from. He suggested a couple of ideas but didn't wait for her to say which was correct. He didn't cross-examine her about her sister's disappearance. He trusts her absolutely. And he doesn't trust the Seychellois police. I'm too scared to ask what he means about the police being different from those in Australia, but his decision to clean up the blood sends an eloquent message.

I'm sure I smell good after my shower at La Belle Romance, but now, while Adam is cleaning, I duck into the bathroom to use some of that apple perfume. I spray it into the air and walk into the mist, breathing in the sweet fragrance.

The girl in the mirror looks much better than she did this morning. Her face will change as the years pass, but it won't matter because no one will be comparing. No one will ask her which twin she is.

Adam fries steak and throws together a salad. We eat in the cockpit. Masts clink and balmy breezes carry the scent of night flowers. Our conversation is intermittent and repetitive, but that's to be expected. Nobody knows what to say to the bereaved.

My new life is falling into place, but the best is yet to come. After dinner, I hurry below to strip the foul, salty sheets off the bed and lay down fresh white linen. I dig through drawers and find a set of clean lingerie. Soft pink satin, never worn; I have to pull off the price tags.

Adam's expecting me back outside, but instead, I slip into bed and wait. My heart beats so fast, I'm sure it's visible through my rib cage.

All day, he's been stroking my hair, clasping my hand, pressing my body to his, but the sexiest thing of all was when he got down on his hands and knees and washed that blood away. Adam is my husband. He loves me.

He saunters into the room, strips down to his boxers, and drops into bed beside me. His warm, firm arms slide around me, and my skin tingles as he draws me close. He nuzzles his face into my hair. 'Summer, my sweet sunshine,' he murmurs. 'I'm sorry about everything. Sleep now. Let me hold you and keep you safe. You and our baby.'

He smells like heaven. My whole body pulses with need. His warm skin presses against my back, and his muscled legs curve in against the back of my thighs.

I wait, breathless, for him to make the first move, but there's no pressure against my hips. Adam is not aroused. This is a comforting hug, a platonic hug for a grieving woman.

Play along, sister. Be patient.

I try to calculate dates, but the numbers jump around in my head. All I know is, they won't fit. Everything is perfect, except for one thing. There is no baby.

CHAPTER 12

THE WASHING MACHINE

Of course I know who I am. I haven't forgotten. I can't forget. But I can't let myself think it, not for one moment, not with these relatives circling and Adam, Adam, Adam everywhere.

I know who I am because, although Adam's family is kind, I want, *need*, to get away from them. Summer would have slept at La Belle Romance, surrounded by Romains, each of them her newest, dearest friend. She would have slept with Tarquin curled up in her arms.

I know who I am because I didn't call Annabeth or Ben myself. Summer would have faced up to them. Isn't this how she snared Adam, because she didn't shy away from his grief?

I know who I am because, as Adam spoons me in the warm night, his sleepy, trusting left hand snakes across my torso and nestles against my right breast, and I watch the right side of my chest pulse with each beat of my wayward, loveless, twisted heart.

I'm Iris, the spiky purple flower, not the sweet round rose. I'm the irises in your eyes, the twin rings of aqua around the two black pupils, the windows to my own missing soul.

I wake in the darkness, jolted into sweaty awareness not by a nightmare but by the stark truth of my waking life, piercing my sleep like a hot blade. *Bathsheba* rocks in the breeze, and I imagine I'm still at sea. I'll make landfall today and tell Adam the truth. Of course he'll help me. He'll deal with the police and call his cousin, Dr Romain. And I won't have to refuse to be examined. I'll let the doctor check me over.

How can I carry on like this? I'm bound to slip up. If only I could get back to Wakefield. Summer's wardrobe holds files of her whole life. I wouldn't make mistakes with those to guide me. I'd read every page. Adam's Favourite Meals. *The Millennial Kama Sutra.*

If only I hadn't covered myself with that apple perfume. Or was it the sarong or the wedding rings that I was already wearing when Adam swept me into his arms? But I could have explained those away. If only he hadn't spoken so lovingly, held me so warmly, smelled so very good.

It went back further, though. Dropping my own ugly green ring overboard along with the notes I wrote, the plans for how this could work. If only I hadn't, out of pure love for Summer, cut open my upper thigh to the groin. Then I couldn't have done this no matter how much I longed to. Without the scar I would have had to tell the truth.

Adam would never marry his dead wife's twin, but maybe there would have been a man, among the many Romains or the other men of the Seychelles, or somewhere in the world, who might one day have loved Iris Carmichael.

No. Right now, she would be lying here alone, the unloved bearer of the worst possible news. Or perhaps, without Adam's intercession, she would be in prison already. Perhaps Adam would have asked Iris, in front of Inspector Barbé, whether that spattered blood belonged to his dead wife?

Even if he hadn't, even if everything had gone as well as it could have, even if Adam gave me *Bathsheba*, even if the first man I laid eyes on when I set foot in the Seychelles fell in love with me, by the time my divorce came through Virginia would have produced the heir.

Francine would have won.

Adam slumbers on as the light turns golden. I slip out of bed. I'm sure there's nothing left for me to hide, but the sheets I pulled off the bed last night need to be washed. Adam might not be able to tell, but I know that they smell of Iris.

The laundry hamper is full of Summer's beautiful new underthings and Iris's faded old knickers, which I suppose I can throw away. Now that we're in the marina, there's unlimited power and water. It's time for me to start being Adam's perfect wife.

I yank open the door to the laundry closet, and the big machines gleam at me. The things Summer loved most on the boat. She was always so content with ordinary things: tying on a sweet pinafore and washing Tarquin's nappies, cooking Adam's favourite meals.

There's a whiff of old clothes, a scent like skin and decaying fruit. The laundry hamper is sitting on the top-loading washing machine. I move it to the floor and tug at the lid of the machine, but I can't get it open. Summer said something about locking it so it didn't bang open and shut at sea, but surely it won't be hard to figure out how to release the lid now. I push my head into the shallow space above the washing machine and below the dryer. Everything is cramped on a boat. I'm bent over the machine, reaching to the back, groping for some kind of release lever, when it happens.

He presses against me. His muscled thighs are hot against the backs of my legs, and I feel a hardness pushing against the strap of my G-string.

'You little cocktease,' he says. There's a sharp edge to his voice. 'Wiggling your sexy little butt at me.'

I can't believe it's Adam's voice. This isn't how he talks to Summer. *He knows. He knows it's me.* Gritting my teeth, I try to turn to look in his eyes. If the game is up, I'm going to face it.

But he grabs my hair and jerks my face away from him. My body slams against the lid of the machine. My chin hits the control panel.

'What are you doing?' I cry. 'You're hurting me!'

'You want it,' he says. 'I'm gonna sexyrape you and you're gonna love it, you dirty little whore.'

Pressure on my G-string. He doesn't even bother to pull it aside. He thrusts against the fabric, and I feel it give way. Adam is inside me.

I can't breathe. I'm not ready. I'm jammed between his hard body and the grim machine. He pushes with such force that the whole yacht seems to move. Hot spikes shoot up my spine into my brain. My feet lift off the cabin sole.

I don't care about being Summer. Maybe I'm meant to play along, but I don't care. I don't care about anything. This isn't how it's supposed to be. Adam's not supposed to hurt Summer.

He's pulling my hair, and my hips are jammed against the steel edge of the machine.

'Stop!' I cry. 'You can't do this! You can't do this to me!'

'You love it,' he says. He doesn't stop. Somehow, he's still holding my hair as his hands force their way under my bra. His palms are calloused, and my nipples respond to their texture, even as my face grows hot with shame.

'I can feel that you want it,' he says. 'You know you love it, little whore-wife. I saw you looking at those policemen yesterday. Do you know how hot you would look fucking a policeman?' His voice is close to my ear now; he's leaning into the space between the two machines. 'Him in his uniform and you naked. I saw you staring at his handcuffs. He's gonna lock you in one of his cells and then he's gonna take you up against those prison bars, and I'm gonna watch.'

Maybe he doesn't know it's me. Maybe this is some sick role-play. What happened to Summer's stories of candles and romance?

I have to play along. 'Hmm, you're so hard,' I moan in my most Summer-ish voice. It seems like a safe thing to say, but it breaks his rhythm. This isn't what I'm expected to say. I'm not playing my part. I don't *know* my part.

Is there a safe word? I don't want this. I want my husband to hold me in his arms. I want my husband to make love to me.

I try something else. 'I'm a good girl,' I lisp. 'Let me go and I'll be good.'

'Too late,' says Adam. 'You should have thought of that before you wiggled your naked butt at me, you hot little slut.'

So this is what he wants me to say. Relief mingles with hot shame. This was Summer's sex life. This is the truth.

'I'm sorry,' I whisper. 'I'll be good next time.'

He picks up speed, thrusts harder, digs his hands into my breasts. The filthy words fly at me—whore, harlot, minx, slut. I don't seem to need to say anything more. I close my eyes and pretend I'm not here. I'm a body leaning over a washing machine. I'm doing the laundry.

I forget to do anything but hold still, but Adam doesn't seem to care. He lets go of me as his body's rhythm takes over. He's nearly done.

And then my skin catches fire, and my body pulses in an agonising release. I can't hide the hot waves of pleasure that wash over me. And Adam comes so volcanically, I swear I can feel his fluid shoot right into my womb. It's over.

My mind is my own, but my body is Summer's body. When Adam pins her against the washing machine and ravishes her, she climaxes. Maybe this is why it's her favourite thing.

———

Adam's in the shower. He's shut the door between the bathroom and the saloon, and I don't want to find out if it's locked. Maybe Summer would sashay in and join him.

There's no way I can go in there. I drift into the stateroom and throw myself on the bed.

I feel I will never be clean again, but Adam doesn't know anything's wrong. He's singing in there, out of tune and cheerful.

I shouldn't be so surprised. People don't tell their kinky secrets to their sisters. What did Adam call it? Rapey sex? No, sexyrape. The word is sickening, but it was obviously part of a shared fantasy. Men don't say that sort of thing, surely, when they're actually raping you.

Adam loves Summer. They're having a baby together. He talked dirty, but his hands roamed over Summer's body in a good way, and he was rough, but not rough enough to hurt the baby. Sure, Summer told me a censored version of their sex life, but what she told me had a kind of truth. They're crazy for each other. Just in a sick way. I should have known no man is perfect. The poetic words, the grand gestures. They were too good to be true.

The worst part is, I didn't want him to do it. I've never been into BDSM, never seen the need to pretend I don't want sex or to be slapped around while making love. I nearly stopped him. A few words would have done it. *I'm not Summer. I'm the wrong twin.*

But being Summer won out over everything. Adam wanted me. He was inside me. It was *my* body that made him hard, *my* body that made him move like that. And even if I didn't want it, my body did.

Adam was doing what Summer loved. They even had their own creepy little word for it. *Sexyrape.* They must have a safe word too, but she didn't say it. He wasn't surprised when she came. He kissed her tousled hair and peeled off into the shower.

I'm the one who put myself here. I made Adam do something he would never do. He's a good guy. If he knew what he'd done, he'd die of shame. And he'd hate me as he's never hated anyone.

I can never tell him now.

I can never ever tell him.

I lie on my back and lift my legs over my head. Might as well get gravity to help out. Virginia will be sixteen in less than a month. This might be my only chance.

I don't know Summer's safe word.

I don't know any of her passwords. How am I going to get into her phone, her email, her Facebook, her bank account?

Can you forget a safe word? Is that believable?

I swing my legs down into a normal position as Adam emerges from the shower. He struts around, casual and preoccupied, while I try to catch my first glimpse of his naked body.

I'm still wearing the porno-pink lingerie. There's nothing innocent about this colour; in Summer and Adam's world, pink is the shade of sex. I slip between the sheets before Adam can catch sight of me. He might start thinking about second helpings. But he's not looking at me. He's pulling on boxer shorts while staring at his phone. 'I need to get Tarq from my aunt's house,' he says. 'I think he was worried by your appearance yesterday—your face is thinner and you're much more tanned. And I could see you found it hard to be with him—'

'No!' I protest, although, of course, he's right. After my initial relief at discovering Tarquin is still a mute, my fear of him has returned. The kid might not be able to spring me, but I don't know how to act around him.

'Hey, it's OK, I understand, beautiful,' Adam says. 'I was the same when Helen died. Looking at this kid you're supposed to love, but you're in too much pain. I could see it on your face yesterday. You couldn't connect with him. Like you'd forgotten how to be his mum.'

I must look as aghast as I feel, because his voice softens. 'Babe, I don't mean to hurt you,' he says. 'Let's take things slow with Tarq. I don't want him on *Bathsheba* anyway after what happened. It feels dangerous. Will you be OK if I leave you on your own for a bit? I'll drop the laundry at the laundrette and pick up some more food. I can get Daniel to come round.'

'Yes!' I say. 'I mean, no! Yes, I'm OK, and no, no need to send Daniel.'

The doctor has to keep away from my body. He can't press his stethoscope against my chest. I can imagine his face as he moves the instrument from my left breast to my right. It's the face every doctor in my life has made after listening to my chest. Not so much surprise as pleasure at the chance to dredge up some phrases they haven't used since medical school. '*Dextrocardia*! Latin for right heart,' they announce, each seeming sure I won't have heard the word before.

Daniel can keep away. I want nothing more than to be alone.

Adam reaches for the sheet and rips it back. I feel naked as his eyes sweep down my body. I still look very different from either Iris or Summer after my ordeal at sea. My skin is tanned and coarse. He presses his face against my abdomen, flatter than it's ever been. I wait for him to comment on my weight loss. Grief, honey, it's the grief.

Instead, he murmurs into my belly. 'How are you, Rosebud?' he says. 'Keep safe, darling.'

Does he have a name for Summer's navel? My face must show my surprise, but he doesn't see. He turns away and I hear his bouncy tread on the ladder to the pilot house.

Rosebud?

I get it. He wasn't talking to me. Rosebud is their foetus nickname. I just about throw up on the floor.

Adam's barely stepped off the yacht before I'm ferreting in Summer's drawers for her iPhone. I find it in a jewellery case along with a bunch of necklaces and earrings, all rose-gold. Adam is taking this rose obsession too far. The jewellery, the rose-pink lingerie and now a rosy name for the foetus. It's too much.

He loves Summer. He went straight from the rough sex to commiserating with her grief and offering to do the laundry and shopping. He was tender and thoughtful. If he realises that his Summer Rose doesn't like the sexyrape anymore, he'll stop. The problem is, I can't be too different from the Summer he knew before.

The phone's flat, but I charge it at *Bathsheba*'s mains power outlet while I shower. Naked in the stateroom, I almost reach for my own clothes.

I'd better not make that mistake. I empty my belongings—clothes, books, make-up, my phone—from the stateroom drawers and jam them into my suitcase, and then I throw on the plainest of Summer's underwear and a modest linen shift. Best to be understated at first. I move Summer's other clothes back to the stateroom drawers. I will get to wear all of them in time.

I turn Summer's iPhone on, and the passcode screen blinks at me, prompting me to enter four digits. Summer will have used something easy for her to remember but, all the same, there are too many possibilities for me to start trying numbers at random. I can't afford to get locked out of her phone.

There's Adam's birthday, Tarquin's birthday—I don't even know it; I must find out how old he is. Our own birthday.

Wait. This is the same phone Summer had before she met Adam, and she's not the type to update her passcode.

She won't use her birthday, not when she shares it with me. She always thinks somebody wants to hack her boring phone. As if I would ever have been interested in doing that.

On a whim I key in 7673, and the phone opens up to me.

It's one of those twin moments that Ben always wants me to explain. But I can't explain what it's like to be a twin, just as he can never explain what it's like not to be. It's always been this way. It's all I know.

It didn't feel like a guess. It's as if I remembered. My passcode is *Rose*.

———

Adam will be gone at least a couple of hours. I charge the phone and the iPad, which has the same passcode. I'm too cautious to write a list of things I need to memorise, but I start by searching my emails for 'birthday'.

Adam will be thirty on the sixth of June, and Tarquin turned two in late January. I remember that it's a badge of honour among mothers to know your kid's age in months right up until he leaves high school, so I memorise the phrase, 'Tarky's twenty-six-and-a-half months.' God, I sound nauseatingly like a mother. Like Summer.

The next question will be, 'And how far along are you?' That's a harder one to answer. I've known enough pregnant women to know the correct answer is always given in weeks, as though anyone gives a shit.

Adam's had a kid before, so maybe he knows pregnancy dating backwards and forwards. On the other hand, Adam's pretty vague about everything, even by man standards.

I'm familiar with female fertility from when Noah and I were trying to conceive. I figure, based on what Summer told me, that she conceived around the seventh of March. Today is the tenth of April.

I connect to the marina wi-fi, switch on private browsing and search for a pregnancy calculator. Turns out Summer's baby is due on the twenty-eighth of November.

And now I calculate the due date if I conceived today.

The first of January next year.

Not even the same year. Just my luck. It's all going to be too late.

I play around with the dates. Adam surely won't remember the date Summer conceived. How much of that story about making love on the deck was true, anyway? Will he know her due date? Do guys remember that sort of thing?

According to Google, it's OK to have your baby a couple of weeks early or late. By the time Summer is overdue enough for the doctors to induce labour, my sprog will be close to term. It might be small, but it won't be obvious that it's early rather than late, since newborns vary in size.

Perfect. I'll have it while it's still nice and small, but it'll look close enough. No one will know the difference.

As long as today's encounter did the trick. Something about my monstrous spasm as Adam spilt his seed inside me made me feel fertile. As though my body was sucking his DNA into my womb.

At the thought, another heatwave surges through me. I feel betrayed by my body. While my brain was insisting that Adam's dirty talk was disgusting, the rest of me was lapping it up. Who cares what he was saying? Summer's perfect husband was having sex with me. Crazy-hot sex. Daytime sex on our luxury yacht.

Adam's an innocent bystander in this mind-fuck, the loving husband I'm blaming for my own fantasies.

The truth is, Adam didn't rape me this morning. I set the situation up; I am to blame. I made him do something he would never do. And there's only one way to stop him from ever finding out. I'm in this game for life.

CHAPTER 13

THE BLOOD

Nobody mourns for Iris.

While I'm calculating due dates, Summer's emails flood in. There's one from my brother, and I'm so eager to read it, I can't even click in the right place. Finally I open it.

Hi Summer,

I'm terribly sorry to hear what has happened. Mum phoned me yesterday, and I couldn't believe what I was hearing. It's awful, so awful.

Mum says the funeral will be in Australia. She called it a funeral, even though there is no body. Unfortunately I won't be able to make it because of my final exams. I hope you understand.

I volunteered to tell Noah. I gather you know that he
left her, but Mum doesn't know and maybe doesn't need
to know. Noah's been in touch with me recently. He's
split up with Lori and moved back into the apartment, so
there's nothing to tip Mum off that they weren't together.
I've already phoned him, so at least you don't need to do
that. I suggested he stay in New Zealand for the time being
to spare Mum the pain of finding out about the marriage
breakdown, which would be bound to come out if he went
to Australia.

Let me know if there's anything I can do. I'm glad you
have Adam to look after you.

All the best,

Ben

I read the email three times.

Ben doesn't even mention my name. This is like an email from a distant cousin, one who met the deceased a few times. A polite expression of sympathy for the bereaved sister.

Tears stream down my face and splash onto the iPad's screen. Ben is the one person I thought would mourn me as much as he would Summer. I haven't seen him since he moved to New York, but we have kept in touch a lot. Not so much on the phone, but through messaging apps. He was upset for me when Noah left, as far as you can tell through typed words.

He isn't coming to the Seychelles. He isn't hurrying to our mother's side. I died, and my brother sent an email.

I'm still mining Summer's emails an hour later when there's a knock on the hull, and I step outside to see Daniel standing on the pontoon, swinging his car keys.

'I know you wanted to be left alone, but Adam's worried about you,' he says. 'He's at my mother's house with Tarquin and he wants me to bring you. I've been looking up flights, by the way. There's a flight home via Colombo tomorrow.'

'Home?' I say. 'Isn't this our home for now? Adam wants to be with his family. We're meant to stay till September.'

Am I messing up, saying this? When Summer and Adam bought *Bathsheba*, they were going to sail the Seychelles for six months, but maybe the pregnancy changed their plans.

'But do you want to keep sailing?' Daniel asks. 'Adam's worried about bringing Tarq on board after what happened. Summer, please would you let me take you to a doctor? I understand if you don't want me to examine you, of course, but I have a lovely colleague, a woman—'

'No,' I say. 'I'm fine.'

But he keeps slipping it into the conversation. He looks and sounds so like Adam, apart from his startling gold eyes, but Daniel's is a different mind, sharp and determined. I need to distract him.

'I need to see my son,' I say at last. 'Please would you take me to Tarquin.'

Ten minutes later we're driving into the hills. Daniel doesn't have a driver today, so we're alone in the car. Being with him is relaxing, despite his hints that I need a medical exam. I suppose it's because he never met Summer. So when he starts questioning me, it catches me off guard.

'Tarquin's language is very delayed,' he says. 'I haven't done a lot of paediatric work. Is that the sort of delay you'd expect with his severe prematurity?'

Oh my God. Doctor–nurse conversation. I have no fucking clue.

'Oh, yes,' I say. 'Absolutely.'

'How many weeks was he?'

'He's twenty-six-and-a-half months.' The words roll off my tongue, but this isn't what he asked. *How many weeks was Tarquin?* It's not enough to know this sort of thing when you're pregnant. You have to remember how early the runt was born, two years later. And Summer was right there in the neonatal unit. There's no way she wouldn't know.

'I've gone blank,' I say.

'Well, what was the birth like?' Daniel asks. 'Was there birth trauma? Or was he born by Caesarean?'

'Dunno,' I say, flicking my hands up carelessly. 'Everything's gone.'

Daniel slows the car right down, and his head swivels towards me. I risk a glance at him. His gold eyes are boring into my soul.

'You don't remember?' he repeats slowly. 'How could that be?' His eyes roam all over me.

He knows. He knows. Or he's about to figure it out.

I say the first thing that jumps into my head.

'Daniel, I'm not pregnant.'

It works. Tarquin goes right out of his mind. I beg him not to tell Adam that I lost the baby, and he reassures me that a doctor's duty of confidentiality is sacred. 'Even if Adam were my brother, I wouldn't tell him,' he says, patting my hand.

He adds, 'To think that you suffered a miscarriage, all alone in the middle of the ocean, on top of everything else.' A tremor seems to pass through him. He's grieving for me, for my loss. He pulls the car over, although there's barely room to stop.

We're on the crest of the hill, almost the highest point in the Seychelles, and the Indian Ocean is laid out before us, a banquet of blue. The colour I thought I could never love again. Even though I'm messing up badly right now, I'm distracted by its beauty. We're higher here than the top of the mast, but the feeling is the same. Everything is blue air and blithe sunshine.

'How many weeks were you when you lost the baby?' Daniel asks. What is it with these medical people and their obsession with weeks?

'It was very early,' I reply. 'I had just found out I was pregnant.'

Daniel hints that I might have ongoing issues from the miscarriage, and I should still get a check-up. 'At the least, you need to tell Adam. You shouldn't try again for three months.'

I'm going to have to ignore that advice, obviously. In an inspired move, I hang my head, wringing my hands as though ashamed. 'I wish I'd known that earlier,' I whisper.

Daniel shoots a glance at me. Is that a glimmer of a smile behind his golden eyes? 'That's understandable,' he says, 'you two getting back together after a long time apart. Don't worry about it too much. So soon after a miscarriage, you're unlikely to fall pregnant.'

Here's another reason not to tell Adam that I'm not pregnant. Aside from the fact that being pregnant proves I'm Summer, Adam won't want to start trying for a baby against medical advice.

There's no way I'm going to go through this charade and not even get the consolation prize. A hundred million dollars seems fair recompense for the sacrifice I'm making. I need the money now, since I can't work either as a lawyer or a nurse.

Daniel starts the engine again, and the car glides forward, descending towards La Belle Romance. 'Now, what were we talking about before, ocean girl?' he asks. 'Oh, yes. Tarquin's health issues. Tell me all about them.'

But questions about Tarquin can never be as difficult as Tarquin himself. I'm already jittery getting out of the car, thinking about how much I've tangled myself up, having one man think I'm pregnant and another that I'm not, and now I have to go straight into battle with the tiny tot.

We arrive at a bungalow set in a luxuriant garden. It's Daniel's mother's house, or as Adam calls her, Aunt Jacqueline. A statuesque woman with long braided hair and a bewitching smile, she ushers us into her living room, where Adam is waiting along with several other Romains.

'Mama's here!' Jacqueline cries to Tarquin as we enter, but the little imp shies away from me. He burrows under the sofa cushions, hiding his face and squawking. Adam looks from one of us to the other, nonplussed.

I had planned to pick the kid up and hug him so tightly that it would smother his protests, but I'm frozen to the spot.

Jacqueline comes to my aid. She plucks Tarquin from his hiding place and plonks him in my arms. Before I can drop him, she winds a colourful strip of fabric around my abdomen, binding him to me.

'This is how children punish their mamas when they go away,' she says, her voice warm and musical, as though your kid punishing you is oh-so-adorable. 'He has to learn to love you again. He was in hospital and you weren't there. He doesn't know what you've been through.'

Damn. I haven't asked a single question about the surgery. Would Summer have taken off Tarquin's nappy by now to see how the circumcision has healed? Or would that be a weird thing to do?

Tarquin writhes inside Jacqueline's makeshift baby wrap, and I break out in a sweat. There's no way I can carry on with this thrashing beast strapped against me. My clothes are oily and rank within seconds. The smell is nauseating. Did I step in dog turd?

Now the flailing stops. Tarquin relaxes and starts cooing. Jacqueline laughs and slaps me on the back. 'This is why he was so grouchy, huh?' she says. 'Now he has Mama back, he can let everything go. The bathroom's through the hall, to the left.'

'The bathroom?' I say.

'Is there something wrong with your nose?' she asks with a puzzled look. 'You need to change his nappy, Mama. There's a change table in the bathroom. I use it for my grandson. Everything you need is there.'

I'm strapped to another human being who has just crapped himself, and I'm meant to clean it up. 'This is the worst day, this is the worst day,' I repeat as I stumble to the bathroom, where I improvise my way through the loathsome task. Why didn't Adam volunteer to do it for me? Do mothers not get a break even when they're pregnant and grieving? Not to mention that my right hand is still healing. Does anyone care that I might pick up an infection?

At least no one is watching me, no one except the mute brat, anyway, and the pack of disposable nappies that I find under the change table comes with instructions in English.

I hold my breath and force myself to glance at the results of the recent surgery. Ouch. The kid's definitely been circumcised.

Things have got to get better. How many more nappies will I have to change? Tarquin must be old enough to be toilet-trained. I'm sure there are day care centres that toilet-train your kid for you back in Australia. Or we could leave him with Aunt Jacqueline until she's sorted him out. She looks like she could get the job done in a couple of days.

I can't hold my breath any longer. I breathe in and nearly die. Can I use morning sickness as an excuse not to change any more nappies? I can't mention my pregnancy in front of Daniel, though. I don't want him to watch me lying to Adam.

Things are turning to shit fast. Adam's into BDSM, Daniel is onto my fake pregnancy, and I don't know the first thing about mothering Tarquin.

I need to get the kid into day care, but first I need to get through today. And right now I need to get through this nappy change. Why the hell does anyone have children?

You're learning fast, I tell myself. One day, I'll know the answers to all the questions. I'll know Tarquin's health issues and which way round a goddamn nappy goes. I'm stepping into someone else's life, but day by day, it will become my life. A year from now, will there be any pretence?

With a clean nappy on, Tarquin—*Tarky*—kicks his legs joyfully and reaches for my neck. I stuff the used nappy into a bin and lift him into my arms.

'This is the worst day,' I mutter.

'Mamamamama,' he says.

It's meaningless babble, but I'll take it for now. As I wander back into earshot, I say, 'I love you too, baby. It's good to have you back.'

———

Jacqueline's house is not far from La Belle Romance, and it seems family can turn up whenever they like. Romain after Romain bursts into the house without knocking. Jacqueline has food for everyone. It's not until I recognise a suited manservant from the hotel that I realise that she has called in catering from La Belle Romance. Soon waiters are everywhere, keeping everyone's drinks topped up, setting tables for lunch. Along with copious side dishes, there is roast ham, turkey, oysters and lobster. We eat *al fresco* in a garden lined with coconut palms, with the same doubled coconuts dangling above our heads.

I ask about the coconuts when Adam has wandered away, in case Adam's already told me about them. It's easier to be Summer among people I've just met.

'The *coco de mer* tree,' Daniel explains. 'Native to the Seychelles. Thought to be an aphrodisiac, because the double shape is like the form of a woman.'

Now that he's pointed it out, I can't unsee it. The coconuts look like a pair of buttocks, unmistakably a woman's. Daniel's language is so delicate. The thought flashes into my mind that Daniel wouldn't jam me against a washing machine and sexyrape me. But then, I didn't think Adam would, did I?

There are more cousins. The Romain line runs to boys, and the family resemblance is strong, so Adam and Daniel's doubles are everywhere, along with pretty, well-dressed wives and children. Everybody's taken time off work at a moment's notice for this lunch, to honour Adam and his bride. There are glasses of wine everywhere, and it's very hard not to pick one up.

But it's also, I realise slowly, a farewell lunch. After many interminable conversations about babies and children, people start to leave, and the women's goodbye hugs are lingering. They say, 'I wish we could see more of you,' and, 'Till we meet again.'

I make my way to Adam, who's kicking a ball around with Tarquin in a corner of the garden.

'Why does everyone think we're leaving?' I ask him.

'Because I already booked flights,' he says. He doesn't even look at me when he speaks.

Blood rushes to my face. I feel like a child, like Daddy is telling me how things are going to be. Do I not get a say in which country I will be inhabiting? I was just starting to relax and enjoy the Seychelles. Adam's family never met Summer, and they're so welcoming, so sharing, so generous. Nothing like the Carmichaels.

I force myself to stop and think. There isn't a hint of apology or doubt in Adam's voice. Is this what Summer meant when she referred to Adam as masterful? Maybe he's masterful outside the bedroom as well as inside, and maybe my sister lapped it up. Maybe this is the way Adam and Summer operate. He makes decisions, and she goes along with them.

Still, I have to ask. 'Why? Why the hurry?'

'I can't keep leaving Tarq with my aunt.' He shrugs. 'And let's face it, after what's happened, neither of us will ever be able to sleep with him on board again. You were scared enough before this tragedy. And then there's the other thing.' He takes me in his arms and draws my face near. He's about to kiss me, right in front of everyone—no, he's whispering in my ear. 'The blood.'

'The blood?' I repeat. I want to look away, to avoid his eyes, but Summer wouldn't do that. I force myself to keep my eyes on his face.

'The blood in the cockpit. What if someone saw it?'

'But the police didn't see it,' I say. 'You said that yourself, that you're sure they didn't notice. If they had, they would have said something before we had a chance to clean it up.'

'What about those sailors who moved the boat for us?'

He's hissing into my ear. I can't remember the order things happened yesterday, but he must be right. The sailors moved the boat before Adam cleaned up the blood.

I remember the female sailor's piercing blue eyes. She seemed sympathetic at the time, but now I can imagine her accusing me. The fact that Adam cleaned up the blood so thoroughly might make it worse.

Could the disc be retrieved if I needed it? Maybe with scuba divers, although the marina water is murky, and there's a strong tide running through. And I would have to explain why I threw the footage of my sister's death overboard.

I'm not even sure the footage proves it was an accident. I might be accused of gybing the boat deliberately. Grabbing my chance when my sister was standing on the aft deck. Using the autohelm to slam the boat to port.

'The story's in the *Seychelles Nation* today,' says Adam. 'The Seychellois are big gossips. Imagine if something came out about your dad's will. People would think all sorts of things, maybe that Iris was pregnant, further along than you. *I* know it's mad, but nobody else here knows you. What if someone mouthed off about what a freak Iris was? I want you safely out of here, babe. I've got tickets. First class. We leave tomorrow.'

The grass beneath my feet is rocking like the ocean. I gasp for words. Freak? Blood? Tickets out of here?

But he's right. We have to leave. Adam thinks so, and he doesn't even know the truth. What if I were unmasked? Who would believe jealous, *freakish* Iris if she said that her pregnant, soon-to-be-rich sister fell overboard, and she'd just happened to step into her life?

CHAPTER 14

THE ANNOUNCEMENT

Adam takes me for dinner at a French restaurant in the marina. I'm settling in to read the menu when he asks me a question I don't know how to answer.

I've persuaded Adam that we should sleep on the yacht tonight. Despite what happened on *Bathsheba*, I still love her. I'm grateful to her for getting me to land. I want to spend one last night on board.

Adam agreed, but insisted on leaving Tarquin with Jacqueline. His vehemence surprised me; I had never given a thought to what life was like keeping a toddler safe on a yacht, how vigilant he and Summer had to be. I've met plenty of people who live aboard with small children and they've always seemed relaxed.

But Adam is a man who has lost his sister-in-law overboard, and his wife is pregnant. I can't challenge his decision to get off *Bathsheba*. The only way to leave the Seychelles is by air.

The menu at Chez Marie-France is fabulous—*escargots, cuisses de grenouille*—but Summer's taste in food is less adventurous than mine, so I've promised myself I'll order the steak. A year from now I can order whatever the hell I want, but for now I'm playing it safe.

'So, when's the baby due again?' Adam asks between sips of merlot.

I gape at him, waiting for some cue that this isn't a trap. Did Daniel tell him? But his demeanour is too genuine to be faked. He looks at me intently and then hangs his head. 'I know I should remember this stuff. I should pay more attention.'

No, honey, you should not remember this stuff. The last thing you should do is pay more attention.

'December,' I say. I can't risk saying January. If I can get him to believe December, it's a mighty step in the right direction. Then I just have to hope the foetus makes its appearance at an appropriate time.

If I conceived this morning.

'Oh, yeah, December,' Adam mumbles. 'I knew that.' He's a terrible liar, but it's kind of adorable. 'A Christmas baby.'

I beam at him. 'You got it.'

———

Adam joins me in the shower the next morning. I'm sure I locked the door, but I must be mistaken. He's naked, and I try not to react to my first glimpse of his impressive erection. Summer has seen it a thousand times.

'Mm, come in, I'm all soapy,' I say, opening the shower door. I'm trying to set a different tone.

A hand gropes at me, and I'm turned and slammed against the shower wall.

Not this again. Once more, I have the fleeting fear that he knows, but I force myself not to panic. This is role-play. I just need the safe word.

'Babe, I'm not in the mood . . .' I begin.

'Shut up, you sexy bitch,' he says. His fingers push inside me. 'I can tell you're in the mood, all right. I saw the way you were flirting with my cousins. How many of us do you want at once?'

What's his obsession with me doing other men? I want to laugh, but now he's pushing inside me again, and a hot blush spreads all over me. Everything is against me. Even my body seems to join with him, making him think that I want this.

His hands wrap around me, pinning my arms to my sides, gripping my breasts. The water courses over us both, too hot. The dirty words already sound tired—to think that they turned Summer on—but soon they give way to grunts. As if he wasn't a bad enough lover, Adam is also a two-minute wonder.

But I can't just go limp in his arms. I make some Summer-ish little-girl moans. I try to move with him, but he's pinned me so tightly that I can't. And now it's happening again. My body's on fire, and a sound escapes me that I've never made before. It's like a seizure. There's no way he didn't feel *that*.

I'm still shuddering as he rinses off and grabs a towel. He mutters some compliment, 'You're so gorgeous, sunshine,' while running his hand down my spine, then he leaves me alone in the bathroom. It's weird how the rapey shoving gives way to tenderness the moment he's satisfied. It was the same yesterday; he was all, *sorry* and *I love you* moments after jamming me against that damned washing machine.

I step out of the shower and rub the condensation off one of the mirrors with my towel. Summer appears before me, her breasts still showing red fingermarks. Her eyebrows are two neat dark arches, and the curvy red line on her inner thigh is a trail leading to paradise. She's still skinny from her ordeal at sea, with protruding ribs and visible abs, but she's beautiful. No wonder Adam can't keep his hands off her.

Daniel turns up soon afterwards. We're leaving *Bathsheba* in his hands, so Adam shows him over the yacht while I walk up and down the marina. When Summer invited me to Thailand, I longed to be in a grand marina with rich men, but now *Bathsheba*'s berth seems confining. It feels wrong to be leaving her here, not knowing when I'll return. She is unnaturally still, bound fore and aft to the pontoon. A yacht ought to be swinging at anchor, gracefully aligning herself with wind and tide.

It's not too late. I could evade Adam, steer *Bathsheba* out into the open harbour and head for the ocean. Who cares where I go? They would know, instantly, when they saw the yacht departing, her sails flying in the free air, that it was Iris on board. With twins, it's always behaviour, not appearance, that gives you away.

By afternoon, we're on the plane, flying towards the night. In a few short hours, weeks of sailing are undone. In Colombo, we're whisked by taxi to a glorious hotel, where I'm relieved to find that, despite the luxury, we share a room with Tarquin. No sexyrape tonight. The next day we board a flight home.

Flying first class contrasts starkly with steering a boat across an ocean. It's lavish, even if you have to pretend to be someone else. I'm starting to relax into my role. Adam's the only person I need to fool, and he is blessedly distracted. Most of our conversation is about the here-and-now: is Tarquin hungry, where is a taxi, do you have the boarding passes? I don't need to know much to keep up my end of the conversation, but I have to remember not to be surprised by the exquisite service. No doubt Summer was used to not having to queue, having everything done for her, and being greeted by name by a dedicated flight attendant. I try to ignore another passenger who is turning everybody's head, a stunning redhead who seems to be flying with an entourage. She must be a model or an actress; I bet Summer would recognise her.

I also have to feign an interest in my son's biological rhythms. Do I really need to monitor the kid's fluid intake?

Surely he would grab the sippy cup that we keep within constant reach, rather than die of thirst? Hell, if we didn't anticipate his every whim, he might even learn to speak. How hard is it to say 'cup'?

When Adam talks about the past, it's a little more challenging. He reminisces about the friends we left in Phuket, but I barely need to get straight whether Brian was the boozer and Greg the groper or the other way round. If anything, I mustn't be too attentive. I'm a tired, grieving, pregnant woman travelling with a young child. Vacant smiles and nods are all anybody could expect.

Tarquin is a handful, though. I can change a nappy without gagging now, but I forgot to pack any in carry-on, so I have to stealthily scrounge a few from a flight attendant. Adam raises an eyebrow when I offer Tarquin a glass of water instead of his sippy cup of special toddler juice.

The hardest part is the pretence that I find joy in observing the kid's antics. I realise a beat too late that the way he cocks his head to the side while stuffing food in his gob is the sort of thing Summer found cute. I gush, but it sounds phoney. I've always secretly doubted that Summer did find *Tarky* so adorable, but now I know that she must have. Keeping up this level of enthusiasm is exhausting.

After another enervating nappy change in the plane toilet, I look up at the mirror, two inches from my nose, and say, 'day care'. Right now, 'day care' is the most beautiful phrase in the English language.

'Day care,' says Tarquin.

Jesus. I'm going to have to watch my mouth around this kid.

'Daddy, Daddy, Daddy,' I say. 'Can you say Daddy?'

'Daddy,' says Tarquin.

'Daddy! That's right! You said Daddy!' I say. I force the foul used nappy into the rubbish receptacle and pick the kid up.

'Daddy,' he says.

'Wow! You said a new word, Tarky! Well done! Can you say Mummy?'

'Daddy.'

'That's right. Daddy and Mummy. Tarky loves Daddy and Mummy.'

I carry him back to Adam and slip into my lush seat. I'm so relieved at my escape that I keep the kid on my own lap for once and snuggle him against my body like I find him just-so-squidgy. Adam is sprawled in his booth with an empty champagne flute in his hand, scrolling through pictures of sports cars that he seems to have downloaded onto his iPad. The bottle, sweating in its bucket of ice, is calling to me. I sip my orange juice resentfully. At least I don't have morning sickness, or I might have had to turn down the bluefin tuna that the attendant is now bringing out.

'Tarky said Daddy!' I say. 'Say it again, Tarky!'

Tarquin turns and looks his daddy in the eye.

'Day care.'

———

Everything is fine. Adam listens to Tarquin even less than he does to his wife. But I've learned my lesson. I'll never again say anything in front of the kid that I wouldn't want the world to hear. I settle back in my seat. I'll keep my day care fantasies private from now on.

Once I'm back in Australia, I'm going to start living Summer's life for real. The dream will come true. There'll be no more glaring police inspectors, no more blood to mop up. I won't have in-laws popping up everywhere. I won't have to fake medical chit-chat with Daniel Romain. Adam will be at work most of the day, and there will be day care. All I will have to do is lie by the pool all afternoon, growing Adam's baby. Every day will bring me closer to the money.

Adam is going to get me pregnant, if he hasn't already. I close my eyes and let myself imagine the things I will buy once the money comes through. Dresses, shoes, lingerie . . .

I'm drifting off to sleep when Adam nudges me with his elbow. I open my eyes. He's pointing at his iPad, which reads, 'Annabeth Carmichael Video Call'.

'Stop!' I cry, but I'm too late. Adam is swiping the screen. My mother's face appears, blurry and too close to the camera.

'Darling heart,' says Annabeth, 'I'm sorry to be a bother. Have I made a video call?' She taps at her screen. 'I don't know how to turn the camera off. Well, at least you can see your home.' I catch glimpses of the living room at Seacliff Crescent: the black piano, the high white ceiling. She's flashing her device around the room. 'Now, I need you to know I won't be at the airport. I can't bear to wait for you all alone.'

'We're on a plane,' I say. The comment is redundant, but I'm stalling for time. The sight of my mother, materialising on Adam's screen as if by magic, electrifies me. She's never been able to tell me and Summer apart by appearance or voice, but the sight of her is confronting. Her eyes are bloodshot, with huge bags under them. She looks so sad.

'Oh, yes, I knew you would be flying,' says Annabeth. 'Sri Lanka is five and a half hours behind us, did you know that? Your plane's a little early according to the internet, but if I allow half an hour for you to get through customs, and then you might have to wait for a taxi, and there'll be traffic on the car ride from the airport . . .'

Annabeth keeps talking. She's analysing every possible variable in order to pinpoint the moment we will arrive at Seacliff Crescent, as if her ordeal will be over when that happens. Thankfully, Tarquin distracts her by smearing the remains of his latest snack all over the screen.

'We need to go,' says Adam. 'Tarq's getting overstimulated. The plane will be landing soon. We'll be walking through the door in no time, Annabeth.' He hangs up.

Annabeth's face disappears, and with it, my sumptuous dreams. I thought I had overcome my biggest hurdles, but a huge one lies ahead. My mother.

I had thought everything would be OK because of Annabeth's poor eyesight. I would walk into Seacliff Crescent with Adam by my side and Tarquin in my arms. Why would she question my identity?

It's hard enough to impersonate Summer, but to fake a pregnancy as well is a step too far. Annabeth is obsessed with grandchildren. She's a pregnancy groupie. She'll want to know the kind of details you only know if you're pregnant for real, all about morning sickness and God knows what else. I wish I had researched the symptoms I would be having.

Faking a pregnancy is easy enough with Adam. He's taking it for granted. It's not news to him. He's not interested in gynaecological details anyway. But with Annabeth it will be a major topic of conversation. She's the kind of person who will count back the dates and figure out when the foetus must have been conceived, and then thoughtlessly drop some clanger in front of Adam. He's been parroting the 'Christmas baby' line ever since I planted the idea in his brain, but if Annabeth does the sums, she'll figure out that my due date ought to be November.

Only a moment ago, I was thinking this would work. I was looking forward to lying pregnant by the pool, awaiting my riches. Why didn't I face up to these problems before we got on this damn plane? It would have been so much easier if we had stayed away. So we had to leave the Seychelles because of the blood and the yachties and Inspector Barbé, but couldn't we have gone somewhere else? Back to Thailand? Hell, right now I would happily jump on a plane to Siberia.

For the rest of the flight, I flipflop between different strategies. Tell Adam what I told Daniel, that I lost the baby at sea. Fake a miscarriage right now. Book Adam and me a romantic getaway in Fiji, leaving tomorrow. Announce that I want a trial separation.

Then again, if I *could* fool my mother, and if I could train Adam out of the rough sex and book Tarquin into day care (Is there such a thing as boarding school for toddlers?), then maybe it would all work out.

As the plane begins its final descent, I still haven't made up my mind what to do. All I know is I must persuade Adam not to tell Annabeth that I'm pregnant. It's essential to keep my options open and to keep my mother's prying questions at bay.

———

We're making our way through immigration and I'm still trying to decide how to persuade Adam to keep my pregnancy secret. It's going to be a hard sell. He's already made a few comments about how badly Annabeth needs this good news, and I'm distracted by the sudden thought that somebody might want to fingerprint me—identical twins don't have identical fingerprints.

Maybe I'll wait until the last minute to raise the subject so he won't have time to argue. I'll say it in the taxi on the way home, perhaps as we pull up to our house.

We get through immigration without catching sight of a fingerprint scanner. Adam carries Tarquin through customs, and we stroll into the arrivals lounge.

I can't believe who's here.

'Isn't this nice of your uncle?' says Annabeth, who is holding a bouquet of white roses. 'I told him I couldn't bear to wait alone at the airport, so he drove me here himself, and look who else came to keep me company.' My mother's tone is even, but the dismissive way she flicks her hand over her shoulder betrays her indignation. 'Wasn't that so nice of them?'

Arrayed behind Annabeth, all in black like a Gothic wedding, is the rest of my family. Colton, Virginia, Vicky, Valerie, Vera and Francine. What the hell are they doing here, acting like my sister's death is an excuse for a party? I don't believe for a second that they came to keep Annabeth company. Was Francine closer to Summer than I realised, or is she here to be nosy?

This is my worst nightmare. I have to be Summer in front of my entire family. I have to be perfect. There are eyes everywhere.

They rush me, surround me, smother me with hugs and kisses. 'Oh, Summer, darling Summer, my poor baby!' I can't even tell who's saying what, and there's never been such a clash of perfumes. My half-sisters are acting like I'm some kind of tragic queen. Somehow I end up in the death-grip of my stepmother. Francine looks dainty in her bolero and pencil skirt, but she's strong enough to strangle me. I'm sure that's her hand on my belly, feeling for telltale signs of growth.

'Whoa, steady on!' says Adam. 'It's awesome to see you guys, but be gentle with Summer.'

I turn to him to signal, *no*, but he's not looking at me. He's looking at Annabeth.

'Oh, I know, it must have been hideous for you, my darling,' says Francine, pressing her cold cheek against mine.

'It's been harder than you think,' says Adam. 'On top of everything else, Summer's pregnant.'

CHAPTER 15

THE TEST

Francine is holding me so tightly I swear she is trying to squeeze this baby out of me. The six females around me are all emoting their hearts out, and it's one hundred per cent fake.

My half-sisters are screeching for joy. Francine is murmuring sweet nothings in my ear. And my mother is trying to look serene, when I know she wants to turn cartwheels through the airport or crow like a rooster.

Adam was right that Annabeth needed some good news. The baby has driven Iris right out of her head—either that or she's medicated. She is floating on a glowing cloud. Her embrace is as soft as gossamer, and her eyes are misty like she's looking at a celestial being.

I can't believe I thought she would be onto me. No one questions winning the lottery.

This is the best moment of my life. Forget winning a beauty pageant you didn't deserve, sucking up the adulation while your sister is adorned in humiliating bronze. Nothing beats this.

Francine is dying here. That'll teach her to turn up where she's not wanted. She's crying, covering it up as so-happy-for-you tears. She can't even form proper sentences and keeps saying, 'Happy baby! Happy baby!'

This time, there is no chance my sister's going to let the cat out of the bag. Never, ever again am I going to be shown up by my twin.

I'm not even a twin anymore. I'm Summer Rose, wife of Adam Romain, mother of the Carmichael heir.

Annabeth is singing, some sort of baby song, a lullaby of pure joy. She takes Tarquin from Adam's arms and rocks him as if he is a newborn himself.

I'm loving this so much that I hug each of my half-sisters three times, forcing more congratulations out of them. As I let go of Virginia, I glance at her hand, but she's not wearing a ring. She doesn't want to tip us off to her plans, but I can taste her disappointment. Her smile is way too toothy and fixed. She could at least be grateful that she's found out in time that she's out of the running. Her sixteenth birthday is two weeks away. She was a whisker away from a hillbilly-incest marriage.

That's when I remember that there's still one flaw in my plan. Like at the pageant, I'm only pretending to be Summer. I can almost hear my brother's voice, the voice of unwelcome truth: *There's blood running down your leg, Iris.*

Adam wraps his arms around me, and I breathe in his sweet spicy aroma, but it doesn't do its usual magic. Part of me wants to push him away.

But I can't. There's no way I can turn my back on this triumph. Even if I knew Summer's safe word, I wouldn't use it. Not until the last piece of the puzzle is in place. As soon as I'm pregnant, everything will be perfect.

The first days in Australia are tough. Annabeth leased her penthouse out till November when Adam and I left to sail around the world, and it turns out that she thinks she can keep living with us until the lease is up. I try to persuade her to book into a hotel, but it isn't easy. I have to spin all sorts of shit about needing to grieve in peace. If I were Iris, I could have got her out of here in half an hour, but as Summer it's much more difficult. How do nice people get other people to do what they want? I'm reduced to hinting that Adam wants her to go, even though, in truth, Adam has some weird ideas about extended families living together which I can only blame on his Seychellois heritage.

At first, I hide from my mother, using the size of the house to keep her at bay. One morning, she fixates on how Noah will be coping with his grief, and insists on sending him a care package, but by the afternoon she has forgotten all about him and has moved onto worrying about the effect of all this stress on my unborn child. At one point, I jump in the pool in my clothes and swim over to the far side to evade her questions about my lack of weight gain.

But within a few days, I begin to relax. This is the woman who doesn't acknowledge that Ridge cheated on her even though his will declares that Virginia is his biological daughter. Annabeth's reality is whatever Annabeth wants it to be. On top of this, losing Iris has addled her brain. She glides around in a fog of confusion, floating from joy to grief and back again in the space of a single sentence.

'How lovely to have you home, Tarky,' she says to the kid, 'only it's for a dreadful reason . . . but your mummy needs to be back for baby's sake . . . oh, just think, a newborn in the house for Christmas!'

I still need her out of here. Even a zombie can stumble upon the truth, and besides, she has become super-annoying lately, the way she talks about Iris.

'Iris was such a lost soul,' she bleats, in the middle of wiping Tarquin's filthy face. 'I had hoped, Summer, that with this sailing trip you'd set her straight, that you might rub off on her a bit.'

Another time she bursts into tears in the middle of break-fast. 'At least you and Adam and the children are safe,' she sobs. 'It would have been worse if it was you. It's not that I loved her less, really, but you and I have always been so much closer. I never understood Iris.'

'Do you know,' she adds, 'when Adam told me the news, he sounded so distraught, that for one awful moment I thought it was you?'

So she had to go. But as I close the door on her taxi and walk back up the driveway, it hits me that I have no one to help me with the kid anymore.

Sure enough, with just me and Tarquin at home all day it's unbelievable how clingy he becomes. Tarquin is only happy if some part of his skin is touching me, unless we're near a busy road, in which case he wants to run away from me faster than I would have thought possible.

I wouldn't mind the constant cuddles, but he's hungry for my attention too. It's as though he believes that if I think about anything other than him for a second, he might cease to exist. I was never keen on motherhood, but I thought at least I would get to take it easy for the stay-at-home years. I thought I could sit and read as long as the kid had a toy to play with. Turns out no. You can't read in the same house as a small child. The child will sense that Mummy is relaxing and will hunt you down.

Whenever Tarquin sees me with my feet up he fetches a picture book and waves it in my face. If I ignore him, he wails and hits me over the head with the book. The kid who can't talk wants to read books all freaking day. And picture books are so predictable. The baddies get caught, the truth will out, and right will triumph. Yawn.

One of Tarq's books I don't mind so much—it's a story about a girl who goes to live under the sea. The illustrations are eerie; the ocean is black and gleaming, and as the girl slips below the surface her legs transform into a fishtail bejewelled with sapphires and emeralds. Everyone assumes I want to forget my ordeal at sea, but when I read this story, I dream of *Bathsheba*; I ache for heaving swells and salt spray. But Tarquin hates the book; when I ignore his protests and keep reading, he rips a page.

Summer's life is a lot more boring than I imagined. She has beautiful dresses but no occasion to wear them. I can't do the housework in chiffon.

I can't read her *Millennial Kama Sutra* while Tarquin is awake thanks to his maternal-relaxation radar, and the kid barely naps. Summer must have accepted her fate, since she seems to have chucked out all her books, even her leather-bound copies of *Frankenstein* and *Dracula* and the other Victorian thrillers that used to hold pride of place on her bookshelf.

As I search for them, I have the urge to dwell on Summer's flaws and sins, as small as they were. Not that her taste in books was really a sin, but I disliked it when I was a kid. Her books scared me to death. Her love of horror stories, so at odds with her otherwise girlish tastes, was perhaps the one thing she shared with Dad. Maybe it stemmed from the time he took us to Carmichael Bridge after it was taken out of commission and dropped a live chicken onto the crocodile-infested riverbank.

I remember the crocs lay still and cold and patient in the sun as the chicken came nearer and nearer. So, so close. The leap and snap were like a bolt of electric current. Croc thrashed against croc, fighting for the prize, tearing it to pieces. The bloody frenzy haunted my dreams for years, but Summer insisted that it was 'the natural way of things' and that the chicken 'had a more painless death than most of the food on your plate'. I could see her point of view, but I was still angry with Dad for making us watch, and I wished I could forget the incident. But Summer kept bringing it up.

It's one of the few times I remember being angry with Summer, when she waxed lyrical about the chicken's dramatic demise. She would read me gory scenes from her books too, unable to believe that I was frightened by them. From her short lifetime of selflessness, these are the moments I find myself remembering. I hate myself for it.

Each day I am more bewildered by the thought that Summer didn't have a maid, even though Seacliff Crescent is filled with glass and marble that shows the dirt, and keeping this peach carpet clean with a toddler around is a full-time job in itself. When I put Summer's Australian SIM card back in her phone, I start getting her reminders. The phone pings multiple times every morning, reminding me to swing by the Little

Gourmand to pick up Tarquin's organic blueberry mush or to start marinating the beef for tomorrow's *boeuf bourguignon*. The reminders are great for a day or two, but then they start to drive me up the wall.

It's a nightmare getting Tarquin out of the house, but once I've strapped him into his car seat, I do enjoy cruising around town in Summer's immaculate white BMW. I drive to the far side of Wakefield to buy pregnancy tests, even though it's probably too early to start testing, and I take one every morning straight after Adam leaves for work. I time one minute on my phone, forcing myself not to look at the result until the timer goes off. Then I wrap the test in toilet paper, hide it in my pocket and walk to our outdoor rubbish bin, where Adam never looks. I stuff it down as far as I can reach.

Adam comes home one evening to find that the pool filter is clogged with leaves and I've ironed burn marks into three of his business shirts. Tarquin and I are lying on the unmade bed, surrounded by picture books and browning apple cores.

'What's got into you?' he asks when I point out my handiwork; I've left the shirts on the floor with the burn marks strategically facing upwards. 'You used to be so good at this stuff.'

I try to squeeze out a tear. 'I'm so tired these days,' I say. 'I have to choose whether to put my energy into cleaning the house or meeting Tarky's complex emotional needs.'

'I guess we need to rethink having a maid,' says Adam, 'but I don't want hired help touching Helen's piano. Please promise me that. I've always appreciated the way you care for it.'

'Of course not,' I say.

'All right, then,' he says. 'You organise it.'

I waste no time.

The Steinway's black lacquer shows every mote of dust, so even after I hire the maid, I polish it every day, while resisting the urge to play a single note on the damn thing, even when no one is around except Tarquin. One moment of weakness could give me away.

As well as single-handedly cleaning the mansion, polishing the piano and maintaining the pool, Summer must have spent hours making dinner for Adam every evening. His favourite recipes are annoyingly complicated and use ingredients from about six far-flung specialty shops. Adam doesn't like eating out. I'm keen to re-educate him, but I can't change things too quickly. He and Summer were in a comfortable routine.

Then there's the rapey sex. Adam wants it morning and night. Every time, I'm more humiliated, not by what he's doing to me, which, despite everything, my body always responds to, but by the thought that he has done this to my sister. I know things she never wanted me to know.

I could stop him if I had to. I have guessed the safe word, I think. According to the web, most couples choose 'red' or a fruit, and Adam and Summer were so unimaginative that I am sure they would have chosen the most obvious red fruit, even if they hadn't already been crazy about the way she smelled of apples. The word hovers on the tip of my tongue, but I never say it. Each time is one more chance to conceive.

Worse than the sex is the day care, or rather the lack of it. At least the sex is over quickly. Each day at home with a toddler is an eternity.

I phoned around the day Annabeth moved out, only to find that all the local day care centres were full. Now I try some centres further afield. At last, a centre half an hour's drive away offers to emancipate me for six hours every weekday, for a very reasonable rate. The hours are a bit disappointing, but beggars can't be choosers. No boarding school in Australia takes kids before the age of eight.

When Adam gets home, I present him with the good news over a meal of *confit de canard*, paired with a gorgeous Burgundy that I have stolen a few sips of in the kitchen.

'But is it worth you going back to work now that you're pregnant?' Adam asks.

I nearly choke on a mouthful of duck. My spine prickles at the thought of going 'back' to work. If I ever find myself in the neonatal unit, expected to display my nursing expertise, it will surely be my Waterloo. Another reason I need to get pregnant fast.

'Of course not,' I say. 'We can't afford to risk this pregnancy with night shifts! But what about Tarky? He needs to get used to classrooms now, or he'll be behind when he starts school. I wish I could keep him home forever.' I hug my arms to my chest in a can't-let-go gesture. 'But he needs more than I can give him. Other kids his age are reading and writing already.'

Adam screws up his face. 'Seems like a waste of money to me,' he says, 'paying for someone to look after our kid while you sit at home missing him. Besides, you're the one who says premmies should stay home with their mothers.'

God, I hate it when he plays the premmie card. Tarquin has to have the best of everything—homemade food, useless 'natural' cleaning products, a cot made of beeswaxed jarrah—because he was premature.

'But that was my ignorant opinion,' I say, 'and we hardly need to worry about the money—'

'Let's not count our chickens until they're hatched,' Adam interrupts. He seems allergic to any mention of the Carmichael fortune, seldom joining in my fantasies about spending it, as if we might jinx our future by talking about it too much. 'And it wasn't your opinion, babe. You said Walter and Michael and Catherine all told you premmies should stay home.'

I nod as though I know who these people are. Their names sound frighteningly authoritative. Doctor names. God, I must look up the names of all the doctors and nurses at the neonatal unit and memorise them. My old colleagues. I might run into them in the supermarket. And is Tarquin due for a check-up?

'You swore you would never hand Tarq over to a stranger,' Adam continues. 'We agreed on this. You persuaded me we should homeschool him, so how does day care fit into that?'

We should homeschool him. Oh my God. What was Summer thinking?

But how can I argue? Adam is right about one thing, more right than he knows. We can't count a chicken that might never hatch.

———

Two weeks after we get to Australia, I plonk Tarquin in his high chair for afternoon tea, set him up in front of the TV and open a kiddie pack of strawberry yoghurt. The smell hits me like a wave of cloying death. I run to the bathroom, fighting the urge to throw up.

Am I coming down with something? The pregnancy test I took this morning is already in the outside bin, and I've promised myself never to take more than one a day. But those yoghurts are fresh, and they smelled good yesterday. It's me that's changed, not them.

I reach into the bottom of the bathroom cupboard. There are three tests left. I've crumpled the boxes so that they look like they've been lying around here for ages. *Just this one time*, I promise myself. *Then back to one a day.* I rip open the packet, dropping the wrapper on the vanity, and scoot over to the toilet to pee on the stick. My hands are trembling so much I can hardly hold the sensor strip in the right place, and I forgot to bring my phone in here, so I don't have a timer. I close my eyes and start counting to sixty, forcing myself to go slow. How many times now have I heard that smug beeping and opened my eyes to a blue minus sign?

Noah always stayed with me when I took a test, back when he and I were trying to conceive. He waited outside the bathroom while I peed, he timed it for me, he looked at the stick first. He broke the news gently. He held me afterwards and whispered that we would try again.

I count so slowly that I decide I can open my eyes at fifty-five.

The result is faint, but it's there.

I'm pregnant.

———

The air around me is full of golden bubbles. Shiny and joyful, they bump together and froth like spindrift or champagne. I have won the race. I have everything that Summer had. I am truly Summer now.

In the wardrobe, I trail my hand over Summer's luscious gowns, diaphanous silver, radiant gold, but I'm drawn to a white dress adorned with red roses. It's a simple sundress; Summer probably wore it with sandals and a straw hat, but I pair it with her highest red heels. I paint my lips red and drench myself in apple perfume. I twirl, and the dress flares, full and round. I feel ready to float away.

Downstairs, Tarquin is still watching TV. I pluck him from his high chair, strap him into the back seat of the BMW and drive him and his portacot over to Annabeth's hotel. I'm so entranced by that blue plus sign, I can barely keep to the speed limit. Outside the car window is sunshine and bright colours.

'Adam and I need a date night,' I tell Annabeth, dumping the kid in her delighted arms. Her room is strewn with half-finished knitting projects, booties and beanies in pastel pink and baby blue. I don't rush away as usual; I don't care now if she asks nosy questions about my pregnancy. She can even moan about Iris for all I care.

She doesn't, though. She's already moulding her memory of Iris into a more comfortable shape. She tells me that they 'never argued', slipping the comment between equally delusional remarks about me 'blooming' with pregnancy and Tarquin being 'very advanced for his age'.

I stay a generous half-hour. I ask her lots of daughterly questions about her boring hobbies and boring friends. Then I head for Romain Travel. 'Come on,' I say to Adam, 'knock off early for once.'

We saunter down the main street hand in hand. I can't help but imagine telling Noah my news. Noah thought it was my fault that we didn't get pregnant, and now I can never tell him that I wasn't infertile, he just gave up too soon. We just needed to try to conceive for a little longer—or perhaps *he* was sterile.

I can barely stop myself from skipping into a cosy Malaysian café. Perhaps Adam is curious about my high spirits, but I doubt it. I've never felt more like Summer in my life. Happy, kind, spontaneous. It's good to be alive.

When Adam queries my choice of meal—the spiciest item on the menu—I blame it on the pregnancy. The only sour note of the evening is my realisation that I can't drink wine now. I've been sneaking a glass or two most nights before Adam gets home, but now that I am pregnant for real, that has to stop.

Strangely, though, the moment when I turn down the wine is when I get it. I'm pregnant. Not just won-the-race pregnant, not just got-away-with-it pregnant, not just fuck-you-Francine pregnant.

I am growing a baby.

I drive Adam home and rush to the loo as soon as we get in the house. Pregnancy bladder. I'm almost pleased with the idea. It's part of what makes this real.

As I wash my hands, I look at myself in the double mirror. The true image in the middle, the two reversed images on either side. Summer, Iris, Summer. I hold my hand to my right breast. Despite the evening's events, my heartbeat is stable.

Can anyone really feel which side my heart is on? I move my hand to the left. I can still feel a beat on that side. Perhaps it's fainter. Perhaps not.

I study my face. Is it really all that asymmetrical? I always thought my left cheek was fuller, the left cheekbone higher, but apart from Summer, nobody else could see it.

I've fooled everybody. Adam, Tarquin, Annabeth. None of them could tell us apart before, and none of them can now.

It's as though I've been Summer all along.

Sitting in plain view on the vanity is the wrapper for the pregnancy test. Although it was a mistake to leave it here, I don't feel panicked at the thought that Adam might have seen it. I'm sure I've been through the hardest times, and I've had lots of practice. I can explain away anything now. All the same, no need to create problems for myself. I scoop it up and wrap toilet paper around it. I'm shoving it down the bottom of the rubbish bin when Adam pushes through the bathroom door.

'You sexy whore,' he breathes. 'Who have you been fucking while I was at work?' My skirt is still up round my waist; he grabs my underwear and yanks it to my knees.

'Really, Adam, in the *toilet*?'

The words leap out, and I forget to use my breathless-little-girl voice. Damn, I sound exactly like Iris.

Adam stands stock-still. Jesus, I think. Be Summer. You have to be Summer. But I can't bear to have him sexyrape me here. Not in front of this mirror.

'Babe, can't you see, everything's changed?' I purr. 'I've been meaning to tell you. Ever since I got pregnant, it hasn't felt the same. I'm going to be a mother. You have to be gentle with me. No more rough sex.'

But he grabs me with his strong hands, and next thing the door is shut and I'm pushed face first into the mirror. Adam is already hard, and he's fumbling with his fly.

'Apple!' I cry. 'Apple!'

He lets go. I turn. He gapes, and emotions roll over his features: surprise, frustration, embarrassment. A hint of intrigue.

'Don't sulk, baby,' I say, pushing my hand inside his jeans. 'We have the house to ourselves for the evening. Let's take our time. My body's soft and round these days. I'm gonna take a shower to give you time to dream up a new way to seduce me. Do you realise you haven't kissed me lately? You haven't kissed me since . . . since I don't know when.'

It's true. I still haven't had a single one of those kisses I used to dream of back when I was Iris.

I stand on tiptoe and kiss him now. His lips stay closed, and he stares at me as though I've slapped him. I take advantage of his surprise to pull my hand out of his jeans, push him out the door and lock it behind him.

I don't have to have sex with Adam anymore. If he wants it, he's going to have to seduce me.

I smile at the girl in the mirror. She smiles back.

'Tomorrow, you're booking that brat into day care,' she says.

'I know it, sister,' I reply.

CHAPTER 16

THE RACE

It's a mild spring morning, and as I stroll across Wakefield Beach, my bikini shows off my beautiful baby bump. My body is sleek and voluptuous. I'm a double D at last.

The last seven months have been a happy dream. The pregnancy test changed everything. No more rapey sex, and Tarquin started day care the next day. When a space came up at a closer day care with longer hours, I switched the little tyke right away. Adam protested, but he didn't have a leg to stand on. I'm gestating the heir, and let's face it, Adam's last wife didn't survive her pregnancy. My mother told him to pull his head in and let me get some rest.

I'm Summer. Everything works out for me.

Adam thinks I've been having piano lessons. For a few months, I banged away on Helen's piano, choosing easy pieces and making deliberate mistakes. Only when nobody was home would I play properly. Recently, though, I've been able to play in front of Adam. Perhaps not the most complex pieces, but challenging enough for me to enjoy myself. He's no musician, so he doesn't know to question how quickly I've learned. All he says is that it's nice to hear music in the house again.

Playing the piano is the only thing that gives me the feeling I had at *Bathsheba*'s helm, a feeling of joining with a great and ancient rhythm. The instrument seems to hold *Bathsheba*'s soul, the soul of the ocean. It gleams, big and black, in the otherwise blanched living room. There's so much glass in our house that sunshine blazes everywhere. Sometimes I pull the curtains to rest my eyes, and then I play songs of the sea and feel the ocean's movement through my fingers.

I think of *Bathsheba* more and more, but I can't figure out how she can fit into my future. Adam keeps making noises about selling her, but I've managed to dissuade him for now.

Any time I trip up and do something un-Summer-like, I can blame Iris. I wanted to learn the piano, despite not having been interested before, 'as a tribute to my sister'. For the same reason, I swim each morning at Wakefield Beach, as Iris did when she lived in Wakefield. Not only does everyone accept this, but they honour me for it.

'It's so touching, the way you've found to remember your sister,' Letitia Buckingham gushed when we caught up for coffee after one of my swims. Letitia was as lissom and lovely at twenty-four as she had been at fourteen, and just as daft. 'You never used to like the sea.'

'Iris had a lot to teach me,' I replied. 'I don't think anyone realised how wise she was until we lost her.'

'But remember her creepy obsession with copying you?' she said. 'Ever since you won that pageant, and she was humil—'

'I was having you on,' I said. 'Iris and I used to dream up nonsense to tell you, to see how much you would believe. The truth is we loved to dress alike.'

There were no more coffees with Letitia after that.

Inch by inch, I've turned Summer's life into my own. I've taught Adam how to please me in bed, ascribing the change in my sexual tastes to pregnancy hormones. I've trained him to eat out more and to cook dinner for me sometimes because pregnancy is so exhausting. I've replaced our super-soft mattress with a futon, and the photo of Summer holding newborn Tarquin has been relegated to the guest bedroom. I don't look my best in nurse's scrubs.

Even Tarq is not the nightmare he used to be. He's older, and he uses the toilet at last, thank God. And now that I'm not stuck with him all day, I don't feel so desperate for space. I've long given up on Summer's regimen of gourmet toddler meals. He's thriving on baked beans and ham sangers.

The thing that used to annoy me most about Tarquin, his silence, I've come to appreciate. There's something relaxing about being with someone who can never open his mouth and criticise you, who adores you. And everyone thinks I'm mother of the year because I'm not panicking about his delayed speech. He says the occasional word now. *Mummy* or *Daddy*, that sort of thing. Everybody thinks he's damaged by his premature birth, but the more time I spend with him, the more I've come to see that he's quite smart.

So this is my life now. I drop Tarquin at day care each morning on my way to the beach. I eat lunch in one of the Asian cafés in the backstreets of Wakefield, blowing off Summer's dull friends when they seek me out for coffee dates. Adam and I joined an antenatal class but dropped out after two sessions, sick of the judgey comments about my choice not to have any ultrasound scans. I agreed with the comments, of course. Playing the hippie birth cultist is a drag, and my midwife, chosen for her dislike of medical interventions and her enthusiasm for home birth, is the human equivalent of nails on a blackboard. The fact that she changed her name from Colleen to Skybird says it all.

I haven't seen hide nor hair of Francine or her daughters since they found out they were beaten, even though the beach house is not far from Seacliff Crescent and only minutes from Wakefield Beach. So much for Francine's concern for me at the airport. I've checked up on Virginia a few times via Adam's Facebook account, and I'm pleased to see that the kiddie wedding hasn't gone ahead. Virginia is blossoming. She's always posting selfies in her gym gear or a sexy crop top and cut-offs, hanging off the arm of a new boyfriend each month. Every day she looks prettier.

In the afternoons I play the piano for hours at a time or hang out by the pool, stuffing myself with cake. My belly is satisfyingly round, but no matter how much I eat, people still comment that I 'don't look eight months pregnant'.

Summer's due date is looming.

My daily swim is my penance, my way of honouring Summer, of grieving for the girl whose death otherwise goes unmourned. Each day, I dive under the water into Summer's world. No matter how many people are on the beach, under the water you're always alone.

I did love her so much. I know what I've done is wrong, but I think she would understand. I saved her mother, her son and her husband from having to grieve her death, and who wouldn't want that? Wouldn't it be the worst part of dying, to know that your loved ones would suffer bitter grief? I wouldn't know; I didn't have anyone to mourn me. Even my brother has never suggested coming home to commiserate with me about Iris's death. In fact, I barely hear from my surviving sibling at all. I feel like an only child.

I swim early, when the sun has just sprung free of the horizon. I dive deep and turn, as I once did under *Bathsheba* in the middle of the ocean, and I look up through the water at the living world above. I don't understand the physics—I guess it's something to do with light refracting through different media—but although the sun is small and low in the east at that time of day, when I look up from the ocean floor, it seems to be overhead, great and golden. The water shimmers blue above me, and the sun seems to swell and blur into the whole sky. It's perfect, round and joyous. And in this moment, I can imagine that things are as they should be. I, Iris, am buried at sea, and my sister, beautiful Summer, is the noon sunshine that lights up the world.

But this morning the sky is thick and grey, and the ocean is moody. I wade into the water and dive down as always, but I can't see the sun from under the waves. I pause on the white seabed, waiting for the underwater silence to grant me peace. Instead, last night's dream flashes back into my head, a nightmare. I dreamed that the sea surface was solid, a solid black thing, like lacquered wood. In my dream, I dived deep, but when I came back to the surface, I couldn't break through. At first I thought the blackness that I pressed against was *Bathsheba*'s hull, but however far I swam, I couldn't get away from it. The water was hard as lead. I was trapped.

Now, my heart pounds wildly and the baby struggles inside me like a creature in a snare. My belly muscles spasm. Is this what a contraction feels like? I must be calm; this can't be good for the baby. I push against the sand and swim upwards, expecting to crash into this nightmarish barrier. Instead, I burst into fresh air. I gasp for breath. I'm in deep water, and a wave breaks over me, filling my nose and mouth with brine. I tumble downwards again. I'm shivering, nauseated and so very tired.

I fight back to the surface and force myself to breathe evenly, to make slow, calm strokes towards the beach. Soon

I'm in the shallows again, trembling as I make my way back to the warmth of my towel.

It's time I stopped this stupidity. I'm a heavily pregnant woman. I'm not a free agent anymore; the lives of my husband and our two children are bound up in mine. This is motherhood. However fake the rest of my life is, my baby is real. From now on, I'll swim in the pool.

———

In the afternoon I'm poolside, drooping in a deckchair, my baby bump pointing skyward, when there is a frantic banging on my door. Through the glass panels, I glimpse a hefty arm, a woman's meaty fist.

Is she one of those crones from my antenatal class? Has she come to scold me again? But no. As I approach I see her through the glass. Virginia.

She's hacked her hair as short as a boy's. She's dressed like a slob. She's as big as a bus. And she's crying.

I open the door and Virginia bursts inside, pushing me out of the way before shutting and deadbolting the door behind her. It's just a careless shove, but the image flashes through my mind of her pushing me to the floor. Is she here to hurt my baby?

And then I realise why she's so enormous.

She's pregnant. Very pregnant.

'Is my mother here?' she asks. Her voice is tremulous. 'Is Uncle Colton or anyone here?'

I don't want to say I'm home alone. 'The maid's here. And the gardener,' I lie.

'Are you in touch with any of my family?' Virginia asks. 'Are you in touch with my Uncle Edgar?'

'Never heard of him.' At least this is the truth.

She sinks to her knees, sobbing and shaking, wrapping her arms around my legs. 'Summer, despite everything, we're sisters!' she wails. 'We're flesh and blood. You have to help me. You're the only one who can. I won't let them do it!'

———

Ten minutes later, we're sitting on the couch together, while Virginia stuffs her face with snake lollies from a pink backpack. She's still crying, but she's starting to make some sense.

Turns out she did get married on the first of May.

'I thought I was in love,' she says. 'We had so much in common. We both like manga, and Richie's even better at drawing than I am, but after the wedding night, after, you know, *we did it*, everything changed. I realised the reason we have so much in common is that we're family. He might not be a blood relation, but I grew up seeing him as a cousin. He almost feels like a brother! You have a brother, don't you, Summer, so you would understand! However much you love him, you don't want to fuck him!'

The word sounds obscene in her baby mouth. She hardly needs to invoke my brother to make her point. I get it.

'What was the purpose of all this?' I ask. 'You knew I was pregnant.'

'Mum told me you had miscarried,' says Virginia. 'She even got me to write you a sympathy card.'

So the marriage went ahead in the hope I would miscarry, or perhaps in the hope that my pregnancy was a lie. Francine had not given up without a fight. And she was a lot closer to the truth than she had realised.

'But what about all those photos on your Facebook page?' I ask. 'Two weeks ago you were tanned and toned and taking selfies at the gym!'

'Mum knew you would find those photos,' says Virginia. 'They're from months ago. Mum took them all in one day with a bunch of male models. She told them it was a fashion shoot.'

'Why did you go along with all this?' I ask.

'I have to be honest. They didn't force me,' Virginia says. She tucks her feet under herself, a girlish gesture at odds with her matronly bulk. 'I stood there in that registry office in Auckland and swore my life to him. It was my sixteenth birthday, and it was raining so hard that it soaked through my shoes. I got married with cold feet, literally.' She snorts, but the sound becomes a sob. 'Mum took us to a hotel room and then she and my gross uncles feasted in the restaurant below while Richie and I, you know.'

'God, I'm so sorry,' I say. The gross uncles must be Colton, and Francine's brother—the 'Edgar' Virginia is so scared of. I don't remember him, but I imagine a red-faced goblin with a bulbous nose, huddled with Francine over a banquet of greasy roast pig and several bottles of expensive port while Virginia and Richie are upstairs. At the thought that Colton was there, I feel a pang for my mother. Does she love Colton? And the thought of these teenagers fumbling their way through the act like a pair of child prostitutes is enough to make me gag.

'The next day was worse.' Virginia opens a bag of Pods and practically crams them all in her mouth at once. She talks as she chews. 'Mum had one of those ovulation-detection kits and she made me pee on a stick each day. She said I was having my LH surge, so she made us have sex three times. Breakfast, lunch and dinner. And each time, afterwards, she made me stand on my head!'

'I don't get it,' I say. 'Wasn't he basically raping you?'

'No,' she says quietly. 'That's the thing. I love Richard. He loves me. And the sex was nothing like I expected. I realised something that people had told me all my life but I had never understood. I'm sure I don't need to tell you. You and Adam, I understand now why you didn't want to conceive to get money.'

For a moment, I forget that I'm Summer and that I'm supposed to know what she's talking about. Because the truth is that I don't know. This is the thing that I have never understood.

'What did you realise?'

'That it's like the nuns at school say, isn't it? It turns out they were right after all. God knows how *they* know.' Virginia's voice grows husky. 'Sex is a sacrament. Sex, the best sex, is the moment when you connect with another soul, and maybe you create a new life. That's why they call it *making love*. If it's right, if it's special, then you're making the holiest thing. You're creating love.'

'Is that how you felt with Richie?' I ask. I don't know if I want to know the answer.

'No!' cries Virginia. A light passes across her face, as if she's some kind of priestess or angel, but now she frowns again and rips open another bag of Pods. 'We both knew that sex should feel that way, but it didn't! It was all wrong! And how could my mother understand? She's been doing it with Uncle Colton since God knows when! I don't think our father was even cold in the ground. It wouldn't surprise me if she did it with Uncle Edgar too! They're barbarians, the pair of them. Richie loathes his stepfather.'

Virginia fixes me with her daisy-blue eyes. 'You were right, Summer,' she says. 'No baby should ever be conceived for cash. This money is a curse! And that's what I've done to my baby! I've cursed him!' She is wracked by such heaving sobs that I fetch a bucket just in case. I don't want regurgitated Pods on my peach carpet.

There's more. Virginia and Richie, after their day of epic lovemaking, locked the witch out of their hotel room and agreed that their love could never be. Richie gallantly spent the night on the floor. Or perhaps he was out of juice. The next morning, Virginia tried to run away, but Francine caught her and demanded she do her duty to her family and hop back into bed with incest-boy.

Virginia was unwavering. She and Richie had agreed never to have sex again, never to see each other again, as some kind of purifying sacrifice, a bargain with the gods. After two days, Francine relented, and she and Virginia flew home to Wakefield, leaving the bridegroom to his father's wrath.

It was too late. Virginia's uterus turned out to be on Francine's side. She was pregnant.

She didn't want an abortion, but she was miserable, especially after she spotted me at the beach, bulging out of my bikini, and Francine admitted that I hadn't miscarried. Ashamed to see her schoolfriends or even her sisters, she hid in the attic of the beach house watching TV and eating herself sick.

'That's why I'm so much fatter than you,' she says, staring enviously at my neat baby bump. 'By the way, I know you're at least thirty-six weeks. Mum's counted.'

I start. Francine must have assumed that Summer didn't know she was pregnant when she set out to sail to the Seychelles, so she has miscounted by two weeks. Summer would be thirty-eight weeks pregnant, only a fortnight shy of her due date of the twenty-eighth of November. I've had to tell my family Summer's real due date and give up on my early attempts to nudge it into December, because, as I feared, my mother asked me too many pointed questions about when the baby was conceived. So she and Adam and my midwife believe I'm thirty-eight weeks pregnant, but I'm not. I'm only thirty-three weeks.

'How many weeks are you?' I ask. For the first time, I share the world's obsession with exactly how pregnant everybody is.

'I'm thirty weeks tomorrow,' Virginia says. 'I've googled it. If the baby's born now, he'll go on a ventilator or at the very least CPAP. He'll probably have a hole in his heart and haemorrhages in his brain. He could have lifelong problems. He could die.'

I can't risk getting into a discussion about this. I don't know what CPAP is. Virginia is staring at the space on the wall where the photo of me holding Tarquin used to hang. I have no idea whether what she said is accurate, but the photo was always a scary reminder of how birth can go wrong.

'But why would the baby be born now?' I ask. 'You might be a bit on the large side, but you're young and healthy.'

'That's why I'm here, Summer. Don't you see? Mum doesn't care about me or the baby. She just can't stand to lose that money.'

'But it's out of her control, isn't it? I'm way further along than you.' I feel a chill as I say it. I have to be nonchalant, like my baby is ready to be born.

'It's not who conceived first,' says Virginia, 'it's who's born first. They can still win if they force me into labour. I don't know what they might do. Mum kept talking about taking us to Thailand, although she had sworn she'd never return after Dad died, and then I found a page open on her laptop, a private maternity hospital in Phuket. Schedule your C-section, choose your baby's birthday. Isn't it true you can get anything up there for the right price?'

'But they can't do this now that you're onto them, can they?' I ask. 'So why are you so scared?'

'They might think of something else. Maybe slip something into my food that puts me into labour. Uncle Edgar is the worst. I honestly reckon he would kick me in the guts! Hide me, Summer, hide me and keep my baby safe! I know you won't let him be born too soon. I don't expect you to love me, but I know we want the same thing. You'll want to keep my baby inside me. And you deserve the money. You and Adam married for love.'

Uncomfortable words roll through my head. CPAP. Haemorrhages. Holes in the heart. In all the days and weeks and years I spent obsessing over the will, I never thought about what would happen if the Carmichael heir died.

All those years, right up until I learned that Summer was pregnant, I believed that my baby was going to be the heir. I was going to beat Summer. I would have one baby and collect the cheque. Although I never wanted the kid, I'm not so evil as to plan for its death.

Now, words from my law school lectures come flying back into my head. The law of inheritance is ancient British law, adopted by Australia centuries ago. We had to learn words like *bequeath* and *issue* and *testatrix*.

A miscarriage or a stillbirth won't count, but if a baby's born alive, even for a moment, it inherits. And then if it dies, its parents are its heirs. Virginia is a minor, so her guardian will gain control of the money. Francine.

The words fall out of my mouth. 'It only has to take one breath.'

Virginia shrieks, as though I've pronounced her baby's death sentence. But it's not Virginia's baby I'm thinking about. It's my own.

I've blithely reassured my lame-brained midwife that I'm happy to 'go overdue'. The plan is to induce labour in mid-December, if I don't go into labour naturally, which I shouldn't, since I'm not really due until next year.

It all seemed perfect. Adam would think the baby was overdue, when really it would be early, but not early enough to be sick like Tarquin.

But there is a flaw in this plan. I've put up with a crappy midwife who doesn't make me get a scan (or, as she describes it, 'put your baby in the microwave') even though the foetus is super-small for eight months. Skybird is almost as desperate as I am to deliver the baby at home, safe from all those doctors and their prying stethoscopes. She seemed like a godsend, even if her drab dreadlocks and distrust of deodorants made her visits not entirely charming. But what if something goes wrong?

I've had phone calls and emails from Summer's old work-mates, aghast at my apparent turn against medical science, and I've ignored them all, deleted their emails, hung up on them. But their warnings come back to me now. Nina, whoever she is, was so persistent that I blocked her number, but she kept emailing. *Please, Summer, anyone but Skybird,* she wrote. Months after I deleted her emails, she left a handwritten card in my letterbox. *I'm trying to support your choice to have a natural birth, hon. Please have one quick scan to rule out placenta praevia so you don't bleed to death.* The note went on and on, but I didn't read the rest.

Skybird was the ideal choice, full of nonsense about feng shui and lotus births. When I told her that I thought stethoscopes stole energy from the foetus, she promised to leave hers in the car during my labour.

I have chosen the worst midwife in Wakefield.

There's a loud rap at the door.

Virginia clutches me, her face frozen. 'It's Mum!' she hisses.

CHAPTER 17

THE ALBUM

I look around the room for somewhere to hide my giant half-sister. I have a crazy image of bundling her inside the grand piano.

An alarm sounds on my iPhone. I glance at the screen. *Get Tarquin from day care*, it reads. Whoever is at the front door will have heard my phone, even if they haven't spotted us through the glass. We can't pretend not to be home.

I can't get off the couch. Virginia's fingernails digging into my arm have frozen me to the spot. Her cowardice is infectious. My belly seems to be spasming, the child itself rigid with fear.

But the next sound is so welcome that it's beautiful. It's Tarquin singing. 'Mama-sama-mama-sea,' he warbles.

'It's not Francine,' I whisper. 'Someone's brought Tarquin home for me, maybe Annabeth.'

'No!' says Virginia. 'Don't let your mum see me like this!'

I glance down at Virginia's swollen body. From her double chin to her elephantine thighs, she's quite a sight. Her skin is sickly and pitted with acne.

'My mother won't care what you look like!' I say. 'She'll want to keep that baby inside you, right? Our family are your best friends now!'

Virginia nods. My abdominal spasm dissipates, and I go to the door. It's Adam.

'What are you doing here?' I ask.

'Why did you deadbolt the door?' he replies. 'Remember I was picking up Tarq today? Annabeth's coming for dinner so we can talk about Iris's birthday and the christening.'

I don't remember any of this, but now Adam spots Virginia. She's glued to the couch, her arms wrapped around her belly, her eyes as wide as a rabbit's. Adam's eyes narrow. Another jittery convulsion passes through my body. For a split second, my husband looks like a predator watching prey.

'You're pregnant? How can you be more pregnant than Summer?' he demands. 'Are you married? When did you conceive?'

What has happened to Adam's fuzzy memory? He's jumped to the heart of the matter in seconds. It seems there's a limit to his diffidence about the money. It's one thing not to care whether you get it or not. It's another to have it snatched away after you thought you'd won.

Tarquin toddles over to me and pokes me in my abdomen. 'Baby's back,' he says. 'Baby's back.' He runs his little hand down the curve of my belly.

You can feel the bumps of my baby's spine through my abdominal wall, to the right of my midline, but I have no idea how Tarquin knows this. Stringing two words together is a linguistic advance for him, but I have bigger things on my mind.

'She's not more pregnant than me,' I say. 'Women vary in size when they're pregnant. I'm on the petite side—'

'And I'm fat,' says Virginia. As if to emphasise the point, she pulls out a king-sized bar of chocolate and snaps off a chunk. 'Yes, I'm married, but don't worry, Adam, you've won the race.'

Virginia explains Francine's evil plan as she chews the chocolate, and reiterates that she's determined to carry her baby to term. I'm waiting for Adam to drop the thousand-yard stare and show his usual chivalry, but instead he says, 'If you care so much for your baby's health, stop scoffing all that junk.'

It's as if a different man has walked in the door from the husband who left this morning, but perhaps Adam has a point. Virginia's ballooning weight might trigger early labour, mightn't it? I can't think straight. Tarquin is still touching my belly and chanting, 'Baby's back,' and pain shoots across my body.

'Stop it, sweetie,' I say. 'Mummy's hurting.'

'Where's dinner?' Adam asks. 'Annabeth will be here any minute.'

'It's four-thirty in the afternoon, I had no idea she was coming, and I have a guest!' I retort. 'And I'm heavily pregnant! What are you expecting, a five-course banquet? Can't we get takeaway for once?'

Adam looks from me to Virginia to Tarquin, who is still chanting merrily at my side, although he's stopped touching me now.

'And why do we need to talk about my birthday—Iris's birthday?' I ask.

At last, my husband comes to his senses. The Adam I've conjured into existence over the last few months—the house-trained helper hubby—reappears.

'My bad,' he says, scooping up Tarq and planting an apologetic kiss on my cheek. 'Of course we can get takeaway. I'll feed Tarq.' He wraps his warm arm around my shoulder. 'I guess I'm more stressed about this baby than I realised. It brings back a lot of memories, you know.' He nods towards the piano. He has a habit of gesturing towards it whenever he mentions Helen; sometimes I feel that thing is her coffin, standing in the middle of our living room. 'We don't need to talk about your birthday if you don't want to, but Annabeth wants to do something to remember Iris, and it's only a couple of days away now.'

'It's fine, honey,' I murmur. I lean into his muscular frame and press my face into his neck. 'Sorry I snapped. I think we're all a bit stressed right now. And we all want to help you, Virginia.'

Virginia nods, all grateful and tearful. Adam stands with one arm around me, the other holding his son. We must look superb, the ideal family, about to become very rich. As long as Virginia doesn't go into labour.

_____

Several hours later, Annabeth, Adam, Tarquin, Virginia and I are sitting in a mess of empty takeaway containers, magazine spreads of christening photos, and empty Pods packets, when I realise the truth about Adam.

Our sex life has been amazing ever since the pregnancy test. I had to let go of Summer's bullshit stories about candlelit seductions, and Adam had to let go of the sexyrape, but since we have both done that, things have blossomed between us. The baby bump has not been a turn-off for Adam, and as for his body, it's a series of roped muscles, honey-gold and sublime. Adam still doesn't kiss me, but apart from that he's a great lover, thoughtful and playful and just plain hot.

But something is wrong, and his wedding album forces me to face it.

Who knew that you have to consult your wedding album in order to sew a christening gown? It wouldn't have occurred to me, but Annabeth says she wants the lace to match. She has brought a ton of fabric samples with her, which she is now spreading out on the coffee table. Her conversation has meandered all evening between how to keep Virginia safe from Francine and what sort of gown she should make. My mother regards these topics as equally enthralling.

'Grab your wedding photos, Summer!' Annabeth cries.

Sometimes I think this will be the rest of my life; I'm just relaxing, my belly full of vindaloo, when someone demands something, right now, that I have no idea how to do. I don't have a clue where Summer's wedding photos are, but I have learned some techniques over the last few months. Grief and pregnancy are my go-to excuses for not remembering, not knowing, not doing the right thing.

'I'm too pregnant to move,' I say. As if in sympathy, my belly goes rigid, as it has been doing periodically all evening. 'I swear if I get out of this armchair, the baby's going to drop out of me.'

Adam takes the hint and strides off to find the photos. I do have him well-trained.

The album is old-fashioned black leather. It's big enough that when Annabeth places it on the coffee table in front of the sofa, we can all see the photos from our chairs around the living room. It doesn't look like Summer's style, and when Annabeth opens it, I see why.

Inside the front cover are two full-page photos of bride and groom. From one side, Summer's smile radiates through the room. Her golden hair tumbles down her shoulders and over her dress so that I can hardly see the intricate lace of the bodice. Summer's eyes are pure aquamarine; her sweet expression hits me like a slap in the face.

Then there's the other photo. This gown is plain satin, and the bride's auburn hair is piled on top of her head. Her eyes have a mysterious expression, almost mournful, as if she knows she's not long for this world. It's Helen.

Adam and Summer don't have their own wedding album. Adam has a combined album for both of his wives. Did Summer do this? Did she add her photos to an existing album? Or was the combined album Adam's idea?

Annabeth turns the pages, and I see photos of Helen and Summer jumbled together. The two weddings were only two years apart, and Adam wore the same suit. In photos that don't include the bride, it's hard to tell which wedding is which. Both took place in Adam's garden, when the flowers were at the height of their bloom, and both wedding parties are surrounded by a swirl of rosy, soft-focus colours, with an azure sky as backdrop. The floaty tangerine tulle that Summer imposed on her bridesmaids—there were six of us—is only a shade brighter than the peachy pink Helen chose for her attendants. In fact, if it weren't for her bronze complexion and auburn hair, you could almost mistake Helen for Summer. Summer's prettier, but they were made from the same mould. Adam definitely has a type.

Maybe men don't spend much time reminiscing over their wedding day, or days, but does he really want to look at photos of me and his dead first wife at the same time?

Adam is hunched over the album beside Annabeth, looking at the photos with an expression of complacent pride. I could swear he is thinking that two wives are better than one.

Adam and I are supposed to be so close. I'm supposed to be the wife who helped him get over his grief. We make love in the bed he shared with Helen. I thought about replacing the mahogany frame, but it was too hard to get it moved down the stairs.

It's always seemed weird that Summer spent her wedding night in Helen's bed, but I figured Adam was so open about Helen and his relationship with her that there was no awkwardness. When you meet your one true love, you talk about your ex-girlfriends and there's no jealousy; you laugh together about how crazy they all were. But Helen isn't an ex-girlfriend. She isn't an ex-wife. They never broke up.

Adam's silence about Helen suggests loyalty. It suggests he loved her as much as he loves Summer. Maybe more. The wedding album certainly doesn't consign Helen to history.

I've always seen my sister as the ultimate prize, but maybe to Adam she was just another pretty girl when he found himself single. And Summer was happy to be the second wife. She would do the girl jobs, and he would make the decisions. They had fun with the sexyrape, and she loved Tarquin.

It's not that I expect to be the only woman Adam has ever loved, but I don't want to feel like I'm interchangeable. I almost feel that Adam doesn't care which wife is which as long as she cooks and cleans, looks after the kids and puts out.

Adam's not a bad guy. I've made our relationship work. Our sex life is great, he's good company, he loves his kids. He's not the idol I thought he was, but I had started to think he could be the right guy for me. But he's not. He never will be.

I'm not even any good at the things Adam loves me for.

I sit in my plush armchair and gaze through the window at the infinity pool, watching the line between water and air dissolve as darkness descends. Did Summer love her life because it was perfect or because she was Summer, happy with her lot?

'Summer,' says Adam, 'isn't it time you put Tarquin to bed?'

Tarquin has toddled over to the album and is rubbing his fingers over the photos. He turns and points at me and speaks up loud and clear.

'You're not my mummy.'

Everyone is staring at me. Virginia, Annabeth, Adam. I can't think of a single thing to say.

It's happening.

'You're not my mummy.' Tarquin is delighted by his words. He says it again. In between his pronouncements, there is clanging silence.

If any of them suspects, it's over. They could easily ask questions I couldn't answer. All Adam needs to say is, describe the day we met. Describe our first kiss. Describe our wedding night.

And my mother doesn't need to ask a question. She doesn't need to say a word. She could walk across the room right now and place her hand on my heart.

Tarquin's eyes bore into me. He knows. I don't know how he knows, but he knows. You nailed it, kid.

'Tarquin is talking!' Annabeth exclaims. 'Listen to his clever new words!'

'I didn't know he understood about Helen,' says Virginia.

'He doesn't,' says Adam. 'We agreed not to tell him yet.' He turns to me, that wolfish look in his eyes again. Is he angry because he thinks I told Tarq about Helen? Or is he starting to doubt?

'He must be able to see the resemblance,' says Annabeth. 'The red hair.'

'Speaking of first wives,' says Virginia, 'did you know, Annabeth, that my mother is obsessed with the idea that Margaret had a baby, after Dad left her for you? Mum thinks that this baby, who would be older than Summer, obviously, could have had a kid by now, and so maybe the Carmichael heir is already born. Mum also reckons that Ben is secretly having a baby in New York. I know he's gay, but he could still marry and have a kid for the money—'

'Francine is preposterous!' says Annabeth. 'Ridge left Margaret because she couldn't have kids. They were both over forty. If she'd been pregnant she would have told him in order to save the marriage.'

'Not necessarily,' says Virginia. 'She might have figured out what a cunt he was by then.'

'Young lady!' cries my mother. 'That's no way to speak about your father!'

Virginia continues unabashed. 'The reason he *was* my father is that he was screwing my crazy-bitch mother while he was still married to you,' she says. 'Why can't you face the truth, Annabeth? He left you, after all. And who did he leave you for? My mother, who's been slyly banging his brother all these years, while Uncle Colton strings you along! My mother, who pimps out her own daughter!'

I want to throw my arms around Virginia. She's provided an awesome distraction.

Virginia and Annabeth start debating why Margaret's kid, if he or she did exist, wouldn't have claimed the money already. Virginia mockingly outlines Francine's paranoid theories, which all contradict each other. Maybe Margaret and her kid don't know about the will. Maybe they don't want it to rule their lives. Maybe they're laughing up their sleeves watching us have babies for no reason.

Virginia out-argues my mother, even though she clearly doesn't believe any of it. I think of Dad's words. Nice is dumb. Virginia is neither. She's opinionated, cynical and smart.

And yet despite her cynicism, Virginia has turned her back on the money and walked into the lion's den, as she sees it, in order to do the right thing.

She loves her baby. Nobody could blame her if she hated the inbred spawn, but she doesn't. Virginia's been raised by a greedy lunatic, but she's still chosen to do right. She has told the truth.

And there's a truth Virginia doesn't know. My baby isn't legitimate, and that means Virginia's baby is the true heir. Virginia deserves the inheritance that she has come here to give up, regardless of which one of us is first to give birth.

'I think you're going to get the money after all,' I say. I push myself out of my armchair. I don't know what's got into me. The words have come out of my mouth before I know what they mean.

'Summer, what are you saying?' asks Adam.

I don't know what I'm saying. I'm forgetting to be Summer. A spasm wracks my frame, and I writhe in sudden agony. Tarquin lets out a wail.

'Something's wrong,' I say. 'I think I'm going to lose the baby.'

'I knew you were in labour!' Annabeth leaps off the couch. 'Don't panic, sweetie! I'll call Skybird for you. I've got her number on speed dial.'

'No!' I cry. If there's one thing I know, it's that this baby needs a better midwife than Skybird. 'Don't call her! I don't want that crystal-waving moron!'

Everybody converges on me, trying to calm me down. 'You can do this, Summer,' they all say. 'It's natural to panic, but you love Skybird.'

I've been avoiding thinking about my body all evening, but the pains in my abdomen have got worse. My mother has spotted it from across the room. I'm in labour. My baby is coming seven weeks early. The idea of a stoned hippie who needs a good scrub delivering my child was crazy enough if the child had been full-term, but now it would be a disaster.

I look at Virginia. The money is slipping away from her right now, money that is rightfully hers, but her eyes show sympathy for me. How is it that she has her head screwed on right and I don't? She's known all along that a healthy baby is the most important thing; I've only realised now. Maybe I wouldn't have ever realised if she hadn't come here with her selfless plea for help.

But it's not too late to fix things. I couldn't care less about all the money in the world. I'm going to save my baby.

'I'm not having a home birth,' I say. 'It's too early for that. We have to go to hospital!'

'You're fine, darling,' Annabeth says. 'Thirty-eight weeks isn't too early. Baby will be fine. Anyway, we can ask Skybird.'

'No!' I cry. 'I haven't told the truth! I'm only thirty-three weeks pregnant!'

That stops the room dead. Everybody gapes at me.

Adam wraps me in his strong, calm arms. 'You're thirty-eight weeks, Summer,' he says. 'Don't back out now. You've dreamed of having a home birth. And you're having'—he lowers his voice—'you're having *the Carmichael heir.*'

'Adam, I lost the baby,' I say. I try to keep my voice low, but Virginia and Annabeth are standing right beside us. 'I lost our first baby in the middle of the ocean. It was a nightmare. I kept trying to tell you, but I couldn't. And then I got pregnant again, and I thought you didn't need to go through that grief. I thought a few weeks wouldn't matter, but it does. I'm seven weeks off my due date. We've got to get to hospital now!'

Adam stares at me and stares at Virginia. At her belly. 'Can they stop the labour?' he asks the room.

'I think they can,' says Annabeth. 'Her waters haven't broken.' She looks at Virginia's belly too.

Is Virginia really only thirty weeks pregnant? She's twice the size of me. Virginia's eyes are fixed on Tarquin, who has picked up the carcase of the tandoori chicken and now drops it on the carpet. An orange-red stain spreads across the lush peach pile.

'Adam, bring the car around!' I cry. 'And nobody call Skybird!' I need real doctors and nurses to deliver my baby, and I need them now.

Adam dashes out the front door.

A freight train of pain hits my belly, and something pops deep inside me. I lurch against the piano and scream. The image flashes through my mind of my father's coffin, of scrambling beneath it to hide. But there is no hiding from this pain.

My legs are wet and there's a bloody puddle at my feet. Tarquin ploughs the chicken carcase into the blood. 'Snap snap snap,' he says. 'Crockie eat a birdie.'

The pain ebbs. I breathe deep and look outside. I glimpse car tyres. Adam must have already pulled up.

The doctors will check my heart. I've lost the money and Adam and everything, but I don't care. All I know is I have to get into that car before the next contraction comes.

'Look after Tarquin,' I say to my mother.

I stumble outside into the rosy evening light. It isn't the right car—it's a silver sedan—but I still expect Adam to be inside. Then the driver's door opens.

Francine steps out. In her ice-blue suit and pearl necklace, she looks as impeccably venomous as ever. She spots me and slams the car door.

'Where is my daughter?' she demands, striding towards me. 'I know you've got Virginia in there. You're harbouring a runaway. This is against the law.'

'Get out of my way, Francine,' I say. 'I'm in labour.'

Francine's face distorts. 'You liar!' she cries. 'Don't try to distract me!'

Another wall of pain slams into my body. I double over, almost sinking to the ground.

'Adam!' I call.

Where *is* Adam? For an instant, nothing exists outside the pain, but when I come to myself, Francine is digging her talons into my shoulders. Her scowling face is an inch from mine. 'You little witch,' she hisses, 'don't give me this holier-than-thou routine. Where is she?'

'Adam! Adam!' I cry. Where is his car?

I can't muster the willpower to fight off Francine. Is she going to hurt my baby? But now I'm free. Someone has dragged her off me.

Adam's red Mustang pulls up. He jumps out and runs towards me. He lifts me into his arms.

I glance back towards Francine. Uncle Colton has her pinned tightly. He must have been in the car with her. She's struggling in his arms, her face purple with rage.

'Face it, Francine, you've lost,' Colton barks. 'Summer's in labour. It's time to give up.'

'You're just like your mother!' Francine shouts at me as Colton drags her backwards onto the lawn, snapping the heel off her shoe. 'You act so saintly, but you just want the money! I pity your baby, having you for a mother!'

I turn away, and Adam carries me effortlessly to his car.

As he lowers me into the passenger seat, another contraction hits. Every fibre of my being screams *push*, but I know I must not push. The car door slams shut, and Adam jumps into the driver's seat and takes off. We don't have time to look behind us. We drive towards the setting sun, glowing bloody in the sky.

CHAPTER 18

THE BABY

We barely make it to the hospital before my daughter pushes her way out of my body. No time for the medical exam I've been dreading. They rush me into a delivery room. She twists like a corkscrew as she emerges, and her eyes meet mine as she enters the world.

'Born facing upwards!' the doctor exclaims. 'A stargazer!'

He places her on my chest straight away, and she wriggles and purrs like a kitten. I wrap my arms around her. Through her fluttery movements I sense the warm steady throb of her heart.

My baby might be small, but she is strong. She's alert, eager, bold. And her eyes are like two stars shining into my soul. I know things are different now. I know I can never lie to her.

'She's a star!' I cry. I forget that she's the Carmichael heiress. All I know is that I love her. And that everything has changed.

—

The morning after the birth, Adam brings Tarquin to meet his sister. We're in a private room. It's windowless and cramped in here, but I don't mind. My baby is safe and I've avoided the neonatal unit. After Annabeth appeared unannounced at eight o'clock this morning, I've said no more visitors except Adam. I don't want Summer's nosy workmates.

All I want to do is hold my baby in my arms and gaze at her perfection. My body is a wreck, my breasts are leaking, and I don't want to think about what's going on with the rest of me. Everything between my neck and my knees hurts, but I don't care. She's worth it.

I know what I want to call her: Esther. It means star.

Adam stands in the doorway with two bouquets, one of irises and one of roses, and his smile is wider than I've ever seen. Tarquin is clinging to his legs.

I'm almost startled to remember that Adam is Esther's father and Tarquin is her brother. It feels as though she fell out of heaven, as though she is just herself, not related to us. She has green eyes and fine black hair, and she doesn't look like anyone else in the family. I thought Adam would prefer sons, but the look on his face when he takes his daughter from my arms is pure joy.

'Watching you give birth was amazing,' he says. 'You were so strong!'

I remember that Adam wasn't allowed to be present for Tarquin's delivery, which was an emergency caesarean section. After we dropped out of antenatal classes, Adam didn't seem too interested in the upcoming birth, but now he can't stop talking about it.

'Watching you bring our daughter into the world . . . I can see why people used to worship pregnant women. You were like one of those fertility goddesses!'

'What do you think, Tarq?' I ask. 'Is Mu—am I a goddess?' I was going to say 'Mummy' but I stumble over the word. Calling myself 'Mummy' is one of the lies I've been telling.

And yet, I am a mother now. For the first time, I deserve the name. And I'm the only mother Tarquin knows. Telling the truth will rip that away from him.

Tarquin climbs onto my bed and nuzzles against my belly, murmuring, 'Mama, Mama.' The labour must have made me crazy last night, to make me think he knew the truth. The kid adores me.

'What do you want first?' Adam asks. 'Renovate or buy a new house? Build our dream home? Or we could buy a holiday home somewhere, or a new car each? I'm thinking a Ferrari convertible for you . . .'

'I like the house for now,' I say, 'and I don't really care about cars at the moment, but I do want to bring *Bathsheba* back to Australia. Let's pay a crew to sail her home.'

'Is this the right time to do that? We have two kids now.'

'I'm not suggesting we move aboard,' I say. 'I just want to know she's nearby.'

'I'm surprised,' says Adam, 'but I'll think about it. In any case, this is the last thing we need to do to secure the inheritance.' He hands me a form. 'We need to prove that the baby's surname is Carmichael. Then Colton will have no choice but to sign everything over to us.'

I squint at Adam. 'How do you feel about that? Our kids having different surnames? I know we have to do it, but it's odd.'

Adam shrugs. 'Let's just get it over with,' he says. He hands me a pen. I take it in my right hand.

Summer Rose Romain, I scrawl. I've been practising Summer's childish loops for months, but this is the first time I've signed her name in front of someone. I'm so intent on getting it right that I sign first and then I read the form.

Adam has already filled in the baby's name: *Rosebud Carmichael.*

'What is this?' I say. *'Rosebud?* Is this a joke?'

'What are you talking about?' says Adam. 'We've been calling her Rosebud since the day we found out you were pregnant. It's the name you always wanted for a girl.'

He skips over the whole losing-the-baby-in-the-middle-of-the-ocean thing. He's clearly not ready to talk about that. Not with Tarquin in the room.

'I think you misunderstood,' I say. 'People use a whimsical name for the foetus, but they don't put it on the birth certificate. Frankly, *Rosebud* was a little nauseating even before she was born. It sounds kind of sexual, like a nipple.'

'Come on, Summer, we agreed on this ages ago,' says Adam, slipping the paper into his briefcase. 'You get Carmichael, I get Rosebud.'

'What do you mean, I get Carmichael?'

Adam lays our daughter in her bassinet and picks Tarquin up. He looks ready to hightail it to the registry office. I've just about had enough of this husband-knows-best routine.

'I don't care if her name is Carmichael!' I shriek. 'We're not naming her that for me! Give her whatever surname you want, but I'm not calling her Rosebud!' Tears fill my eyes. I have a sick feeling that if Adam leaves the room, I'll have lost this argument. My daughter will be Rosebud Carmichael, like a little bud of Summer Rose.

'I suppose you want to call her Iris,' says Adam.

'No,' I say. 'Iris hated her name.'

Adam slumps down in a chair and puts Tarquin down. Tarquin toddles over to the bassinet and gazes at his baby sister. 'Baby's out,' he says.

'OK,' Adam says. 'Fair enough. What do you want to call her?'

'Esther,' I say. 'It feels right for her. No more flower names. Iris grew up never feeling good enough because her name was like an offshoot of mine, like she was an afterthought. And "Rosebud" feels like that too. This baby is new, she's our chance for a fresh start.'

Adam studies the wall. My speech probably makes no sense to him. Are we going to have a stand-off over this? And in the meantime, I suppose, we don't get the money. Do I care?

At last Adam opens the briefcase and takes out the form. He tears the paper right down the middle.

'Esther Carmichael,' he says. 'I like it. I'll go and get a new form.'

He stands to leave, but before he reaches the doorway, he turns and walks back to me. He looms over the bed; his face is so near. The air is heavy with cinnamon and cloves.

He kisses me.

For seven months, Adam hasn't kissed me, but now he kisses me as though our children are not in the room, as though no one else exists in the world. His lips are firm, and they push against mine as though he's thirsting for me.

'It's like kissing the night sky,' he whispers. 'Thank you so much for giving me our daughter.'

Now we're both laughing because Tarq is wriggling his way between us, determined not to be left out of the family hug. He pokes my jelly-soft belly with his little paw. 'Baby's out,' he says. 'Baby's out again.'

'And Tarq's suddenly talking.' I smile at Adam. 'Isn't it great? It's like everything's coming together.'

Adam nods, gives me one more fervent kiss and hurries away. *Like kissing the night sky.* I thought Summer's stories about Adam's romantic speeches were fantasies, but perhaps I haven't been doing the things, the Summer-ish things, that got him in the mood. Until now. I roll his words and his kisses around my memory.

But it's typical Adam, wandering off and leaving Tarq here. I want to call after him, but he'll be out of earshot. The birth was straightforward, but I can barely get out of bed. What'll I do if the kid decides to do a runner?

Luckily, Tarq is all snuggly and soft, and he pushes his head under the blankets, as though he wants to be a baby again himself. 'Put baby back in,' he says.

'You funny thing,' I say. 'How sweet it is to hear your thoughts at last. Babies can't go back in.'

On the white hospital sheet, there are smears of orange. No one's washed Tarquin's hands since last night, when he spattered tandoori chicken all over the carpet while Esther began her dramatic entrance into the world. What had he said? *Snap snap snap. Crockie eat a birdie.*

What was he talking about? *Crockie.* He must mean crocodile. It's as though he knows the story about Ridge throwing a live chicken to the crocodiles at Carmichael Bridge. Could Annabeth have told him about it? It isn't the sort of story she would repeat.

It's possible that Summer told him the story or even did the same thing herself with Tarquin in tow. It's not everybody's idea of family fun, but I can't think of any other explanation. Was Summer crazy enough over the crocodile-versus-chicken thing to have re-enacted it in front of her own kid? This would have had to have happened a year ago, before they left Australia to go sailing. Could Tarquin remember that far back? He was a baby the last time he saw the real Summer. Surely he can't remember.

I've been assuming that Tarquin's memories of Summer are all tangled up with his memories of me, that it's all a babyish blur. I thought when he finally did learn to speak, he would only talk about the present. Surely he can't dredge up the past.

Perhaps Adam took Tarquin to the bridge recently. Perhaps they swung by on their way home from day care, and Adam forgot to tell me. And Adam happened to have a live chicken on hand? No way.

They must have just talked about it. It's a gruesome enough story to stick in a kid's mind.

'Tarq,' I say, 'did you see the crocodiles eat a birdie?'

'Snap snap snap,' says Tarquin. He writhes like a little lizard.

'Tarq,' I say, 'I need to know. Did Daddy take you to the bridge to see crocodiles? Did you see crockies?'

Tarquin's mouth clamps shut, and he stares up at me with big eyes. Has my urgent tone scared him? I force myself to take a breath. I rub his little back. If I want to get the truth out of him, I need to take it slow.

The door opens and Adam saunters back in. 'So sorry, leaving you with both kids,' he says with a grin. He scoops Tarquin up, and they're gone.

But not before I've seen that look in Tarquin's eyes again. *You're not my mummy.* This time there's no mistake. He knows.

He remembers. And it's only a matter of time before he makes himself understood.

————

We don't announce Esther's birth online; I don't text anyone. I can't face the deluge of Summer's bosom buddies. I have to let Annabeth visit again at some stage, and Adam's parents will want to fly up from Sydney, but that will be all. I always imagined I would invite Francine, to watch her trying to hide her gall, but I've moved past that now. She embarrassed herself enough yesterday.

Adam drops by in the early afternoon with a new form for me to sign. He's going straight from the registry office to Carmichael Brothers to sort out the paperwork. Annabeth is looking after Tarquin. Esther sleeps the day away like a dream of a baby. Although she's tiny, there is a satisfying weight to her in my arms. She's cosy and downy and soft. Her eyes are so pretty, I'm impatient for her to wake up.

In the meantime I craft an email to Ben, typing one-handed on my phone while I cradle Esther. It takes me a long time because I don't know how to talk to him as Summer. I try chatty, earnest, teasing, but I can't strike the right tone. The email I would write, if I could be myself, somehow appears on my screen.

The sprog is out, and she's gorgeous! You're an uncle! Come home and see me. Can't wait to tell you all the news!

I hold down the delete key until it's gone. Ben would instantly know this came from Iris, and of course I can't risk inviting him to see me. How should Summer phrase the news? Since that first dispassionate message from him when I was in the Seychelles, I haven't spoken to my brother, and there have only been a few brief emails, which I haven't replied to.

Why has he been so quiet? I laughed last night when Virginia said that Francine thought Ben was secretly having a baby. Now I wonder. Why have I always assumed Ben wouldn't chase the money, just because he is gay? He could get married and get his wife pregnant if he wanted to.

In seven months, he hasn't picked up the phone. In seven months, he hasn't come home to see his mother, who lost her daughter, or his sister, who lost her twin. I know he takes his study seriously—he worked his butt off to get that scholarship—but hasn't he had a semester break since then?

Would Ben tell me if he had beaten me to the money? Perhaps not. Perhaps he is married, with a pregnant wife, but he didn't want to tip me off until his baby was born. I remember enough trust law to know that if I get the money, and it turns out that Ben had a baby first, I'll have to give it back.

My phone rings. It's Colton.

'Congratulations! My favourite niece!' His voice is smooth. 'How's the little heiress? Does she have a name?'

'Esther,' I say. 'Esther Carmichael.'

'Beautiful name for a beautiful girl.'

What a super-friendly guy. I guess he knows which side his bread is buttered on.

'Adam's organising the birth certificate today,' I say.

'Oh, take your time,' he says breezily. 'I'm not concerned about that. Francine is demanding a DNA test and all sorts of nonsense, but she needs to get over herself.' He pauses. 'Summer, I guess Virginia's told you that Francine and I had a thing going on, but I want you to know I broke it off with her last night. Her performance at your house woke me up. I should never have got caught up in the row between her and your mother. I want to sign off on my brother's will. It's the last thing I can do for him, and to be honest, it will be nice to have this job off my hands after so many years. Your little girl has so many stocks and shares that I had to pay two people to run her portfolio. In fact, I thought I might drop by now to give you access to the first tranche of income. There's a slush fund that you and Adam can spend right away. Fifty grand or so, and then the share transfers will dribble through over the next few months.'

My head is buzzing. Can it be this easy? Part of me wants to say no. Wouldn't it be better never to get the money, than to get it and have to give it back? This all seems too good to be true, and yet I'm not even having to tell any lies. My life and Summer's are one and the same at last.

'Yes, come now,' I say. 'Good to get things moving. Adam and I have been talking about bringing our yacht back to Wakefield, and that will be expensive.'

'You just had a baby, and you're already dreaming about sailing away?' Colton asks.

'I just want to bring *Bathsheba* home,' I say. 'I'll want to teach Esther to sail one day. And Tarq.'

'Well, you might have to wait a while,' Colton says. 'I spoke to Adam earlier, and he was pretty clear that the first pile of cash goes straight into Romain Travel.'

'What? No,' I say. 'We get money *out* of the agency, we don't put money *into* it.'

Colton cackles. 'OK, well, you're the boss now, Summer. You and Adam. He told me not to worry you with this stuff, anyway. You two can do whatever you like. I'll see you soon.' He hangs up.

Esther dreams on. What a mess I am; I'm not fit for visitors. I haven't showered today. I gingerly climb out of bed and lower Esther into her glass-sided bassinet, taking care not to wake her. She makes quiet grunts as she breathes, the sweetest sound I've ever heard. I hobble on stiff legs towards the ensuite bathroom. Adam forgot to put the bouquets in water, and the irises, lying on the meal trolley, will be wilting in no time.

I pick them up. I have a feeling that today I get everything I want. The irises are bold purple, a dazzle of colour splashed with gold. They are tall and proud and unashamedly themselves.

Perhaps they are not as beautiful as roses, but they are my flower and I love them. All my life I have tried to smell them and smelled nothing. Why not try one more time? I bury my face in the bright blooms and breathe deep.

I'm sure there is a faint scent. It's green and warm as springtime, and it fills my lungs. I exhale and breathe in again. I smell everything good: honey, spice, fresh-cut grass and morning.

Why today of all days? Perhaps I'm imagining the fragrance, but it doesn't matter. It's the smell of happiness. It's the smell of everything being OK. I have a daughter. Adam loves me. I've done it at last.

I've got my back to the door, my face deep in my namesake flower, so I hear his voice before I see him.

'Hey.'

I wheel around. Ben is standing at the door in crumpled clothes, a travel pack on his back. 'Am I the only sane person on the planet? How the hell did you manage to fool them all?'

CHAPTER 19

THE MONEY

The game is up. There's no question this time. Ben knows. My brain is screaming, *deny it*, but I can't. It's no use.

It's the first time in months that anybody has looked at me and seen me. He didn't need to question me or hear my voice. He knew. It feels as though he's woken me from a long dream, and I've remembered at last who I am.

Ben looks older, tired and bewildered. He shrugs his backpack off his shoulders and dumps it on the floor. I want to run over and hug him, but the look on his face stops me.

'Iris, you crazy cow,' he hisses. 'What the fuck are you doing?'

'Would you please shut the door?' I hiss back. 'And don't wake Esther or the nurse will come.'

Ben shuts the door. His form, even with his back to me, is so familiar—tall but slight, with those long, angular limbs—that

I could pick him from a line-up of thousands. How could I ever have thought he wouldn't know me?

'How could you do this to Mum?' he asks, turning to face me.

'What have I done?' I ask. 'Annabeth *prefers* Summer. If I didn't know that already, I would now. You should hear what she says about Iris now that she's dead.'

Ben's eyes meet mine.

'About me, I mean,' I find myself saying. 'What she says about me now that I'm dead.'

Ben looks aghast. 'Jesus, now that you're *dead*. OK, maybe you're right about our mother, but what about Adam?' He sinks into a chair and buries his head in his hands.

'Um, Adam obviously prefers Summer. As does Tarquin. As does, actually, everybody.'

'Except me,' says Ben.

'Well, you weren't too cut up, were you? Don't forget, I read the email you sent Summer when I died. You didn't even mention my name. In fact, let's go back a step. You sent an *email*.'

'So you think I didn't care? Iris, for a bright girl you can be freaking stupid. I didn't phone or visit when you died, and you think it's because I didn't care about *you*. I lie in bed every night thinking about you lost out there in the darkness. You who loved the ocean, who were always so powerful and brave. Did you suffer? Were you alive, injured, struggling to stay afloat? Were you terrified? Despairing? What got you in the end, the cold or exhaustion? Or a . . . a . . .'

He sticks his fist in his teeth and bites down. I know what he can't say. The thought that a predator took our sister. It haunts me too.

'But all that did happen to your sister, just not the sister you thought.'

'Oh, and that would make no difference to me?'

'Well, if anything, it's worse that it was Summer.'

Ben's face screws into a scowl. I can feel his fury. 'You know what, Iris? Fuck you and your obsession with Summer. I know you think the sun shone out of her pristine little butt, so you'll just have to wonder why I didn't rush to her grief-stricken side. No, you know what? I will tell you. I thought it was murder. Just so you know. I thought she pushed you. And I couldn't do a goddamn thing about it. I knew she would have covered her tracks.'

My scalp prickles. Is this how Ben thinks about his family, that we would kill each other over the money?

'Why would Summer ever want or need to kill me?' I ask. 'She had everything.'

'Maybe you were pregnant.'

'No,' I say. '*She* was pregnant.'

Red spots appear before my eyes. I can't bear what my brother is about to say.

'I didn't do anything, Ben,' I say. 'You have to believe me. She fell.'

Ben rolls his eyes. 'Would you quit already, you moron? I know you, Iris. I've spent my life watching you watching

Summer. You kill her? You'd as soon cut out your own heart. But who else will believe you? She was pregnant, about to get a hundred million dollars. The press will dig up the whole sordid story. They're gonna love how you rushed out and married Noah the day after Summer and Adam got engaged. You've framed yourself perfectly. You know Noah's in town, by the way? Don't you think he might recognise you?'

All I can see is blood. That blood in the cockpit. Adam washed it away. Has he forgotten it?

Ben's right. I've framed myself perfectly. What a mistake to throw that CCTV footage in the sea. If Adam ever finds out who I am and starts wondering about that blood, I'm done for.

And the memorial service is tomorrow. Annabeth explained to me this morning that she had delayed the memorial service for her lost daughter until my birthday 'so that we only need to live through one dreadful day'. She had avoided consulting me about the service because she didn't want to stress me out during my pregnancy, but it should have been obvious to me that Noah and Ben might attend.

'And what about the sprog?' Ben gestures contemptuously towards Esther's bassinet. 'Is it Adam's or Noah's? Do you even know?'

'How dare you bring my daughter into this!' I cry. 'I'm sorry you missed out on the cash, but if you tell anyone, it won't help you, because Virginia's married and pregnant too. Or are you ahead of us all? Have you had a baby?'

'Is that what you think?'

'I don't know,' I say. 'Francine thinks so. Have you? Is that why you're here, to claim the cash?'

Ben glares at me with such a look of pain, anger and hatred, that I have to look away.

'This is bullshit,' he says.

Esther stirs in her sleep. My body tells me to go and pick up my baby, but I don't want Ben to look at her. Not when he's so enraged.

'I'll give up the money,' I say.

'It's too late for that.' Ben speaks slowly, coldly. 'Think, Iris. Think hard. If anyone does spring you, the money is the only thing that could keep you out of prison.'

I look down at the irises, now crushed and pulpy in my hands. I slam them down on the trolley.

'Is that how it's going to be?' I say. 'Is that how things are between us? After you laid it on so thick about your grief and anguish, lying awake at night—'

The door opens. Colton hurries in.

'Summer! My princess!' I'm caught up in a bear hug. 'And Ben! My man! What are you doing in Australia?'

Ben hastily smooths his hair and shakes Colton's outstretched hand. 'Um, I—I'm here for the memorial service Mum's planning for Iris's birthday. My visit was kinda meant to be a surprise for Summer, but ... well ... I'm not going to be able to make it. I've got to catch the first flight back to New

York. So, maybe don't tell Mum that you saw me. It's a long story. I don't want to upset her. I'll tell her that I never got here, that I missed my flight.'

'I understand, of course,' says Colton, looking like he clearly doesn't. My uncle is in a suit and tie and carries a slim leather briefcase. 'I'm sorry you have to leave so soon. I hope it's not serious? If there's anything I can do?'

'No, no,' says Ben. 'Just a thing with uni, with my studies. I've got to get back. The only thing you could do is not talk about today. And I know Summer can keep a secret.' He can barely keep the contempt out of his voice. 'Take care, Summer. I have to go. Don't know when I'll see you again.'

He walks out the door.

I've lost my brother. I can tell from the look in his eyes, from the tone of his voice, that he's gone. I'll never see him again.

I don't want the money anymore. I'm tempted to send Colton packing, to send him straight to Virginia, wherever she is, to put her name on the paperwork. She deserves the money. She is carrying the true heir. She's been through more shit than I have, and none of it was her fault.

I wouldn't care if I had to work every day of my life to make ends meet, as long as I could hold my head up high and look my brother in the eye. Look my daughter in the eye.

But Ben's right. This isn't just about money. How could I think I would escape a murder charge by leaving the Seychelles? What about the Australian police? They would hardly let this lie. I can't remember which country has jurisdiction if a murder happens at sea. It's something to do with where the ship is registered—

'Summer,' says Colton, 'the baby's making a strange noise.'

I start. Colton is picking up my baby, whose grunting is getting more forceful, though she's still asleep. I snatch her out of his arms.

The door opens, and Ben walks back in. 'I almost forgot the most important thing. I've sent you some emails, *sister*.' The last word drips with meaning. 'You need to check them. Then you'll know how things stand.'

And he's gone, this time for real.

Colton looks perplexed. I shrug, as if to suggest that this is mere sibling banter. But I know what it means. This is it, then. An email setting out 'how things stand'. Because the money's the only thing that can keep me out of prison.

Hush money. Ben is blackmailing me.

I ought to be relieved that Ben's not planning to expose me, and no doubt his demands will be reasonable, but that's not what I feel. Everything around me—the room, the flowers, my uncle—seems a bare outline, like I'm living in a hollow world. It was bad when I was never going to hear from Ben again, but this is worse.

Colton pulls a pile of papers out of his briefcase. 'I know this isn't a great time,' he says. 'I'll try to be quick.'

'I don't understand,' I say. 'Adam's on his way to your office to pick up the paperwork. Didn't he tell you?'

'Yes.' Colton hesitates. 'Adam was keen to sort it all out

for you, but I felt I needed to speak to you in person. As I said, I'm determined to do this properly. I know you don't like handling money, but you do have certain responsibilities now as trustee. Ideally, you and Adam should both be signatories on the slush fund account.'

'Of course,' I say.

'Well, that's not how it's set up at the moment. And you do have the right to spend it as you see fit, but you should be passing formal resolutions before you divert it to Romain Travel. Is that noise she's making normal?'

Esther is grunting with each breath, though she still hasn't woken up. 'I expect she needs a feed,' I say. 'And I kind of need privacy for that. She's been sleeping all day, so she's probably starving. Maybe you could leave the papers with me?'

'Adam seems to want to sort this ASAP,' says Colton. 'I thought babies never slept? She's tiny, isn't she?'

The grunting has become a groan, as though Esther is trying to tell me something. Is it cute, or is something wrong?

'What's the time?' I ask.

'Three, no, nearly four.'

She's slept nine hours. And I'm really not sure if she should be making that noise. I turn my back on Colton and focus on my baby's face. Her colour seems to have changed in the past minute, even in the past few seconds. She's almost grey.

'Wake up, baby,' I whisper. I jostle her gently and kiss her little forehead, but she doesn't wake up.

'Something's wrong,' I say. 'I can't rouse her.'

Wind is rushing in my ears. The room darkens. I pull back Esther's wrap, push up her gown to expose her tiny chest. Her rib cage is distorted, like she's straining for air. Each breath she takes, she makes that noise.

It's not contentment. It's her last-ditch effort to breathe.

'Ring the bell!' I cry. 'Get a doctor!'

———

The room is full of people. Colton is holding me. I want to go to my baby, but there are too many people in the way.

'What's happening to her? Let me go to her!'

'No, Summer, you must stay back,' says my uncle. 'Let the doctors take care of her.'

I catch glimpses of Esther on a table. Naked, something being forced into her mouth, medical gear all over her. No one is talking to me. I can't understand half of what they're saying, but words jump out. *Acute. Distress. Prematurity.*

A nurse approaches. 'Your baby is having trouble breathing, Summer,' she says evenly. 'It would help us if you could be precise about her due date. We have on the file that she was thirty-eight weeks, but she seems like a younger baby. Are you sure about your dates?'

'I thought you knew! She's only thirty-three weeks!' I say. 'Is that why she's in trouble?'

The nurse is distractingly pretty, her eyes heavy with kohl. I glance at her name badge. Nandini Reddy. I don't think Summer knew a Nandini, but the way this woman is looking at me—

'Oh my God, Summer, what are you doing?' she says. 'Thirty-three weeks? Why isn't she in the neonatal unit? What's got into you? First Skybird, and now you have a thirty-three-weeker and you don't make sure we admit her to the unit? How could you not realise this could happen?'

I have to go on the offensive here. I draw myself up. 'I just gave birth, Nandini!'

'Nandini?' she repeats. 'You're calling me *Nandini*?'

She steps forward and places both of her hands on my face. This is someone who knows me well. Very well.

'I don't understand what's happened to you, my friend,' she says. 'Your baby will be fine, but she needs to be in the unit. We'll call you when she's stabilised.'

She and the other doctors and nurses wheel Esther out of the room.

———

Colton is kind to me. He offers to phone Adam, to go and get Adam. But I can't let go of him. I don't care that he's been Francine's lover, that his friendliness might be fake. Hugging him is like hugging my dad, and right now I miss my dad. If Ridge were here, he would tell me what to do.

Nandini will be telling everyone in the neonatal unit that Summer didn't recognise her. All it takes is for someone to say, 'You know she has a twin? Are you sure it wasn't her twin?'

Even if nobody says this, in the neonatal unit, I'll be surrounded by dear friends I've never met. Doctors and nurses talking medical talk, expecting me to understand.

It's impossible.

Yet I have to go there. There is no excuse. My baby is there. My sick baby.

There's a taxi rank right outside the hospital. I can whip home, grab my passport, head to the airport. I can't bear to lose Esther, but I know that I already have. She'll probably be fine—the doctors weren't panicking just now—but once they decide I'm a murderer, I won't be allowed to see my daughter. It's all over.

If I don't go into the unit, they'll still guess. Why would Summer stay away from her baby? People will be curious. People will speculate. Someone will figure it out.

My choice now is to run away or face my undoing.

I won't have money. Even if I persuade Uncle Colton to leave the papers behind, Adam hasn't signed them yet, and in any case, the money's not coming into my bank account. It's going to Romain Travel, because Adam calls the shots in this marriage. A while ago that seemed worth getting upset about. Now I don't care.

'Shall I call your brother?' asks Colton. 'Tell him that Esther's unwell?'

'No,' I mutter. I pull out my phone and refresh my emails, but there's nothing from Ben. A sob escapes me at this reprieve. I'm losing everything here, but the last straw is my brother's betrayal.

'She's going to be OK, sweetie,' my uncle says. 'They said she would be fine. I'll stay here with you until they tell you that you can see her.'

'Thanks,' I say, 'but I need to be alone right now.'

Colton makes a few more useless offers of help and then slips away.

This is my last chance. I need to make a break for freedom.

I slip into a chair and scroll through the 'N' section of Summer's phone contacts. There is no Nandini Reddy, no Nandini at all. But there is a Nina Reddy. The nurse who kept begging Summer not to use Skybird as her midwife. I had pictured a petite blonde, Russian or Spanish, but when I blow up her profile pic, I see the pretty face framed with black hair, the thick eyeliner. It's her. Nandini is Nina.

I find Nina's emails in the trash on my phone. What once seemed rude now strikes me as the confident directness of an intimate friend. Although I deleted all her emails and blocked her texts, Nina's words got through to me. I knew Skybird was a menace. If I had gone through with the home birth, where would Esther be right now? I should have thanked Nina for her warnings.

Between reading Nina's emails, I keep flicking back to my inbox, refreshing and refreshing, waiting for Ben's message,

Ben's demands. His email doesn't arrive, but by the time I've looked a dozen times, I know the truth.

I'm not leaving. I'm hanging on till the bitter end.

There's no way I can fool so many people at once. They will unmask me. This is the end. But I can't go.

I can't leave my baby.

CHAPTER 20

THE NIGHT SKY

'**M**rs Romain, you can see your baby now.'

The nurse invites me to follow her. We walk out of the maternity ward together. I fall behind a little, trying to memorise the route as she turns one way and another. We come up against double doors and I read the sign. Neonatal care. This is it.

I push against the doors, but they don't open. The nurse swipes a card against a control panel at the side. An automatic lock clunks. 'We'll get you a parental swipe card today,' she says as we push through the doors. 'Don't forget the antibac.'

She pumps fluid from a bottle fixed to the wall and smears it over her hands. I do the same.

We walk through more corridors. I catch glimpses of what look like stillborn foetuses in glass cages. Tall machines loom above them, blinking and beeping. An antiseptic smell mingles with the odour of sour milk.

Which baby is Esther? I'm afraid I won't recognise her.

A muddle of voices. People converge on me from all sides. 'Summer! Welcome back! It's so good to see you! I'm sorry it's not under better circumstances.'

They're upon me. I am hugged, squeezed, smothered.

I can't speak. I can't think. I should be sneaking glances at name tags, listening out for names. At the very least, smiling at my old friends. But I can't.

'Where's my baby?'

It comes out shrill. Everybody backs off, apologising. 'We'll give you some privacy,' they mumble.

The nurse leads me on.

I spot Esther at once. She lies in an incubator, plugged into a mess of wires and tubes. She is sweet, vulnerable, and unmistakably mine.

'Forgive me, little girl,' I whisper.

Nina is nearby, tapping at a touch screen. She greets me with a sad smile. 'Baby's sats are up,' she says.

What does this mean? It's clearly significant news, but good or bad? I make a noise, 'Mm-mm,' my tone calibrated to work for both.

'Her O_2 is at ninety-eight and her pulse is around one-twenty.'

'Mm-mm.'

She takes my arm. 'We'll take her off the ventilator this afternoon.'

'No!' I cry. 'Please! There must be something you can do!'

Silence. Nina stares at me. 'Summer, this is hardly the time for jokes,' she says at last.

No more words will come out. I have no idea what is going on. Why are they taking my baby off the ventilator? Is she going to die? Or is she being discharged?

I just need to know.

'Please explain everything as though I'm not a nurse,' I say. 'Why are you turning off the ventilator?'

I don't want to be discovered. I don't want to go to prison. But I can't do this. I can't be Summer anymore.

———

The hospital staff are patient. A lactation consultant shows me how to use a breast pump. A paediatrician explains Esther's condition. She needs to grow; she will be discharged in a week or two. She's going to be OK.

The late-shift nurse, who doesn't seem to know me, sets me up in a recliner beside the incubator and settles Esther on my chest under a baby blanket. Esther's monitors are still attached to her body, but I can feel her soft skin against mine.

'This is kangaroo care,' the nurse explains. 'It's better than the incubator. Your touch helps baby to grow.'

It takes a while to get hold of Adam, but when I do, he rushes back to hospital. I overhear the nurse telling him that they want to keep me in overnight. She is whispering, but the sound travels. 'We think her memory has been affected by stress. We need to tread carefully. Even after your wife is discharged, you'll need to drive her to hospital every day. She needs to spend each day in here with baby. They need time to bond.'

Adam comes and sits with me, observing the precious bundle on my chest with concerned eyes. He places his hand on Esther's back. Our daughter is cocooned between her parents, warm and safe.

I fill Adam in on Esther's condition. He's sorry for not being here earlier, but I won't let him blame himself. 'It's my fault,' I say. 'I should have realised she needed special care.'

'I can't believe Colton was here,' Adam says a little later. 'I chased all over town trying to track him down.'

'Why are you in such a hurry to sort out the money?' I ask.

Adam shrugs. 'Esther coming early has messed up a lot of our plans.'

'*Our* plans?' I say. 'Who do you mean?'

'Annabeth and me.'

'Since when do you make plans with Annabeth?'

'Since you've been pregnant, and since you've not been yourself after losing your sister.'

'So what are these plans?' I ask.

'Well, it's your birthday tomorrow, and we haven't told you everything about Iris's memorial service. I had a surprise planned, but now I'm not sure if you'll like it or if it will bring back bad memories. Or maybe you don't want to do anything at all.'

'Just tell me.'

'OK,' says Adam. 'I guess I have to now. Part of the surprise was that Ben was coming for the service, but don't get excited, because he isn't anymore. He missed his flight and now something's come up at uni and he can't come. And the other part of the surprise is something I was meant to do while you thought I was at work, but now that's difficult, since I need to be here to look after you.'

'Tell me,' I repeat. 'I hate surprises.'

'And I hate keeping secrets,' says Adam. 'I felt like you nearly guessed this morning. It's the venue for the service.' He leans close and strokes my hair. 'We almost got her here in time. She's less than two hundred miles away in Cairns. I could have sailed her here in less than twenty-four hours. There's a fresh nor'east breeze—'

Who is he talking about? *Bathsheba*?

I close my eyes and I'm back on the water. I feel the lilt of waves through my feet. I smell the ocean, the blueness, the salt spray.

'Wait! Did you bring her back for me already? For my birthday?' My voice is almost loud enough to rouse Esther. If she wasn't so fragile, so tangled in tubes, I would leap up and dance around the room with her.

'Yes.' Adam's voice is warm. 'A delivery crew sailed her most of the way, back to Thailand and down through Indonesia, but they've flown home already. I was going to sail the last leg myself. I had this brilliant plan. Ben was going to take you to

Carmichael Bridge and then you were going to spot me sailing up the river! But now Ben's not here and we can't get *Bathsheba* here in time for your birthday, and it's not a surprise anyway.'

'Do it,' I say. 'Go now. Go tonight. They're keeping me in hospital overnight. This is your only chance! Once Esther and I are home I'm going to need you all the time. A newborn waking at night, Tarquin to look after too. It might be months before we get around to it.'

Adam demurs. What if I need him, what if Esther needs him, how can he leave us alone? But I won't be dissuaded. It's not that I care about my birthday, although Adam's plan is the kind of gesture from my husband that I always used to dream of.

It's the thought that she is so near and yet so far, still a day's sail away. I feel as though when I stepped off that boat, I left myself behind.

'Esther's going to be OK,' I say. 'They want me to lie here with her on my chest for hours every day. I can't think of anywhere I'd rather be, but what can you do, sit around all day and watch me?'

'They think that you're really stressed,' he says. 'You're the mother of my children. I think I should stay.'

'I've had a tough time,' I say, 'but I'm OK now. Esther's going to be fine, and that's all that matters. And it's about time I had some good news. Go, Adam. I need her back. Go and bring me *Bathsheba*.'

He stands but doesn't leave. 'There's one thing I never understood about Iris's disappearance,' he says. 'Why did you search so long? She couldn't have lived for more than a few hours. Maybe there was a ghost of a chance on the second day, but a week? You must have known there was no hope.'

I remember the blood pouring from my hand. The sunburn. All I could think about was water.

'I loved her,' I say. 'I didn't realise how much until she died. I was so petty, so selfish, and then she was gone and it was too late. You ask me why I searched so long, but it's the wrong question. The real question is, how did I ever bring myself to stop?'

I grab his arm. 'Adam,' I say, 'can you forgive me?'

'Nothing to forgive.' He grins.

'No, really,' I say. 'I've made some bad mistakes, and I put our daughter at risk. I need to make sure everything's right. I need to tell you everyth—'

'I forgive you,' he says. 'You don't need to ask. You don't even need to tell me what you think you've done wrong. Let's not spoil things by looking back.'

He kisses me goodbye. 'Night sky,' he murmurs in my ear.

———

I dreaded the neonatal unit for months, but now that I'm here and nobody is questioning me, it feels as though I have nothing left to fear. Esther's body rhythms seem to sync with mine as we lie snuggled together. We drift in and out of sleep.

In the early evening, the nurse returns Esther to her incubator and sends me back to the ward for the night. 'Get some rest,' she says. 'Don't come back till morning. Baby needs you to be well.'

Back in my room, dinner waits on the meal trolley, gravy congealing around cold beef. The sheets on my bed haven't been changed, and I've been wearing this hospital gown all day. My body feels grimy. I've been so focused on Esther, I haven't thought about what I need. I have only the clothes I was wearing when I went into labour. I hadn't packed a hospital bag, so I don't have a toothbrush or a change of underwear.

I climb into bed and check my emails for what seems like the thousandth time. I keep imagining that I'm chatting to Ben. 'How did you spring me? Did you know it was me before I turned around?' Friendly chit-chat. I imagine us laughing about it.

But this will never happen. Even though he is the only person on earth who knows who I am, I can't talk to him. As soon as I get his email telling me 'how things stand', our relationship will be over. And although I'm the one who did something unforgivable, that isn't what has destroyed it. What will destroy it is his email. His demands.

The longer Ben's silence has stretched out, the more I have allowed myself to hope. Perhaps he has changed his mind.

Perhaps I won't hear from him for a long time. As long as I don't get this email, he hasn't slammed the door on forgiveness.

But now I remember what he said. He didn't say he was going to send an email. He said, 'I've sent you some emails.' He had already done it.

I look through my spam folder, my social folder. I check Facebook and WhatsApp. Nothing.

And why did he call me 'sister'? He had already called me Summer in front of Colton. He said 'sister' so pointedly. Was he trying to tell me something without Colton realising?

Why did he think he needed to tell me to check my emails?

I've been checking the wrong account.

I have to log in as Iris. It makes sense; what could be more secure than emailing someone who is dead? Adam might read Summer's emails, but no one will read Iris's.

I tap at my phone, logging out as Summer, and type in my old email address, but I can't remember my password. I'm afraid to go through the password recovery process. I can't risk some notification going out through the ether that someone is trying to log into Iris Carmichael's account.

In the walk-in wardrobe at home, the suitcase that I brought on board *Bathsheba* has sat, unopened, since we returned from the Seychelles. My old phone is inside, along with my forgotten belongings: my sleazy dresses, my lipsticks in jealous shades of red and maroon. My phone was permanently logged into my email account. The password was autosaved.

The battery will be flat. Perhaps the phone is dead. I'm not sure if I can get into my emails any other way.

Adam was going to drive straight to Cairns. Annabeth will be looking after Tarquin at the penthouse; she moved back into it a couple of weeks ago. Annabeth invited Virginia to stay at the penthouse too.

No one will be home.

I'm clinging to the thought that Ben's behaviour doesn't quite make sense. I'm missing something. He was out of the room for a few minutes before he came in and told me he had sent me 'some emails'. Not just one email.

I have to get my phone.

———

Leaving hospital without my baby is like wrenching my heart out of my chest. I'll be back in an hour, and nobody needs to know I've gone, but it's still hard to make myself leave. I have to force my aching body out of bed and force my feet to turn away from Esther, towards the exit.

I walk out of the ward in my hospital gown and slippers, carrying my dress and shoes in a plastic bag. I've got the house key, the iPhone and some cash. I've left everything else behind, even Summer's wallet. Hopefully, the ward staff will think I'm in the neonatal unit, and the neonatal staff will think I'm on the ward. If I am sprung, I can say I wanted fresh clothes, but I know this will seem strange. New mothers don't care that much about their clothes.

I dart into the stairwell, throw my dress over my gown and switch my footwear. I'm transformed from patient to visitor. Giving birth at seven months has its advantages; I look pretty trim already. I hurry down two flights of stairs and I'm outside. No one has even glanced at me.

In order to make a discreet entrance, I give the taxi driver an address a few houses down the road from our place. I would like to get out of the cab further away from home, but it's a steep walk up to the house and my legs are still weak. It's just over twenty-four hours since Esther was born.

Night is falling as I walk up the driveway. Everything is quiet and dusky, although I can see blue light flickering from the living room. Adam must have left the TV on.

I let myself in the front door and hurry to the alarm, but Adam has forgotten to set it. There are fresh flowers in the entrance, and Colton's stack of papers is on the kitchen counter. I guess Adam has caught up with him at last.

I drop my keys on the papers and glimpse Adam's messy handwriting. It's the birth certificate application form, signed by me and Adam. The name on the form is Rosebud Carmichael.

I look again, willing the letters to spell out 'Esther', willing there to be a mistake. I am sure I watched Adam tear this form in two. When he brought me the second form, did I check that it said 'Esther' before I signed?

TV noise blares from the living room: cartoon voices, a children's program. I walk around the corner. Sprawled on the carpet in the growing dark, his eyes fixed on the screen, is Tarquin.

Damn, Annabeth is here. I'm going to have to pull the fresh underwear excuse. Why hasn't my mother taken Tarquin to the penthouse? Hasn't she been looking after him there all afternoon?

Or perhaps Adam's still here. Annabeth never lets Tarquin watch TV.

'Adam!' I call.

Tarquin turns and spies me. 'You're not my mummy,' he says.

'That's right, darling,' I say. 'Helen is with the angels.' I don't have time for this right now.

'Mummy happy now,' says Tarquin.

'Where's Daddy?' I ask, flicking off the TV.

Tarquin is silent.

'Adam!' I call again. 'Adam!'

Still no reply. I pick Tarquin up and carry him from room to room. Has Adam fallen asleep? I feel a chill at the thought of Tarquin having the run of the house alone. Adam must be exhausted.

I'm at the foot of the stairs when my phone rings. It's Adam. I answer, and there's a burst of wind in my ear. Adam's voice is distant, like he's calling me from space.

'Hi babe!' he shouts.

'Where are you?'

'About four miles south of Cairns!' he yells. 'I'm passing a headland so I might lose reception. The breeze is a bit fresh. I'm really moving! How's Esther?'

'She's great,' I say. I can't decide whether to tell him where I am. Tarquin is snuggling sleepily into my shoulder, but if he perks up and starts talking, I'll have to explain. I try to sound tired. 'I should let you sail. They've told me to get some rest.'

'Can't wait to see you, babe.' Adam hangs up and the noise cuts off.

Annabeth must be here, but where? She never leaves Tarquin alone.

'Where's Grandma?' I ask.

'No,' says Tarquin.

I phone Annabeth. She answers instantly, bursting with questions about Esther. I cut through her words. 'Was Adam meant to drop Tarquin with you tonight?'

'What? No. Why would he do that?'

'Mum, I know about *Bathsheba*,' I say. 'I know Adam's going to get her for me.'

Annabeth starts enthusing about what a great husband Adam is, while also suggesting that this solo sail is a little reckless of him.

Perhaps he got a babysitter. I climb the floating staircase slowly, weighed down by Tarquin and postpartum fatigue. I let Annabeth keep talking, hoping she'll say something that will fill in the blanks for me.

Across the landing from the master bedroom, the door to the baby's nursery is open. We haven't bought a cot yet, but there's a cot in there now, and it's not Tarquin's; it's brand new. I go in to take a closer look. The cot has been made up with sheets and a blanket. Everything is adorned with delicate pink roses.

Rosebud.

'Adam must have decided to take Tarky with him,' Annabeth says. 'I'm sure there's still a crib on the boat.' She gushes about her new granddaughter. She's already started sewing pink lace onto the christening gown, and do I think it's too hot for knitted booties?

The master bedroom is empty. I walk into the wardrobe, put Tarquin down and haul out my old suitcase. Tarquin is tired; he clings to me, rubbing his eyes.

I kneel and open the case. My phone is right on top, lying on musty clothes along with its charger. I crawl across the bedroom to the power point and plug it in. The screen lights up.

'Gotta go, Mum,' I say and hang up. I sit cross-legged beside the power point. Tarquin crawls across the room behind me, like it's a game. He climbs onto my lap and yawns.

'Ginia,' he says. 'Ginia.'

The word resolves into a name. Virginia. Of course!

'Is Virginia looking after you, Tarq?'

'Ginia.'

Of course Adam would ask Virginia to babysit. She must have stayed here last night. I haven't checked the guest bedroom yet; it's downstairs by the garage. She's probably staring at YouTube, oblivious to passing time, or asleep.

I don't need to tell her I'm here. Not yet. Perhaps I can get away without her knowing.

'Lie down, kiddo,' I murmur. For once in his life, Tarq does what he's told. He lies across my lap and closes his eyes.

I stroke his hair with one hand while I turn on my phone. I click on my mail app. The number is bold: 208. Two hundred and eight new emails, dating back to April. Most of them are from one person. Ben.

My hands tremble as I open the most recent one, dated today.

> *I guess you'll be wondering why I've been sending you all these messages. No, I didn't suspect anything. It was therapy, I guess. It's not like I had anyone else to talk to.*
>
> *I want you to know that I don't hate you. I always thought Summer would get the cash, but I think you kind of deserve it. It's just that I can't be a part of this.*
>
> *I was going to have a beer with Noah this arvo, and I guess I still will, but then I'll fly back to New York, and you won't hear from me again. I want you to know that I will never expose you. And that you are the dumbest person I know.*
>
> *Love you forever,*
>
> *Ben*

Tears are splattering on the screen. I wipe them away with my dress. Of course this is the email that Ben would send, that I should have known he would send. I can't believe I was expecting demands, talk of money, threats of betrayal. How could I have thought my brother would do that?

I ought to feel relieved. I've escaped again, and I can carry on as Summer. But all I can think is how much I miss my brother. And all this time he has been emailing me.

I open another email.

It's so crowded here. At rush hour we're packed like sardines on the subway. But I feel like I'm alone in the middle of the ocean. I feel like I'm the only human being left alive.

I read another and another and another. Tarquin lies heavy and hot and still on my lap, and his breathing is slow and even. I have to find out if Virginia is here, but I can't stop reading Ben's emails. They claw at my heart.

You were the only one who understood what it was like for me to be Ridge Carmichael's gay son . . .

You understood that I wasn't interested in competing for the money. Even if I hadn't been gay, I didn't want to jump through Dad's hoops to get money that he should have shared out fairly among all of us . . .

When I was a kid, I always wished you and I were the twins . . .

Over and over, Ben tells me that since Dad died, I am the only person who loves him. When did he fall out with my mother and sister? He doesn't explain. But he can't bear to phone Annabeth. He can't bear to phone Summer. Without me, he feels as though he has no family.

You were always beating yourself up about things that weren't your fault. Look at how they blamed you for the scar on Summer's leg. What were they doing putting you in charge of us anyway?

Ben always had my back. He always said it wasn't my fault that the dinghy overturned that day.

I'm reading too fast to take things in. There's something Ben isn't telling me. These are emails to himself really, and he already knows.

. . . the blood on her leg. I tried to tell you so many times that she did it on purpose . . .

Does he mean Summer? What did she do on purpose? Cut her leg open when the dinghy overturned? Why would she do that? I'm skimming over the words. There are far too many emails to read them all, but I can't risk taking this phone back to hospital, and I don't know when I'll get another chance to read them.

If Virginia is asleep in the spare room, I can settle Tarquin in his cot and slip away. He'll be safe in there till morning. Virginia might wonder how the hell he put himself to bed, but she won't guess I was here.

I tried to tell you so many times that she did it on purpose. She enjoyed your humiliation.

He's not talking about the dinghy.

The pageant. I'm fourteen years old, wearing a swimsuit and a golden crown, and everyone is staring at me, everyone is thinking, *You didn't win. You're the ugly twin.*

I want to argue with Ben. Yes, Summer let me win on purpose, but he seems to think she exposed me on purpose too. How could she have planned for blood to be running down her leg? Does he think girls can get their period on demand?

I don't know the answer. I can't figure it out, but that doesn't mean Ben's wrong.

'You're right, Ben,' I whisper. 'I am the dumbest person you know.'

Tarquin stirs in his sleep. I put the phone down, move my arms under his body and struggle to my feet. He's grown so big.

I creep to his bedroom and lower him into his cot. I place his favourite teddy bear in his arms and tuck a light blanket around him.

Ben's emails describe me as someone who could do things that Summer couldn't do. Handle a dinghy. Sail across an ocean. Earn the love of a younger brother.

Who have I been trying to be?

I have lied to my mother, my brother, Tarquin, Adam. I have lied to everyone in Wakefield. All of this to try to be Summer.

But who is Summer? No one is perfect, but I have never let myself face up to her faults. Teasing me about my name. Taunting me with horror movies. Showing off that she was the firstborn twin, the one whose organs were in the right place. Thoughtless, minor sins. Not things she did on purpose. Or did she?

I pad back to the master bedroom. It's fully night now, but the bay window is silver with light. Outside, the rising moon cuts a lustrous path across the dark ocean. I can almost see *Bathsheba* sailing along this pearly line, her genoa and mainsail outstretched like great white wings. I check my watch. Adam must still be several hours north of here.

Ben didn't like Summer. I'm starting to think he hated her. And Ben is way smarter than me.

I wander into the bathroom and stand in front of the double mirror. I'm a silhouette, backlit by the moonlight flowing through the bedroom.

'I am Iris,' I say aloud. 'I am left-handed, and my heart is on the wrong—no, on the *right* side of my body. I play the piano and I love the sea. My sister died in March, but I still have a brother. A brother who loves me for who I am. And now I'm a mother. I have a baby who needs me to be my true self.'

My father's will was meant to ensure that his kingdom stayed undivided, but in doing so, it divided something much more important: his family. If all seven of the Carmichael offspring had inherited a slice of the family fortune, as the many branches of the Romain clan did, perhaps we would have learned to cooperate to run the business together. The Romains had expanded, opening travel agencies across the globe, working together to build an empire. If the Carmichael offspring had overcome our differences, what might we have achieved?

Ridge's will was meant to reward the child who made him a grandfather, who valued family enough to continue his line.

Instead, his will has poisoned his family. His will has poisoned my life. Things got so bad, I began to suspect Ben of betrayal.

Now I let the poison ebb out of me. I fill my lungs with fresh air.

Summer wasn't perfect. She was an ordinary girl. Sometimes she could be unkind. Perhaps she could be cruel.

I have to tell Adam the truth. I have to risk it all. Even if he hates me, I'm sure he won't turn me in to the police. He'll know that I would never have killed her.

If he leaves me, so be it. He can take the money. He deserves it. He can choose whether he wants Esther to be a part of his life. As long as I'm a part of Esther's life too. That's all I'll ask. Don't take my daughter away.

I hope that he'll give me more than this. I know it's crazy, but I want Tarquin in my life too. He's Esther's brother. After all these months of resenting the kid, he's somehow found his way into my heart.

I can't lie anymore, but perhaps Adam and I can make a new truth together. I can love him and Tarq as Summer loved them. I can love Esther as Summer loved her baby.

It doesn't feel crazy to hope that Adam will forgive me. I even wonder if perhaps he already has. Perhaps some part of him knows. I have always assumed he would confront me if he guessed, if he suspected, but perhaps I judged wrong. It seems to me that he's been distant, that he's never been quite the soulmate Summer described. He didn't kiss me for months. Perhaps he was wondering. Perhaps he was assessing, deciding what to do.

And now, I think, he's decided. He made a plan, organised a grand surprise for me, bringing *Bathsheba* home. And since Esther was born, he's spoken so lovingly, stroked my hair, kissed me again and again. What did he say when I asked his forgiveness? *I forgive you. You don't even need to tell me what you think you've done wrong. Let's not spoil things by looking back.*

Summer told me that Adam said kissing her was like kissing the sun, but that's not what he said to me. I was something different, but just as beautiful. The night sky.

He knows.

We can sail away. We can take *Bathsheba* back to the Seychelles, the four of us together. And we can sail on. Island after island calls to me, day after sunny day of coconut palms and gentle breezes. The African coast with its stormy capes. The sweet Atlantic, the dancing Caribbean. The Pacific Ocean, laced with atolls made of heaven. If we want to, when we get back home, we can set off again.

There's a movement behind me. A black shape, a shadow, in the bedroom. I flick on the light. And that's when I see her.

The girl in the mirror.

Not me.

Summer.

Summer is standing behind me.

CHAPTER 21

THE GIRL IN THE MIRROR

I spin around.

Here she is in front of me. In the flesh. Summer.

Darkness caves in on all sides until I see nothing but my sister. She stands in a golden sphere, alive and well, brighter and more beautiful than ever before.

What the hell happened? Did someone rescue her? How could she not get word to us? Did someone hold her prisoner? Pirates?

'How—how are you alive?' I stammer.

'What's with carrying Tarquin around all night, Iris?' Summer responds, her aqua eyes regarding me coolly. 'I was starting to think you would never put him down.'

'What?' Has she been watching me? 'Why didn't—'

She flicks her hand, as if she can't be bothered with my questions. 'So how has it been sleeping with my husband?'

I can't breathe. My face burns. She knows. She knows about me and Adam. I want to sink into a hole.

'Summer, I'm so sorry,' I say. 'I—I can't explain. I was crazy. It's like I lost my mind. But I'm not trying to make any excuses. I know I made an unforgivable mistake.'

'Just the one mistake?'

'I made a lot of mistakes.' I stare at her, wondering if this is even real. 'My life has been one long mistake. But you're alive! You're OK! And what about—where's your baby?' She's in a loose dress, but I can see the form of her body beneath her clothes. She looks fuller-figured than usual, but she's not pregnant.

'We'll get to that,' says Summer.

'I don't understand,' I say. 'I saw the boom knock you overboard. And I searched everywhere for you. Where the hell were you? How did you survive?'

'One thing at a time, Twinnie.' Summer stands proud, hands behind her back, elbows out. 'Glad you enjoyed my little snuff movie. You never told anyone about it, did you? But I knew you would find it, and I knew you would fall for it. You wanted to believe it so badly. Dumb Summer can't sail straight. Dumb Summer fell off the boat.'

She keeps talking, but I can't hear. My ears are thrumming. My brain is on fire. Everything that's happened since she died—since she *didn't* die—is thrown up in the air, and when it lands it's a different thing. All my sorrow for my sister. The life I've made without her. My life with Adam. Where does it go now?

Summer's words make their way through the fog. She's talking now about sailing, sailing day after day on her own. As though she were the one left behind on *Bathsheba*. 'You'd never have believed I could do it, would you, Iris? I can see you don't believe it now.'

I'm trying to get my head around her words. Where, when, why was she sailing alone? I want to ask but my mouth won't form words. I'm shaking. I grip the vanity.

She's here, she's here, she's alive. The words whirl around my head. I'm stuck on them, but Summer's moved on.

I've never heard her talk like this before. She's so angry. No, not angry. Sneering.

Hateful.

And something else. Triumphant.

This is not an accidental meeting. She didn't just turn up here. This was a plan. *Snuff movie.* She intended me to find that footage.

Summer talks about scuttling a yacht—what yacht?—off the coast of Australia. Opening the seacocks, watching till the tip of the mast sank below the waves. But she's not telling me this to let me in on a secret. She's boasting. She's taunting me.

It's bad enough what she's already said, but she's leading up to something worse. The reason she did this. Her plan.

I want to know and I don't want to know.

And there's something else worse than any words. It's what she's holding in her hand. She's trying to hide it, both hands behind her back, but I can see the glint of black metal.

Summer is holding a gun.

———

The floor lurches like a ship in a storm. I want to crumple to my knees, but that gun behind Summer's back tells me that I can't. This isn't just about humiliation. It isn't just about money. Summer's been playing a bigger game than that. And now we're in the endgame.

I've got to keep my sister talking. I'm hoping, praying that she doesn't know Virginia's here. A pregnant teenager is an unlikely rescuer, not much of a match for an adult with a gun, but she's all I have. If I play for time, maybe Virginia will overhear us. Maybe she'll call the police or sneak up on Summer from behind.

'I saw the boom hit your head,' I say. 'I saw you hit the water. How could you fake that?'

Summer smirks. 'It was tiresome, Twinnie. I *hate* falling in the sea. I had to act it out nine times to get it looking legit, and then splice the footage into the feed. Can you imagine?'

'But it hit you so hard . . .'

'Well, the footage you saw was sped up, and you wouldn't have realised I was wearing a helmet under my hat, but yeah, it still hurt. It put my neck out.' She wiggles her shoulders. 'I'm fine now, though. Thanks for your concern.'

'But where were you? I searched every inch of *Bathsheba*. I even dived off and checked under the hull.'

She laughs. 'I knew you would do that. Everything you did was totally predictable, but you were hours too late. I'd already made my getaway while you were having a nice long snooze. A pharmaceutically enhanced snooze.'

'Pharmaceutically enhanced?' I repeat. 'What are you talking about?'

'I don't have time for this, sweet pea. We need to get moving. I don't know why you turned up here tonight, but now that you've seen what you've seen, we have to make the best of it.'

'Wait, no,' I say. 'This doesn't make any sense. Where did you go? Who picked you up?'

'No one *picked me up*. The big I-can't-sail routine was all for your benefit. Don't you get it? I pumped up a rubber dinghy, clamped an outboard on it, and off I went. It wasn't hard. I didn't need any help.'

'But we were hundreds of miles from land. No dinghy can take you that far.'

'According to all the charts on board we were hundreds of miles from land, yes. And you thought you knew the Indian Ocean so well.'

'But, but—' I'm trying to think what to say next to keep her talking. 'Why would you make me think you were dead? And our mother? And Adam?'

'Can you not figure it out, Iris? Well, as Dad always said, nice is dumb.'

My sister filmed herself nine times getting hit by the boom. She drugged me and climbed into a dinghy and sped off into nothingness in the middle of the night. She went to an island she had deleted from our charts, where, it seems, a yacht was waiting. She solo-sailed all the way back to Australia.

And she did all this while she was pregnant?

It's like being hit with a hammer. I get it at last.

'You weren't pregnant,' I say. 'You were never pregnant. You can't have a baby.'

'Congratulations,' says Summer. 'Clever you.'

She points the gun at me.

———

I'm standing with both hands raised, trying not to sway.

'Take your phone out of your pocket,' says Summer. 'Or I should say *my* phone. Smash it.'

I reach into my pocket and pull out the iPhone. I think about trying to dial someone, but there's no way. I hit it against the corner of the vanity. The screen shatters.

'Again,' says Summer. 'Harder. Hit it against the tap.'

I smash the phone over the tap. Its innards spill out and fall into the sink. When I look up, Summer is holding the other phone. Iris's phone. My phone. She tosses it to me.

'Same deal,' she says.

I smash this phone harder. I'm praying that the banging will rouse Virginia. The sink is a jumble of smartphone parts.

'Don't worry about your rings,' she says. 'You can keep them. They're replicas.'

I glance at her left hand. Her princess-cut diamond engagement ring gleams in the faint light. I've been wearing a cheap fake all this time.

'Tarquin told me that he saw you,' I say. 'You took him to the bridge, didn't you?' Now I understand Tarquin's confusion about the baby. *Baby's back. Baby's out again.* Did he know his mother was two people, or did he think the baby was popping in and out of me? He was asking for an explanation, but no one was listening.

'Poor old Tarq,' says Summer, 'losing a perfectly good foreskin just so I could lure you to Thailand.' She takes a step backwards. 'Now, downstairs.'

I walk out of the bathroom and through the bedroom. Summer is behind me.

I stop at the top of the stairs. Across the landing, the door to Tarquin's room is open. I can see his sleeping form from here. Stray locks of auburn hair stick out between the bars of his cot, only a few metres away.

If I could just get to him. She waited until I put him down. She doesn't want to hurt him. She wouldn't shoot if he was in my arms.

The gun presses into the small of my back.

'If I shot you now,' Summer whispers, 'the bullet would tear a hole in your *uterus.*' She spits the last word out as though she hates it. 'Keep moving, Twinnie.'

Down the stairs, towards the garage. With each step I'm trying to catch up with a world that has turned inside out and back to front. Does Summer know where Adam is? There's no chance he can help me, but Summer might not know that. And she hasn't said anything about Virginia. Maybe she thinks I was alone with Tarquin. She would never imagine that our rival would be staying here, babysitting her kid.

Has she been waiting for me to have the baby? Hiding somewhere nearby? For hours? Days? Weeks?

'Go into the garage,' says Summer.

We have to pass right by the guest bedroom. The door is shut, and there is no light behind it. *Please let Virginia be in there.*

I shouldn't get her involved. What if she gets hurt, what if her baby gets hurt? We can walk right past and Summer won't know she's here.

I stop outside the door. 'Is this what you want to do, Summer?' I ask as loudly as I dare. 'You want to murder your own sister?'

Summer snorts. 'Of course not! Don't be so paranoid, Iris. This gun *is* loaded, and I've practised using it, but that's just in case you're too dumb to figure this out for yourself. If you don't do as I say, I will have to shoot you, but that would be a shame. I'd prefer to resolve this amicably.'

'How can we possibly resolve this amicably? You're pointing a gun at me.'

'Think of it as a partnership,' says Summer. 'You gave me, lent me, your womb, and in return I let you escape with your life and your dignity. Think about it, Iris. If you stick around, you'll lose everything. After what you've done, you won't even be a beautiful memory. Our mother will hate you, and Adam could probably press charges. And think about this: I could kill you right now and it would be the perfect murder. There wouldn't even be an investigation. Everyone thinks you're already dead.'

'So what do you want?' I ask. 'What do you want me to do?'

I turn to face her. We're right outside Virginia's door, but I won't let myself look at it. Not a glance.

'Leave. That's all. Go and don't come back. I'm going to be super-generous. I'm going to give you *Bathsheba*. But don't let there be any doubt in your mind. Any sign of trouble and I *will* kill you. I *will* be stepping back into my life, even if I have to step over your dead body.'

There's one thing that I can't bear to think about. I can't. I can't. But I have to.

Esther.

Wake up, Virginia.

'Move it,' says Summer.

I take a step backwards, away from the door, towards the garage. Still nothing from the guest bedroom. Is Virginia too cowardly to help me? At least, surely, she will call the police after we leave.

But Summer is my twin. It's so hard to hide anything from her.

'Stop,' she says.

I stop.

'Open that door.'

'There's no one there,' I say. 'It's just me and Tarquin.'

'Open it.'

I throw open the door. 'I'm sorry, Virginia!' I cry.

The room is empty. Summer and I look around, and I know we're both thinking the same thing. There's no space under the bed, and the chest of drawers is compact. There's nowhere to hide.

Summer's face is scornful. 'Virginia?' she repeats. 'Why on earth did you think she was here?'

'Someone must be here,' I say. 'Adam wouldn't have left Tarquin alone.'

Summer bursts out laughing. 'He left Tarquin with me, petal,' she says. 'Don't you understand? Adam knows. He knows everything. He's been in on it from the start.'

CHAPTER 22

THE BRIDGE

'm driving north. Summer's in the rear seat of the BMW. I know she's right behind me because cold steel is pressing into the back of my neck. The gun is small, but Summer pushes it against my skin with unexpected strength.

Adam knows. Of course Summer couldn't have filmed that footage by herself; they would have filmed it back in Thailand before I even set foot on the yacht. Adam's flirtatiousness on the phone when he and Summer invited me to Thailand . . . his telling me I was beautiful when he picked me up at the airport . . . the original plan that I would set sail with Adam, which only changed once it was too awkward for me to back out . . . the vagueness that made me confident I could cover up any mistakes . . . Everything Adam did was a ruse. All part of Summer's game. Their game.

'Where are you taking me?' I ask.

'The river,' she says. 'You can get on *Bathsheba* and leave before dawn.'

Darkness presses in as we leave Wakefield. I watch the last streetlight fade in the rear-view mirror.

'Where will you go?' I ask. 'After I leave? Will you come back here?'

'Of course,' she says. 'I wouldn't leave Tarky alone all night. But you don't need to worry yourself about these things, Iris. You'll have plenty of worries of your own. *You* can't step back into *your* life, you know. I always said you didn't have a life, but now you really don't.'

Is she going to let me live? She didn't bother to tidy up the smashed phones. This gives me hope. She's not acting like someone who needs to cover up a crime.

But then, she wouldn't need to. As she said, if she did kill me, there wouldn't be an investigation.

All she has to do is get rid of the body.

'Summer, let me live,' I say. 'I'll do anything.'

'Iris, you're my sister! You know me better than that. Don't judge me by your standards. I said to Adam, once Iris sees the gun, she'll do whatever I tell her.'

She presses the gun harder against my neck. 'Adam wanted to kill you,' she says. 'You're lucky he's not here. I persuaded him to let you live. *Bathsheba* is fully laden. You could go halfway round the world without restocking. There's cash on board, ten thousand American dollars. Enough to tide you over. Make sure you don't come back, Twinnie. I'm scared of what Adam would do to you.'

'Of course,' I say. I don't know whether to believe her, but it feels safest to play along. '*Bathsheba*'s all I ever wanted anyway. I think you're being generous after what I've done.'

Summer gives my shoulder a sisterly squeeze, but she keeps the gun in place. 'I knew you'd understand, Twinnie,' she says. 'I told Adam we could trust you.'

I tell myself to act grateful. Act relieved. Like maybe I didn't want to carry on being Summer. Like all I ever wanted was to sail away.

I want to believe her. Summer gets her life back. She gets everything. Adam. Tarquin. She gets—I can hardly bear to think it—she gets Esther. She has to believe I don't want to come back. She has to believe that I'll do anything as long as she lets me live. She has to believe that the only thing I want is *Bathsheba*.

Summer knows I'm selfish, freakish, unmotherly. She knows I disliked Tarquin. She knows that I know I can't have Adam. She knows I never wanted a baby. So this isn't so bad, is it? I'll live the rest of my life with no legal identity, the ghost of Iris Carmichael, but at least I'll live.

———

We turn off the main highway onto the dirt road that leads to Carmichael Bridge. I glance in the rear-view mirror. Summer is resting back in her seat. She catches my gaze.

'Aren't you wondering where I hid the dinghy?' she asks.

'I suppose,' I say, although, of course, I'm only thinking about Esther. How to make sure she's safe. How to keep Summer thinking I don't care about her. I can't mention her. If I say anything about her, Summer will know. She'll know that I can never leave my baby.

'I knew I had to hide it well,' says Summer. 'You're always poking your nose into everything of mine. I thought the one thing you wouldn't try to do was housework. You've always been so slovenly, but I told you the washing machine was sealed shut, to be on the safe side.'

I'm barely paying attention. 'So the dinghy was inside,' I say.

'Yep. We had to take out all the innards to fit it. And the dryer too, to fit the outboard and the fuel tank. And then you tried to open it the moment you got to port. Adam told me what he had to do to distract you. What a laugh. He tried to be the worst lover he could, but you still couldn't get enough of him.'

'That's not true,' I say. She's trying to humiliate me, and I do feel a pang. Adam knew. When he pushed himself inside me and called me a slut and a whore, it wasn't a sexy game with his wife. He knew.

'Well, you must have super-low standards,' says Summer. 'He never kissed you, not once. I made him promise.'

I open my mouth and close it again. Don't say it, Iris. She's holding a gun.

'You never had a period, did you?' I ask. 'Not even at the pageant.'

'Aren't we the clever one?' says Summer. 'I had to cut myself to make that blood run down my leg. It was easy enough to fool Mum, but I always thought you might figure it out one day. You were always jabbering about how I got the perfect body while you were deformed, jabbering about us almost being Siamese twins. How we might have had to *share organs*. That's what gave me the idea. It was your fault that things were wrong inside me.'

'I'm not deformed,' I say. 'Everything's backwards, but it still works. Everything's in place.'

Summer hisses in my ear. 'I wasn't missing anything either,' she says. 'I was perfect until you split off from me. I was whole. But then you stole from me. You stole my uterus. And frankly, I wouldn't have cared, if it hadn't turned out to be worth a hundred million dollars.'

———

Even without a uterus, Summer is perfect. She is brilliant, glittering, metallic. She is a siren. Now I see what makes her beautiful, what has always made her beautiful. She has never needed anyone else. Her missing womb somehow makes her more self-contained. What is a womb but a yearning for motherhood, a yearning for a baby? But Summer doesn't yearn. Summer doesn't need. Summer takes.

And she knows me so much better than I realised. She knows everything I tried to keep secret from her. She thinks she can read my mind. Can she?

She believes that I don't care about the baby. She believes that I am willing to sail away. Or else she's pretending to believe. As long as I think she's going to let me live, I'll cooperate. Yes, there's a gun pressing into my neck, but if I knew she was going to kill me, I might as well take my chances. Crash the car. Make a run for it. Try to knock the gun out of her hand.

Instead I'm playing along. Buying time. Trying to catch up, trying to think of something Summer hasn't thought of.

The only thing I'm sure that Summer doesn't know is that Ben found me out. I try to think of a way to use this to my advantage. *Ben knows. Ben can tell us apart. You'll never fool Ben.*

I bite my lip. Don't speak. It won't make any difference. It will only endanger Ben. If she is planning to kill me, she would probably kill Ben too before he could expose her crime. I'm thankful that Ben is heading back to New York. I hope, I pray, that he keeps his word and never comes back. If I am going to die tonight, I need to know that the people I care about will be safe. My mother. Ben. Esther.

She's my twin sister. She predicted everything I would do since she disappeared in March. She guessed I would step into her life, get pregnant, beat Virginia to the cash.

I've said that I won't come back, but does anyone believe words spoken at gunpoint?

———

Carmichael Bridge looms ahead. It's closed to traffic nowadays; the main road north is further inland. People only come here to see the crocodiles. No one will come at night.

Random scenes from the last seven months jump into my mind. I have no way of knowing how much of the life I perceived as Summer's was real. Did she really spend her days running around after Tarquin, cleaning Helen's piano and cooking Adam's favourite meals, or were those tasks set specially for me? Those phone reminders, that freaky shared wedding album, were they fakes planted for me? Did Adam make all the decisions and get all the money banked into his account to stop me from having any influence over Summer's life while I was keeping it warm for her? Were Summer's stories about Adam's romantic seductions any truer than the shameful sexyrape he tried out on me? I want to ask, but I know I can't. I don't get to find out.

Some things I do know. Summer doesn't like sailing. Her raptures over *Bathsheba*, over Adam, were lies to lure me in. All the glamorous touches, the lingerie, the jewellery. The grand piano, which they kept even though no one could play it. The stories of spectacular sex. And I fell for it. I fell for it all. She's been as single-minded as a predator, and I have been her prey.

'Pull over,' says Summer. 'We'll wait for *Bathsheba* here.'

The car park is empty. I pull into the nearest spot. I can't quite see the bridge from here, but there's a clear view downstream. The river, gleaming black under an almost cloudless night sky, is sluggish and wide, lazing its way towards the sea. The shore is thick with mangroves. I know what lurks there.

Further downstream, the river twists around a bend, so I can't see the ocean from here, but the river is navigable right up to the bridge. Dad brought *Bathsheba* in here sometimes.

The moon is high. Somewhere out on the open sea, Adam is sailing towards us. Is he bringing me life and freedom, or death?

Perhaps Summer is waiting for him to do the dirty work for her. Or am I really going to be allowed to leave?

Cairns is nearly two hundred nautical miles away. *Bathsheba*'s a fast boat, but not that fast. There's no way she's going to get here before sunrise.

Summer must know this.

And there's no way Summer's planning to wait here all night.

There's something else. Something not right about the way Summer's been talking. She's told me too much. She didn't need to tell me that she faked her death. She could have invented a miraculous rescue. She didn't need to tell me that she doesn't have a uterus. She could have pretended that she'd lost the baby.

There's only one reason she would tell me everything. She doesn't care what I know. It doesn't matter what I know. That's how sure she is that I'm never going to see another sunrise.

My sister is going to kill me.

I feel calm. I've been so stupid, it's like I deserve it. Not just for these past months. For my whole life. Summer has fooled me since we were fourteen years old. Since our father died. She never had a uterus. She managed to keep it a secret not only from me, but from Annabeth. I remember her asking our mother to buy more tampons, complaining about cramps. Nothing seemed amiss. She was meticulous. The last thing on anybody's mind when Summer very publicly got her first period at the beauty pageant was that she might be faking it. What better way to hide a lie than to make it look like a humiliating accident?

She never would have had a chance of getting the money if I hadn't been so jealous of her life. In an alternate universe, Iris Carmichael stepped onto shore in the Seychelles and told the truth. Who knows what future awaited her? The first man she laid eyes on was Daniel Romain. He was a man perhaps better suited to me than Adam ever was, a man who seemed to know me at first sight. A man with golden eyes, with whom I could have sailed away into a golden sunset.

'Now,' says Summer, 'you have to promise you won't come back. I'm scared for you, Iris. Adam has some nasty ideas.'

'I promise,' I say. 'I only ever wanted *Bathsheba*. I'm not cut out for motherhood.'

'Get out of the car,' says Summer. 'Walk up to the bridge.'

I climb out of the car, and I face my sister.

'Summer,' I say, 'I know *Bathsheba*'s not coming. Is she even in Australia?'

Summer's teeth glint in the starlight. Her smile is cold, reptilian. She's thinking about whether she can be bothered stringing me along anymore. Whether she needs to.

'Oh, yes, she's in Australia,' says Summer. 'We're holding your memorial service on her tomorrow.'

The pretence drops away. There is only Summer and me. She looks me in the eye.

No lies.

'Summer, I'm sorry about everything.'

'There's no point snivelling, Iris.'

'I'm not snivelling. I've lost. I know I've lost, but please promise me one thing.'

'I'll make sure you're dead when you fall,' says Summer. 'I won't let them eat you alive, even though I always wanted to see that.'

The way she says it, I nearly sink to the ground. I nearly give up. I can't speak.

'Walk,' says Summer. 'It's time.'

I walk to the bridge. I am cold, but sweat drips down my back. My legs are weak, and my body still aches from the birth. Could I jump from here? The handrail is hip height, and there's a gap at the bottom that I could squeeze through. The fall is probably ten metres. I could survive it, maybe. The water is deep enough, but I know what's down there. I would only swap one death for another. A worse one.

'One more thing,' I say. 'Please promise me that you'll look after Esther. I would have made an atrocious mother, but I do love her. Promise me she'll be OK.'

'Oh, don't you worry,' says Summer. 'I'll *take care* of Rosebud.'

She'll take care of Rosebud. Like she's taking care of me.

I remember my words to Virginia. *It only needs to take one breath.* How Virginia shrieked.

I have to face it. Summer doesn't love Esther. Maybe she hates her. How can I leave my daughter in the hands of this psychopath?

I'm so tired. I'm worn out just walking up the slope of the bridge. But I know what I have to do.

I have to fight.

'You're wrong about one thing,' I say. 'One small thing. It doesn't matter, but I think you should know. Adam has kissed me. He didn't for a long time, and I wondered why, but he has now. He's kissed me over and over. He pushes his lips against mine so hard, and his tongue pushes so deep, it's like he's aching for me—'

'*I told you* that,' says Summer. 'It's obvious you're lying.'

'He's done it in front of people,' I say. 'Ask the nurses at the hospital. Ask Nina.'

Summer's lip curls, and her eyes flash. I've riled her. She's distracted. The gun is off-centre, pointing at my shoulder. It's a poor play, but it's the only chance I've got.

I lunge for her. I grab at the gun.

Summer is taken by surprise, but she doesn't let go. She grips the gun as my hand closes around hers. She grabs my hair, wrenches it back. My chin jerks skyward.

I throw myself at her. We fall together. We both hit the ground hard. I'm on top of her, pinning her down. I'm still holding the gun, my hand enclosing Summer's. I bang our hands against the concrete. Hard as I can. She cries out. I bang again, harder. The gun skitters across the concrete. It stops at the edge of the bridge. I reach for it, but Summer brings her knee up hard into my crotch. I yell in pain and now she's on top of me. She claws at me. I kick back, scratch back, clutch her, tear her away from that gun.

We are both fighting for our lives, and we are perfectly matched.

———

Two girls stand on a bridge. They both have golden hair and eyes the colour of the sea. One of them is clinging to the safety rail. Her body aches from the fight she has lost, the biggest fight of her life. She feels the space beneath her, the long drop to the river below, and she knows what's in that river, but she can't look down. Her eyes are fixed on her sister.

The other girl stands in the middle of the bridge, at the summit. Her eyes are fixed on her sister too. She points a gun at her sister's head.

A shot rings out, splitting the night in two, and the girl at the safety rail screams, but she doesn't fall.

The girl holding the gun crumples, falls. It's a perfect shot through her chest. Her twin's head whips round towards the sound, and she sees her brother standing in the car park, a rifle in his hand.

'Iris!' he cries.

PART III
IRIS

CHAPTER 23

THE BIRTHDAY

'm Iris. I'm Iris. I'm Iris.

My brother runs towards me, still holding the rifle.
I collapse into his arms. 'Thank God!' he cries. 'I got here
just in time!'

I'm trembling uncontrollably. My sister's body lies on
the ground, a scarlet flower blooming on her chest where the
bullet struck. Blood is pooling around her body. I turn to
Ben. He's shaking so badly we can't hold each other up. We
sink to the ground together.

'How the hell did you find me, Ben?'

'It was Noah—I . . . I . . .' Ben's breath comes in short
gasps. His fingers dig into my shoulders. He bites his lip so
hard I expect to see blood appear. 'I can't believe it! I just
killed Summer! I murdered my sister!'

'But you saved me, Ben. You had no choice. She was about to kill me!'

'I know. I figured out her plan.' Ben lets go of me and crawls over to her body. That's Summer there, lying dead beside us. Truly dead. Ben whimpers at the sight of her. He grabs her gun and hurls it over the edge of the bridge, followed by his rifle. They hit the water with a double splash. 'God, I always hated her so much, but now I've killed her!' cries Ben. 'I'm in deep shit!'

'Think, Ben, we have to think! What do we do now?'

'Quick, we have to hide her body! Or do I call the police and confess?'

'No, wait. It's gonna be OK. We can get through this together. Oh my goodness, I thought I was dead! Listen, does anyone know you're here? I don't think she told anyone where she was taking me. Adam's out on the ocean with no phone reception. He's miles away. We've got time. It's the middle of the night. No one's coming.'

'No, I didn't tell anyone where I was going. I didn't have time.' Ben's eyes are wide, but they're blind with panic. He holds his head in his hands and gives a low moan. 'I'm a murderer,' he stammers. 'I killed my sister.'

'But how did you know? How did you save me?' I ask.

'I saw Noah—I told you I was seeing Noah. He told me that you couldn't bear a child. That's why he left you.'

'That makes no sense,' I say. 'We were trying to have a baby the whole time we were married. That's why we got married.'

'I know, but Summer persuaded him that you were so desperate to stop him from dumping you that you pretended you could have children. She showed him proof. She had films, scans, to prove you had no uterus. She swore him to secrecy, saying you would never forgive her for telling him. And I sat there thinking, but Iris just had a baby. So whose body was it on the scans?'

'Summer's,' I say.

'Right, but Summer had told you she was pregnant before she disappeared. Once I figured out she was lying—lying about being pregnant, lying about being able to have a baby—I realised her only chance of inheriting was to pass someone else's baby off as her own. That's when I guessed that she set you up, that she wasn't really dead. Everything she did was designed to make you do what you did. Have her baby for her. And once the baby was born, she didn't need you anymore. She needed you to disappear. Iris, it was the worst moment of my life. What if she had killed you already? I phoned you but it went straight to voicemail. I really started to panic when the hospital couldn't find you. So I rushed to her house. It wasn't locked. I found Tarquin sleeping alone and smashed phones in the bathroom—'

'Was Noah with you?'

Ben shakes his head. 'No, I didn't tell him anything.' He pulls out his phone. 'I'm calling the police.'

'Ben, are you crazy? You killed someone. Wait a minute. Think.'

'No, Iris, I'm not going to get caught up in lies. I'm telling the truth.'

'Stop a second! You're not just exposing yourself, you're exposing me. Everyone will find out about me! If they see me here and Summer's body, I'll have some serious explaining to do.'

I can't get my head around what the police would think, but I know it doesn't look good for me or Ben.

'I don't even understand how you knew to come here,' I say.

'That was the easy part,' Ben mutters. 'As soon as I asked myself, how would Summer kill Iris, I knew the answer. She was fucking obsessed with crocodiles.'

———

The world has fallen to pieces. I'm clutching my brother. I'm alive, but I'm so bewildered I can't even feel grateful to him for saving me. Right beside me is my sister's body. Her corpse.

'Ben, you threw the guns away, like a guilty person.'

'I know,' says Ben. 'I wasn't thinking.'

'You saved my life,' I say. 'I can't watch you go to prison.'

'You can testify that Summer had a gun to your head.'

'Yes, and of course I would, but who am I? Who is your witness? Someone who's meant to be dead! Someone who has lied for months to everyone around her. They won't believe a word I say! They'll think we cooked the whole thing up together!'

'But don't you want to come clean?' My brother's eyes bore into me. 'I really thought once you read my emails, you would want to come clean.'

'Let me think,' I say. 'This is all so terrifying. I was so scared, Ben!'

Ben waits.

'I want to come clean,' I say. 'I desperately want to come clean, but the most important thing is that you're safe. I owe you everything. God, I'm freezing.'

I try to stand, but I can't. I sink back into Ben's arms.

'I tried to tell you, Iris,' says Ben. 'I always knew she played games with you, called you names, taunted you with horror stories. And the beauty pageant. She set you up for humiliation, letting you wear the crown and then exposing your true identity in front of everyone, at the same time as she fooled us all into believing she was having periods. That was only a month or so after Dad died, but she was already laying the groundwork for her scheme. She must have known she was infertile—perhaps Dad knew too—but she'd managed to hide the news from Mum. So she had to make you think she had no interest in the money, to lull you into complacency. She must have panicked when you got married. When I heard she had flown to New Zealand and was trying to save your marriage, I had a feeling she was going to sabotage it, but I never realised how far she would go. Our sister was a monster.'

I nod slowly. The truth hurts. I don't want to think about it. I need to think about Ben, my brother. I've neglected him for so long, but I can't afford to do so any longer. I try again to get to my feet, and this time I manage. Ben moves away from the edge and looks away from me, back towards the car park. This is my chance. I have to make sure Ben doesn't get arrested. I take a deep breath and clutch the armpits of my sister's corpse. One great heave and her head and upper body slump over the edge of the bridge, leaving a trail of dark blood on the concrete. I let go, pausing to catch my breath.

Was that a twitch? No. Surely not. Ben killed her. I'm just cleaning up the mess. I push her legs, and she rolls, and now she's falling.

A splash. She's in the water now. She's with the crocodiles. Instantly, I see movement on the bank. Long dark shapes glide into the water.

'What the hell have you done?' Ben shouts. 'Now we look guilty!'

'It's the only way,' I say. 'I know what I'm doing. We can't come clean. It'll be a disaster for both of us. You'll lose your scholarship. Even if you don't end up in prison, this will ruin your life.'

Ben is as white as ash. 'How can you do that to her?' he cries. 'Think what will happen to her body!'

My eyes are drawn to the river, but I mustn't watch. I don't want Ben to see me looking, and in any case, a cloud has rolled over the moon, cloaking the river in darkness. But I can hear something. A disturbance in the water. The predators striking.

The death roll. Something churns in my belly. Is she still alive? Can she feel that? What does it feel like to be eaten?

I can't let myself think about it now. It doesn't make any difference. The important thing is that there will be no body, no evidence.

'I did it so you wouldn't have to, Ben,' I say, 'because I love you. We need to stick together now. You're the only one who knows who I am, and it has to stay that way.'

I take my brother's arms and pull him to his feet. 'Come on. The keys are in the ignition. I have to get back to Tarky. He's home alone right now. How did you get here?'

'In my rental car,' says Ben.

'And the rifle?'

'It was Dad's.'

'Does anyone know you had it?' I ask.

'No. I snuck into the garage at the beach house and took it from the safe.'

'No one saw you?'

'No one.'

'Good. Now get in the car and go. And never mention this in an email or on the phone. It's best we never talk about tonight again. Go back to New York.'

'You can't be serious,' he says. 'What about Adam? How are you going to handle him?'

'Adam?' I repeat. 'I don't know what to think about Adam. She said he was in on it, but maybe she was just taunting me.

She said that he had dreamed up some nasty ways to kill me, but I can't believe it of him. He's been so kind to me.'

'Come on, Iris, isn't it obvious?' says Ben. 'They've been planning it for years. Everything about Summer's life was designed to pull you in. I wondered why they bought *Bathsheba* when Summer hates sailing. Adam had to be in on it.'

'Even if you're right,' I say, 'it doesn't mean he agreed to the murder. Neither of them knew I was going to turn up tonight. I was meant to stay in hospital. I think Adam's plan was to let me take *Bathsheba* and leave. I'm sure he cares about me. Anyway, don't worry about it. It's my problem, and I'll handle it.'

Ben is so virtuous that he would rather tell the truth even if it ruins his life. I will have to work hard to keep him from confessing. It's the least I can do for him. She was going to kill me.

It's perfect this way. I'll be Iris for Ben and Summer for everybody else. Adam I'll play by ear. Everybody gets the twin they love the most.

I'm in the car, turning the key, when Ben knocks on my window. I roll it down.

'You know, if I had arrived a few seconds later back at the hospital, you would be dead now,' he says. 'And I would never know about it. Summer would have succeeded.'

'What do you mean?'

'I can't tell you guys apart. I've never been able to. If I hadn't seen you sniffing those iris flowers I would never have guessed who you were.'

'I still can't believe you guessed,' I say. 'I thought I was doing such a good job. You're a legend, Ben.'

'Please don't congratulate me,' he says. 'I keep thinking, I didn't give her a chance to drop the gun. I just shot her.'

'That's true,' I say. 'Why didn't you?'

Ben makes a derisive noise. 'If it had been you holding the gun, I would have reasoned with you. But come on. We're talking about Summer. That bitch would have shot you without breaking a sweat.'

———

At noon on my birthday, *Bathsheba* arrives in Wakefield Marina, just in time for the memorial service to be held on board. We have to keep things brief; I haven't made it to the hospital today yet. I had to take care of Tarky and clear away the broken phones.

My instinct last night was to put Ben on the first flight back to New York, but he decided to stay. It's always possible that someone reported hearing a gunshot or finding bloodstains on Carmichael Bridge, and if this were somehow connected with Ben or his rental car, it would look bad for him to have fled the country. My sister's body will be safely disposed of by now, but crocodiles don't eat rifles. It seems unlikely that someone will fish my father's rifle out of the river, but you never know. So Ben changed his flight again and slept the night at Mum's. It's uncomfortable for me, having him here today under false pretences, but it's the least I can do after he saved my life.

We hold the service in the saloon. Nine people in here is a crowd; I'm not going to get a moment alone with Adam until after the service. I'm impatient to find out his true feelings.

Everybody today is telling lies about Iris; it's hard to keep track. A minister who never met her makes an interminable and inaccurate speech about a promising young lawyer whose career was cut short. Mum, in the same black dress that she wore to my father's funeral, talks about her special bond with her middle child. Colton and Virginia espouse regret that they didn't get to know Iris better. Letitia Buckingham says how much fun it was to be best friends with identical twins. Noah and Adam and Ben say as little as possible.

My mother weeps, and I do my best to cry with her.

Nine people to mourn a life. It's not much of a legacy. My spine tingles at the thought that Iris is really dead now. No possibility of resurrection. I've promised Ben that I will keep what happened secret forever.

It's for the best. Ben will go back to New York, I will live as Summer, and no one will ever suspect what Ben did.

Colton approaches me after the service. 'Summer, the money is all in your hands now,' he says. 'I have one question, and it's just idle curiosity. Why did you mortgage yourselves so heavily to buy *Bathsheba*? If you hadn't had the baby, you guys would have been in trouble.'

'But we always were going to have the baby,' I say. Colton doesn't have any power over me anymore. Without the trust fund in his hands, he's just a nosy uncle, the family bore. 'We always were going to get the money. Surely you knew that. I *am* the oldest.'

Colton's eyes widen, but now Mum is calling me from outside.

'Summer, it's time to go! Adam's on the deck waiting for you.'

I say goodbye to Colton. I say goodbye to Letitia and Virginia. I say goodbye to Noah.

On my way through the pilot house, I hug Ben. 'Have a safe flight back to New York,' I say.

There's a bouquet of white irises on the pilot house table. I bury my nose in them and breathe deep. I arrange my face into an expression of bliss. I have to remember to keep sniffing these weeds whenever my brainless brother is around.

Now it's time to get off this floating hellhole and go meet Rosebud.

I step into the blinding sunshine and take my husband's hand.

It feels good to be one person again at last. My clone has been ripped to pieces. Crocodiles are digesting her deformed body: her twisted heart, her leaky breasts, her womb.

ACKNOWLEDGEMENTS

The community of round-the-world sailors is full of generous, resourceful and smart people, and my family and I couldn't have made it across the Indian Ocean without the friendship of the families of the vessels *Gromit*, *Sophia*, *Utopia II*, *Simanderal*, *WaterMusick* and *Totem*. I cherish a hope that one day someone will read this novel and feel inspired to sail away. If so, sailingtotem.com is a great place to start your journey.

Thank you to my friends, readers and fact-checkers, including Jessica Stephens, Cliff Hopkins, Vivien Reid, Greg Lee, Marie-Paule Craeghs, Sarah Heaslip, Nicci Duffy, Behan Gifford and Charlotte Gibbs. Any errors are my sole responsibility.

I am so grateful to everyone at Allen & Unwin and William Morrow, including Jane Palfreyman, Ali Lavau, Elizabeth Cowell, Christa Munns and Angela Handley at Allen & Unwin, and Liz Stein and Laura Cherkas at William Morrow. And to my rights manager at Allen & Unwin, Maggie Thompson, and my American agent, Faye Bender. Thank you, all of you, for believing in my manuscript.

Thanks are due to the New Zealand Society of Authors and Creative New Zealand for awarding me the mentorship with Dan Myers, whose enthusiasm convinced me to keep writing, and to the Michael King Writers Centre for awarding me a residency. Thank you also to my fellow writers at the University of Auckland, including Amy McDaid, Rosetta Allan, Heidi North and Paula Morris. Thank you to the late Elwyn Richardson, who took me on as his student when I was nine years old and promised me I would be a published author one day.

Thank you to my amazing children: Ben, who climbed the mast for me and who hand-steered our yacht through long night watches; Moses, who took solo watches before he had reached his teens and who knew every species of fish; Florence, who fixed so much equipment and who swam with sharks. Thank you, also, to my inspiring aunt Kathryn and my lovely mother, Christina.

Finally, my brother and sister. David, when I lost you, I felt like a twin without a twin. And Maddie, you taught me to live again. What a delicious irony it was to write a book about jealous sisters when surely no siblings have ever been as free from rivalry as you and David and I always were. This novel is yours as much as it is mine.